# ROYAL BASTARD

NANA MALONE

Royal Bastard

Photography: Wander Aguiar

Cover Art by: Amy Daws

Edited by: Angie Ramey, Daisy Cakes Editing

Published in the United States of America

*To all those who believe in fairytales...*

# 1

LUCAS

*WOULD ANYONE EVER LOOK at me that way?*

I don't think I've ever seen anyone look at someone else the way my brother looked at Penny as she walked down the aisle.

He was in awe. Completely dumbstruck.

One second, he'd been murmuring nonsense words to me, telling me to stop fidgeting, while he was the one who was rocking back on his feet and clearly antsy to see his bride. But then the music started playing, and she appeared with her father in the doorway, dressed in some slinky white confection that showed off her body.

Was I even allowed to say that about the future queen?

Either way, Sebastian stopped moving. He was frozen, rooted in place. Staring at her.

I knew fuck-all about fashion unless it involved some barely dressed supermodel, but the dress was pretty. It had glittery stuff on the shoulders and around the waist, and something that looked like feathers along the skirt. And she was wearing a veil.

The cinnamon complexion of her arms practically shimmered under the lighting from the stained-glass windows.

Okay, yeah, she was gorgeous. She wasn't mine, but even my brain stopped for a moment.

But the best part was Sebastian's face.

The big brother I'd never even known I had was completely in love, and I was happy for him. I was going to ignore the big gaping hole in the center of my chest, the one that burned, the one that told me that I didn't belong here, that this was a mistake, that this was some kind of accident. I would absolutely ignore it.

*Ignore me if you think you can, but I'm right. You don't belong here. These are not your people. They will eventually see that you're a fraud.*

I shoved that voice down, stomped on its head, and locked it up. Then I sent my ugliest, scariest demons to guard it. Sebastian *was* my brother. The kind of brother that I'd dreamed of having when I was struggling to survive as a kid.

From the moment I'd been aware that there were families that loved you and looked out for you, I'd dreamed of having one. A *real* family. Not my fucked-up mother and her fucked-up choices. I'd always imagined that my real family would come and get me, liberating me from the hell I was in.

They wouldn't make me steal. They wouldn't make me do— other things. I would be safe and well fed, and I could just be a kid.

Little did I know, that dream family *had* existed, and they had been looking for me.

Now here I was standing next to my brother, and a guy who would turn out to be one of my best friends in the world, wondering how the hell I ended up here. All the while watching my brother marry a girl I genuinely loved. If anyone was deserving of this crazy fairy-tale ending, it was the two of them. Of course, that also meant I was going to need a new roommate.

I'd liked Penny as a roommate. She cleaned, she cooked, and she had excellent taste in TV shows. She loved anything involving superheroes. Where the hell was I going to find someone else like that?

As the ceremony started, I let my gaze drift around the packed church. One thousand people sat in the cathedral. Those of greater importance were closer to the front. My gaze collided with the Queen Mother's. The smile she gave me was warm and bright.

And Christ help me, my eyes misted a little bit. It wasn't my fault. Honestly, it wasn't. But the woman had been really nice to me. Considering I was the bastard son of her dead husband, she was more than accommodating. She was... loving.

The first time I met her, she enveloped me in her arms and told me how happy she was to meet me and how much my father would have wanted to see me home. I hadn't been able to keep it together. I was slightly ashamed of that now, but I would never forget the kindness and love she'd shown me that my own mother never could.

None of the other people knew who I was. All they knew was that I was a friend of Sebastian's from his time in the States, which was true. There were only a handful of them who sat on the Regent's Council who knew who I was, a fact we were all keeping quiet for the time being. All but two of them had voted in favor of me being legitimized and named prince. They were, at best, cold towards me, at worst, dismissive. Which was fine.

In the two additional meetings I'd attended, the plan for the announcement of my title and my knighthood had been met with some arguments. But for the most part, everyone followed Sebastian's lead.

Sebastian commanded respect and allegiance without ever having to demand it.

*That's because he's the king. Even as a prince, they would follow.*

It was true. And who was I to be welcomed into the fold?

*You are the second son of King Cassius Winston, Commander of the Royal Armies.*

My heart squeezed just thinking about him.

It was ridiculous for me to mourn a man I'd never met. I knew that. But still, Sebastian and his mother insisted that I had a right to it, that I could feel sorrow for the man who would have loved me.

And I did. Every time someone brought him up, my heart pinched as I tried to understand who he was. There had been some letters, things he'd written for me and our sister, but I hadn't been able to bring myself to open them yet. And maybe I never would because I wasn't sure how I was supposed to feel about them.

When the choir stopped singing "Ave Maria," Penny's choice of song as opposed to "Pachelbel's Cannon," I lifted my gaze to look at Sebastian. The way he was looking at her, the way he bit his lip and then broke out into the broadest of grins, proved he was a man in love. He was a man who knew his place in life, who knew that he had family.

He was the man who I hoped to be like, because the boy I'd been once knew how lucky I was.

Sebastian had given me the life I'd always wanted, the life I'd dreamed of and never thought I would get. I would do anything to show him that I was deserving of it. I would give my life for my brother. I would give my life for this country. There was no way in hell was I ever going back. The old *me* was dead, and nothing was dragging me back into the darkness.

⚜ ⚜

### Sebastian

I fidgeted with my military uniform, pulling at the hem of it, adjusting the pins. I just wanted to hear the music of "Ave Maria" and know everything was okay.

Roone leaned over. "Relax mate. She's coming."

I shifted my glance over to him, and he gave me a reassuring nod. Lucas, however, winked and gave me a smirk. The little shit had seen me running back from Penny's parents' house on the grounds. Yes, I might have been screwing my soon-to-be bride... on our wedding day.

Not exactly tradition, but it didn't matter. It was almost as if we both needed the reassurance.

*But where is she now?*

*What if it's too much? What if she runs? What if the danger is too overwhelming? What if she doesn't want this life?*

Things had been so crazy in the last year. I didn't want any of that to overshadow how I felt about her. I wanted her to know that she was everything to me. I wanted her to know that my world started and ended with her.

*She knows. Relax. She's coming.*

But once I heard the violin start, the panicked *tap-tap-tap* of my heart calmed to a steady thrum. *She was here. She was coming.* One more glance over at Roone with his wide smile, and my brother, who gave me a full grin this time, and I knew that I was doing this. I was excited to do this. I couldn't *wait* to do this. Penny was going to be my queen.

After everything we went through, we'd found our way to this spot, and I wasn't going to take any of it for granted. It took several moments before I saw her appear in the entrance of the church. The long Cathedral had a thousand guests seated; members of court, dignitaries from around the world, even Hollywood was represented.

Blake Security had a presence of course, some as guests, some as added security. I knew what had happened to my father and what had almost happened to Penny and me. I wasn't taking any chances.

Penny met her father and brother halfway down the aisle, and they both walked her down. I rapidly blinked away the tears. I knew she and Michael hadn't had the easiest of relationships, so to see her with her brother as a unified team... I had to admit, it choked me up.

And the look he gave his sister, one of pride and love, was something she'd always felt like she'd been missing from her brother. And given Michael's relationship with the traitor, Robert, I knew how important it was to her that he also walked her down the aisle.

The closer they got, the calmer I became. The violin playing "Ave Maria," the soprano soloist bringing the house to tears, Roone, Lucas, our thousand guests, my mother sobbing quietly in the front pew, all of it vanished.

And all I saw was Penny, my bride.

*My Queen.*

## *Penny*

*He's here.*

Okay, of course he was here. I knew he would be. I could still feel him inside me. My whole body still pulsed with need after what we'd just done. I still couldn't believe this was my life. A little over a year ago, when I'd been sent to protect him, I had no idea how my life would change.

I had no idea that this was where it would go, or who I would be. How in the hell had that happened? Who in the hell had made it happen? With each step I took forward, I could see him more clearly. He was waiting for me. His smile only broadened as I got closer. And the calm that fell over me was like nothing I'd ever felt before. There was a reason they called me 'Calamity Penny.' I was always a little too hyper, a little too crazy. But with Sebastian, everything slowed down, like he was my center. And I was walking to him, ready for a whole new life.

When I met my father and my brother, both gave me reassuring smiles. I handed Michael my bouquet and hooked my arm into my father's. And then Michael handed my father my bouquet as I hooked my other hand onto his arm. I knew it was unconventional for my father *and* my brother to give me away, but Michael and I had been working on our relationship.

We'd both been working on repairing the rift that had somehow landed us on opposing ends of the spectrum. Neither one of us had ever really understood the other. And that had cost us time, so much precious time. But it was time we had back now, and I was thrilled to have it. As we walked, I saw Robert's parents out of the corner of my eye. Well, his mother and his adoptive father, I guess.

I'd gone to see them once after Robert had been arrested, just to check on them. His father, always a kind, quiet man, hadn't had much to say. His mother had spent most of the visit sobbing. She'd apologized profusely several times.

His father had just looked mostly numb with shock. I'd wanted to offer to do something to help them in some way, but that wasn't appropriate. After all, their son had tried to kill me, so offering to help them wasn't really going to fly. And I didn't want to help Robert. I didn't so much care about what he'd tried to do to me, but I did absolutely care about what he'd tried to do to Sebastian.

For myself, I wasn't fussed. I was used to being overlooked and undervalued, sometimes by the people whom I loved the most. Robert had systematically tried to hurt me and belittle me, but again, I didn't care about that.

What I cared about was Sebastian, my husband-to-be.

The closer we got, the more at ease I felt. My mother was at the front pew, next to the Queen Mother. They were both clutching on to each other, sobbing. What was it about moms and weddings? Ariel was waiting up front, and her grin said it all. *Oh my God, we did this!*

And I wouldn't have been able to do any of it without her. But then my attention fell on Sebastian, and it stayed there. Everything else faded away.

The priest in front of us was asking something. Then I felt my father move away and hand me my bouquet as Michael let me go. They both gave me brief kisses on the cheek, and I couldn't even respond appropriately because my eyes were glued to my future husband.

His gaze swept over me. "Well worth the wait," he whispered. "You look sensational."

I couldn't help the tug of a grin over my lips. He always had a way of making me feel like I was the only person in the room. When he held out his hand, I took it, ready for our new adventure, ready to be his wife, if not so ready to be queen. Either way, together we were going to do this.

But even as the warmth and the bubble of love and light wrapped around us, I could feel the tension, the anger, the enemy at our back. Today was about us, about love, about everything Sebastian and I were to each other.

Tomorrow, we returned to the fight.

## 2

BRYNA

I KNEW what this looked like.

It looked like I was escaping.

Who the hell ran away from a wedding ball? *Me. Little Miss Crazy.* My parents had said it all; I was ungrateful, I was taking this opportunity for granted, I was looking a gift horse in the mouth. But I had to get out of there, so I was making my escape... out of a window... in my canary yellow, satin and tulle ball gown.

I wasn't entirely without guilt. I winced a little when I thought about it. My mother would be disappointed, but what else was new? My father would be furious. Again, not new.

I only came to the stupid ball because they forced me. Dad threatened to keep me from going to New York if I didn't comply. Little did he know, I was way ahead of him on that. I was already prepared for such a threat. After all, my parents and I had been dancing to this tune for years.

I had something I wanted to do, and they would dangle it as

a carrot. When I would do what was asked, *poof*; The carrot vanished or moved.

I had an internship at Turntable Records that started in New York the following week. It was unpaid and had to be done in conjunction with some business courses, but it was a dream internship. I'd worked hard to get it, and finding fresh, undiscovered musicians was a total passion for me.

The plan was to travel with my parents. But, as this was not my first rodeo, I wanted to make sure New York happened.

I stared at the window. Okay, first things first. Shoes out. And then bag, because a girl is going to need her cellphone and cash to get out of this joint. Next, bunch up the dress and climb out.

Except, the office window was slightly higher off the ground than I'd anticipated, so I had to hoist myself up to get on the sill. By the time I swung my legs around, the jump looked downright dangerous. *Suck it up, Bryna. You got this. Either that or suffer here in another situation you don't want. Take charge of your life. Or let someone else do it.*

That did it. Without looking, I jumped... and squealed.

As I fell, I tensed every muscle I had. There might have also been some expletives and silent prayer to every deity I could think of. Then I landed with a thud and a crunching of leaves and branches, with a gardenia up my—*dear Lord*. I'd normally expect dinner before anything got shoved up my ass. Was that too much to ask? Somewhere to my right, there was a giggle accompanied by a low, rolling chuckle.

Then a low, melodic voice said, "Wow, you must be desperate to leave. I didn't think the music was that bad. That's flipping Mark Ronson on the ones and twos."

From my spot in the middle of the gardenia bush, I whipped

my head around toward the male voice I'd heard. The voice was too low to belong to the giggle. *Oh hell.*

"Who the hell is out here?"

"*You're* the one sneaking out a window, and you're asking us who the hell *we* are?" The owner of the voice stepped forward dragging a pretty blonde behind him. I recognized them from the ball immediately. *He* was a friend of the king's.

One of the groomsmen or something. I didn't know his name. But the girl... I knew her name all right. I generally called her *other* names I couldn't repeat in public. Because to be fair, my ex's inability to keep his dick in his pants wasn't *her* fault.

*But her pursuing him, was.*

At any rate, her actual name was Charity Fellows, and it was no surprise to find her out here with some random hottie.

It took a moment, but I was able to prop myself into a sitting position, gardenia still lodged where the sun doesn't shine. Unfortunately, the tulle of my yellow dress was wrapped around my feet and the bushes, and I couldn't extricate myself.

"Do you need help?" the guy with the voice like sin and chocolate asked.

I slanted him a glare. "I got it."

Mr. Tall-Dark-and-Holy-Hotness leaned against one of the pillars. "Oh, sure you do. This I have to see."

Charity turned to him and said, "She's fine. Can we go? I thought you were going to show me the sights of the garden." When she said sights, her gaze drifted over his broad chest.

"I think I just threw up a little in my mouth," I muttered to myself.

"Oh, come on. This will only take a minute since she's got it."

Charity pouted. "You're serious?"

His gaze narrowed at that. Then it was like he was seeing her for the first time, and he found her lacking.

*Yeah, pick your bedfellows wisely. This one is a viper.*

When he didn't budge, she threw me a look that was all daggers and stomped off.

I tried to extricate myself, and I heard a ripping sound. "My mother is going to kill me." Naa Darfoor was the newest 'it' designer, and this dress cost a fortune, I'm sure.

"Sweetheart, do you realize that most women are trying to sneak *into* the ball? Not *out* of the ball?"

I finally just hiked the damn dress all the way up to my waist, kicked my legs over, and hopped out of the bush. I could feel his gaze skim over me as I stood. As the heat spread out from the center of my chest, I dropped my skirt, squared my shoulders, and deliberately glared at him. "Thanks for the help."

"You said you had it," he said with a wide, cheeky grin.

"Little-dicked twat monkey," I whispered under my breath.

His bark of laughter filled the still night like an unexpected firecracker.

I tried to dust myself off and tug my dress into place. For some reason it was pulling in places.

"Can I ask you a question?"

Tall and dark, with a jaw so chiseled it could be labeled as jaw porn, he raised his brows. "I get the impression I couldn't stop you if I wanted to."

He was right, he couldn't stop me. I pointed at the retreating back of Charity Fellows. "Why girls like her? I mean, those girls are obvious. Sure, she's beautiful, because well, guys are visually motivated. I get it. But she's also clearly a viper. There is nothing honorable about a girl like that. And let me guess, you didn't make the approach, she did."

He took a step back, even as his brows furrowed warily. "Well, I—"

I didn't let him finish. What was the point? "You were having a glass of champagne, enjoying the festivities, thanking God that it wasn't you who'd gotten married today, and she sidled on up and, and what? What could she possibly have said that made you instantly think, 'Hey, let's go out to the gardens and bone like minxes?'"

Then he did the unexpected. He laughed. A sharp crack of laughter that transformed his face and make him look younger, more approachable, less smug, arrogant, and charming.

I hated that word, *charming*. To me, it meant liar. Blatant, bald-faced, saying one thing to your face while doing another kind of liar. Heartless.

But with the moonlight beaming down on his face while he laughed unashamedly, he was a gorgeous man, who looked... amazing. If I hadn't been so mad, I might have been awestruck for a moment, even though I knew better than to be struck by how handsome someone was.

"I mean, let me guess, she offered to show you a good time and do something that no one had ever done for you before? I hate to break it to you, but really there's only like a set playlist."

He chuckled then. His gaze was full of—I don't know. Was that wonder? Or maybe he thought I was insane. He was examining me like he'd never seen someone like me before. Or he'd just never seen anyone with a brain before. Yeah, that was more likely it. "Oh my God. Are you like this all the time? Because this is awesome."

I blinked. "Awesome? You think it's awesome that I've clocked that you're completely ruled by your hormones?"

He shrugged. "Well, I am a guy. I'm sure you've met one or two?"

"Boy, have I ever. But I just want to know what makes men susceptible to girls like *that*, when you have perfectly nice girls running around doing good things, being good people, trying to be all things for all people?"

He seemed to chew that over for a moment. Then he scrubbed his hand over the light scruff on his jaw. "Honestly, she's crazy. Guys know that girls like that are up for anything. Absolutely *anything*. It doesn't matter how much you polish them up, ball gown or not, beautifully coiffed or not, there's something crazy in their eyes. She's not the kind of girl you marry or settle down with. She's the kind of girl you'd take out to the garden at a palace and see just how crazy she is. It's that walk on the wild side." He glanced back to a retreating Charity. "The problem with girls like that is that sometimes they have the tendency to be more crazed than you can handle. It's dangerous. But that's part of the appeal. To walk the tightrope and see how far you can go before you fall off or get a bunny boiled. You get the idea."

I stared at him. "So, it's the danger aspect?" I was genuinely curious.

He shrugged and nodded. "Sorry to break it to you. I know you're probably looking for some deeper meaning. But guys like the danger. It's not like we can run out and tussle with a saber-toothed tiger. There are better ways to get your kicks and your adrenaline rushes, but women? Women are the easiest."

I stared at him. So, my life was where it was at because men liked danger? I didn't even have any way to respond to that. "You know what? Whatever. Danger *this*."

I went back to the bush and grabbed my purse and my

shoes. I had to use part of my dress to wipe my shoes off, and I could see the dirt marring the gorgeous canary fabric. I really did love the color.

*There's work to be done. You don't get to play princess.* And then I was stomping off toward the garden. Unfortunately, Mr. Tall-Dark-and-Totally-Worth-a-Bone followed me.

"Where are you off to in such a hurry?"

"None of your business."

"Well, considering you were sneaking out of the wedding reception, and nobody in their right mind who was invited to party with royalty does that, I have to assume that you're up to no good, which means that you're maybe a spy. Or," he smirked at me then lifted a brow, "you're a thief. If so, you have the worse egress route in the history of man."

"A thief?" I stopped and glared at him. My eyes were round, and my mouth hung open. "I've never stolen anything in my life, thank you very much."

The corner of his lips tipped up in a wry smile. "So say all thieves when they get caught."

He jogged to catch up with me as I kept on stomping. Where the hell was the parking lot? Was it that far away?

"I'm serious, what did you steal? Please tell me it was something good. I have been missing a really good lift lately. Diamond necklace?"

I glared at him and ignored his chattering as I made my way out of the garden.

"Tell me, was it a brooch? I'll bet it was something where you can pop the diamonds right out and you wouldn't even need a loupe."

I frowned. "What the hell are you talking about?"

His gaze slid over me again then finally met mine. "You're not a thief."

"Give the man a cookie. He's a genius. Of course, I'm not a thief. Who would dare steal from the king? You know there's a rumor that they have dungeons here, right?"

He shook his head. "They don't."

"Oh yeah? Then where do you think they're keeping the traitor?"

Everyone knew what had happened last year. One of the Royal Guard had launched a plot to kill King Cassius and Prince Sebastian. All because he thought he could somehow take the throne for himself. He'd been successful in killing King Cassius, but Prince Sebastian was saved, all thanks to his Royal Guard, Penny. I wasn't a romantic, but the whole idea of a Royal Guard saving the wayward prince then falling in love... I wasn't immune. That was a fairy tale I could get behind.

The rumor was that Robert Sandstorm was one of the missing royal heirs. There had been rumors for years that the former king, Roland, had illegitimate children. He'd been a bit of a womanizer. It was part of the reason he'd abdicated the throne. There were too many restrictions to being king.

The Regents Council had passed a law to legitimize royal heirs. Now the rumors in the islands ran rampant. Everyone claimed to be a royal now, but so far, the palace had not announced who they were. And no one had actually seen Robert after he had been arrested. Hence, the dungeon theory.

My unwanted companion scowled then. "What do you know about the traitor?"

I blinked rapidly. "What? Nothing. I know *nothing* about the traitor. I *assume* the traitor is in the non-existent dungeons, as would any would-be thief."

He sighed. "Okay, you're not a thief. But where are you going in such a hurry? And why aren't you using the front door? Are you in some kind of trouble?"

He asked a lot of questions. "It's a long, stupid story. This royal thing is just not my scene." I wasn't telling this random stranger the reason I was running. "While I'm sure that King Sebastian is great and all that jazz, I think that he's likely a product of a spoilt upbringing. I don't know the guy, but I can assume."

His brows lifted. "Oh really? Do tell."

I planted my hands on my hips. "Come on. Even you must have seen all the tabloids from before. He was running around acting like a doofus. Granted, when he met Penny, everything changed. And from what I've heard, she's pretty badass. Actually, she's one royal I wouldn't mind meeting. She's like a real person, you know?"

So, I tended to a little excited when I talked about the future queen. She was like a hero. First of all, she didn't need any guy to save her. She'd been the one to save *him* because she was a Royal Guard. Okay, *had* been a Royal Guard.

There was speculation about whether or not she would stay in the Royal Guard or serve in some kind of advisory capacity. As queen, she would obviously have a whole other set of duties. But I kind of liked the idea of her still being Royal Guard. A queen with a job, a real job... in charge of protecting the islands. She was my kind of feminist hero.

Anyway, after she and the king had met, that had been lights out for her. And, even though I despised romances, it was sweet. Then she'd saved his life, and they'd uncovered his murder plot together. God, she was everything I ever wanted to be. Just as soon as I figured myself out.

The guy in front of me laughed. "Wow, you are incredible."

I scrunched my nose. "Why do you say that?"

"You should see the way your eyes light up when you talk about Penny. She's like your 'she-ro' or something."

"You know, when you're referring to her, you can just say *hero*. You don't have to feminize it up or something."

He held up his hands. "Easy does it. Where are you headed in such a rush?"

"I feel like I already said it's none of your business. Besides, stranger danger."

"I promise you, I don't bite." His teeth glided over his lower lip. "Unless you ask *real* nice."

I lifted a brow as I slid him a get-real glance. "Seriously?"

He blinked in surprise then shrugged. "That usually works."

On who? *You. It works on you.* My lady parts started pulsing. "Does it? Well, you can stop it. Seems I'm immune."

The corner of his lips tipped up. And I will admit it was sexy... if you liked that sort of thing.

He clutched a hand over his heart. "You wound me."

I couldn't help but laugh. "I would only believe that if I somehow discovered that you had a heart, Tin Man."

"Ouch." But he said it with a laugh.

I eyed him again. There was something familiar about him. I couldn't place it though. Did he go to the university here? Is that where I recognized him from? "Aren't you going back to the party?" Having him follow me was a little disconcerting.

He shrugged. "I'm just not one for these kinds of parties. No one in there is *real*. You're the first real person I've met all night."

"How do you know I'm real?"

He laughed. The sound was low and rumbling, and it

poured over me like sin and bad judgment mixed in with chocolate and topped with whipped cream. "Well, for starters, I caught you climbing out of the window. None of the debutants in there would dare mess up their makeup or their nails or risk their pretty dresses. So, you're at least a real person. Now, how about you tell me your name?"

I shook my head. "Not a chance. Sorry, see you around."

I took a left, sure I was headed toward the parking lot, but then I heard the chuckling behind me. I turned around and glared at him. "Just what are you laughing at?"

"Are you trying to get to the parking lot?"

"Yes, if you really must know."

The laughter only deepened. "You realize you exited the *South* Tower, right? Parking is the other way."

I blinked at him. "No. No. No. No. I left the ballroom, I made a left, then I made the other right, and then –" *Oh shit.* I'd been in a hurry and I hadn't gotten my original bearings right. I *was* in the South garden, for the love of Christ. He was right. I yanked off my shoes again. I could go faster if I didn't have to avoid the gravels in my heels. The only problem with that idea was that I was *barefoot* on gravel. *Awesome.* "You don't have to laugh, you know."

His chuckle had turned to a full belly laugh as he clutched his hand around his middle and doubled over. "I'm sorry. It's just your face, your expression..."

"Jackass."

"Oh, come on. Play nice. I can give you a short cut."

"A short cut? Why would I trust you?"

He shrugged. "That's the thing about trust and faith. It's sort of a blind thing. Do you want the short cut or not?"

I had no choice but to follow him. "Fine, but first, what's

your name? I'm going to text my friend, just in case you turn out to be a kidnapper or murderer or something. At least my bestie is going to have your name."

"Lucas. I'm Lucas Newsome."

I sighed. "Fine. Let's go Lucas."

He grinned at me, and I was temporarily stunned by his smile.

"So, now that we're friends, is this a good time to tell you the back of your dress is stuck in your thong?"

👑

*Lucas...*

Money, money everywhere, and not a bauble to steal.

I downed my scotch, and man did that go down smooth. My brother had fantastic taste. I leaned back against the balcony, the ocean breezes wafting the scent of hibiscus around me, the lapping waves just off in the distance making me long for the warm, azure blue water.

Had the brunette found her way to wherever she was going? The look on her face and the fury in her eyes when I'd told her about her dress... the thought of it made me smile. She was a sassy pain in the ass, and what a fine ass it was.

I watched Sebastian and Penny glide over the dance floor. He looked happy, like that bone-deep kind of happiness. Meanwhile, I was desperately trying to avoid the one thing that would make *me* happy... or at least feel more like myself.

*Stop thinking about the jewels.*

My brain flashed to the brunette with the wide dark eyes and the pouty, kissable mouth. That yellow fabric had glowed against her tanned skin. It made her skin look luminescent. Alas, this line of thinking was no more helpful. I'd blown my shot at something quick and dirty earlier to chase the brunette, so better not to be horny right now.

The jewels on display were a good distraction,

Gauging the value of things was a hard habit to break. All around me, all I saw was the obvious wealth displayed in pompous fashion. Not necessarily by Sebastian, but by the other members of the court who wanted to show off and impress the king.

*The king...*

The king, how was he my brother?

When all of this went down, he was just some guy.

It was surreal. Fast forward a year, and I'm co-best man at his wedding, and a goddamn prince. *From pauper to prince... never to go back again.*

The events of the last year had been shocking and devastating. I'd found out I had a brother and a father I'd never known. Then I lost that father, and that brother of mine happened to point out that he was a prince and that I was a prince too. It was all a little head spinning.

Thanks to a little plot to murder the family, it was still a secret to the rest of the world that I was one of the 'lost royals,' as the press was calling us. Everyone was under a gag order until we were able to locate our sister. After the murder of our father, Sebastian wasn't taking any risks.

Robert Sandstorm, Penny's ex, had been arrested. Prince Ashton had been exiled. But Sebastian knew there were others involved.

Out of nowhere, I heard someone say, "And how is the would-be prince?"

I worked hard to school my response before slanting a

glance at the pudgy, ruddy older man to my left. He was around fifty years old, with thinning hair, big, wide blue eyes, and rosy cheeks that looked like maybe he drank too much, or like the sun didn't agree with him.

There was a Rolex on his wrist, and he also wore diamond cuff links and one hell of a diamond pin on his lapel. All in all, he was walking around with a hundred and fifty to two hundred grand, easy.

*Stop it. You don't do that anymore.*

No. No, I didn't. Nowadays, I didn't need to steal to survive. Nor did I need to steal to keep my asshole stepfather from beating the shit out of my mom. It wasn't like I was addicted to it or anything. The thrill, the rush, I didn't need that in my life. My life was fucking great. I was a newfound prince.

"Lord Dominic Tressel, right?"

His brows lifted. "You're very good with names, young man."

"Yes, well, I have been getting tutoring." That was bullshit. I remembered all names. It was a basic rule. *Know your mark.* Know who they are. Know who they surround themselves with.

When Sebastian had given me the list of everyone who would be at the Regents Council meeting, I'd done my homework. Not so I could rob them, because I didn't do that anymore, but just so I could have all the information about them.

Lord Dominic's net worth was just over two million dollars. His father before him had lost most of the family fortunes to gambling, but Tressel managed to recover some of it. It seemed that the son had spent most of his years trying to make up for his father's losses. He clawed his way up, made the right alliances, and really worked his father's Regents Council seat to his advantage.

"I don't consider myself a prince yet, or even at all. I don't really care about that."

Tressel chuckled as if I'd said the funniest thing in the world. "Oh, come on now, my boy, *everyone* cares. Those who claim not to are kidding themselves. But you know, considering all the ugliness of the last few months, I'd say it's wise to not be quite so open about your ambivalence. I'd like you to remember that I voted for you."

I lifted a brow. Where was this going? "Yes, I remember."

"I'm not usually one for commoners, but it was what King Cassius wanted. It was what Sebastian wanted."

I worked to keep the chill out of my voice. "I think you mean *King* Sebastian."

His brows lifted more. "Yes, yes of course." He continued as if he had no clue about his casual classism or disrespect. "So, it was a wise choice. I just hope that you can live up to who His Majesty thinks you are."

My teeth gnashed. "Well, all I can ever be is myself."

"Right. But you know, your past... that business with your mother. Despite knowing all that, I voted for you."

Like douche-face here had done me a favor. "Well, I guess this is the part where I say I appreciate it?" *Instead of saying, you're a prick.*

"Good, good, because in this palace, you need allies. And I would like to be one of yours. You're scrappy."

"Forgive me, but you hardly know me." If he did, he'd call the guard to put me in those dungeons everyone talked about.

"Oh, but you and I were the same. Abandoned, left to forge our own way, really coming from nothing, making it up, and clawing our way to the top, by hook or by crook. I like it."

A sense of unease rolled through me. He thought *we* were

the same? Having to buy off-the-rack instead of bespoke was hardly the same as doing just about anything to eat. I guess he didn't know that I actually knew his history. He had stepped on people to get where he was, made business dealings that ruined other people, just so he could get ahead. We weren't the same at all. "Well, thank you for the vote of confidence, I suppose. If you'll excuse me."

He placed a hand on my arm, and I glanced down at it as he spoke, "Just realize, one day I may need a favor from you, just like you and your brother needed a favor from me. I expect that I can count on your support?"

*Douche bag.*

I turned and faced him. It happened so quickly, I almost couldn't believe myself. I patted him on the arm while I was shaking one hand. I palmed his Rolex. Yes, okay fine. I palmed the cufflinks too. They were *diamonds*. I could sell those easily.

"Yes of course. Just as long as it's in my brother's best interest."

"Always. Long live the King. This is a round table here. We're all on the same side. All we want is what's best for the Winston Isles."

"Of course." As if I didn't see that all he wanted was what was best for him. I'd known men like him my whole life. They were takers. "Nice to have an ally in the palace," I said through gritted teeth.

"Yes of course. Allies, absolutely." He grinned, as if he were really believing what I was pitching him.

As I made it back into the reception, I stroked the Rolex in my pocket, somehow feeling a little bit better now that I'd let some of my old self out.

*You shouldn't have done it.* The guy had it coming.

I headed out of the ballroom. I didn't see Sebastian and Penny anymore, but it was likely they were surrounded by well-wishers at the high table. I made it down the corridor and headed toward the guest cottages, needing to be alone for a moment. But before I made it down the hall of the Rose Tower, Sebastian stepped out of nowhere.

I stopped short. "Hey. Um, shouldn't you be pulling off a garter or something?"

My brother held his hand out. "Hand them over."

My brows lifted. "What?"

He waited patiently.

I could certainly wait him out. I tried to stall. "Where's Penny?"

"My *wife*, pointed out that you were with Lord Tressel outside on the balcony. I know the guy is a douche bag, and likely he said something to piss you off. I happen to know what you do when you get pissed-off, so I want you to hand them over."

He had me there. I sighed and rolled my eyes. "Come on Sebastian, he was a dick."

"I know. But you still can't steal from him. Right now, he's an ally on the Regents Council. I can't get rid of him."

"You know," I said, as I fished in my pocket for the Rolex, "he used the same word. *Ally*."

"Yes, well, I suspect we have different definitions of the word." He inclined his head. "Follow me."

I followed him, our polished wingtips clacking on the marble floors that led to his office. When Sebastian was seated, he stared at the Rolex. "God, he really is a dick. I wish I didn't have to give this back."

I chuckled still stroking the cufflinks in my pocket. "I know, right?"

"Listen Lucas, everything is going to change soon."

"I know. You don't have to tell me that. I'm preparing for it."

Sebastian leaned back in his seat. "I know, but you can never really prepare for it."

I shrugged. "Well, good thing I'm a survivor."

He nodded and sat back. "I want the cufflinks too, little brother."

My mouth hung open. "How did you even know? My lift was clean."

Sebastian grinned. "I might have just met you a year ago, but I know you well. Also, I want to ask a favor."

I sat back and waited. What could a king need from me? "It's yours."

"You know the Artistic Trust that Penny and I started?"

I nodded. "Yeah. It's made Penny so happy. Every time I see her, she's trying to get me to see some new artists."

Sebastian's smile was fleeting, but it was so full of love and hope, it even made my heart ache a little bit. Would I ever look at anyone like that? *Not likely. You would need to open your heart first.*

"Yeah. Same for me. Except half the time, she's showing me someone's work on the laptop, or trying to show me some Instagram photo."

"Yeah, that sounds like her. What do you need?" Sebastian shifted in the chair. It was the first sign I'd ever seen from him indicating he was nervous about something. This was his world. I was the interloper. What was making him so anxious? "What's up, man? You're making me twitchy. You know what happens when I get twitchy. You can't afford to lose the crown jewels right now."

He narrowed his gaze at me even as his lips twitched. "I'd like you to audit it. I want to make you a director. When you get back to New York, I know you've still got a couple of classes that you're finishing up, but I'd really like you to take over a full audit of the trust on the charity end. The last set of numbers looked low to me. I'm not sure, but I want a full audit. Something is missing there. Either that, or the charity initiative isn't working the way that we'd hoped, and we need to reconfigure some things. But I need someone I can trust to look after mine and Penny's interests. Maybe I'm the king now, but I am and always have been an artist first, and I really want to give opportunities to other artists. I want this to work. I obviously can't be in New York right now with everything that's happening here, and I'm certainly not letting Penny out of my sight. And well, honestly, I plan on keeping her naked for the foreseeable future."

I scrunched up my face and made a gagging sound. "Gross. Seb, I know what you're asking, but you want a con man to look after your money? I don't think that's the best choice."

He was my brother, and I loved him. I wanted to do something for him, but I couldn't do *this*. If something wasn't right, fingers would point directly at me, and in some cases, they should. But I just didn't want to fuck up anything for him.

"Just tell me you'll think about it. Maybe you are the only one I can trust."

I shook my head. "Send Roone. Hell, send Penny's brother Michael. He'd do anything for you, considering." Penny's brother felt more than a little guilty he'd been best friends and lovers with the traitor and hadn't seen his duplicity.

"Yeah, but firstly, Michael is a Royal Guard. And secondly, he doesn't have a triple major in international relations, poly sci, and economics."

I opened my mouth to argue, but then I snapped it shut. "Yeah, you have a good point there." The thing was, I'd picked those majors because they all sounded sort of like cons in and of themselves. They were ways to put my best skills to use, but not like this. I didn't want to be the face of anything for my brother. Because eventually, my past was going to catch up to me, and there would be shame associated with it. "What about, Roone? Roone is an option. He went to university. He's smart."

"Yes, he did, and he majored in political science, but Roone *has* another job."

"What could be more important? If this matters to you, then Roone should be doing it."

He sighed. "Roone will be your personal guard."

I sat up straighter. "Say what?"

He nodded and put up a hand before I could even argue further. "No arguments. At the end of the day, while we still haven't officially named you as a crown prince, the truth is you are. And there is still a threat out there, so, you're getting a guard. Like it or not. And in this case, two, because I know you."

I sputtered. "You don't know shit. I do *not* need a guard." Most of all I didn't want someone watching my every move. Roone was my boy. We were thick as thieves, mates, as he would say, but I didn't need him watching me and reporting back to my big brother.

Sebastian sighed. "Look, they're not watching you, or babysitting you, or any of that shit. It's not like that. They're strictly there for your security. As a matter of fact, they work *for* you. Look at it that way. They'll only report back if there are any security threats, and that's all. I've made it clear I want nothing else reported back to me. I have zero intention of spying on you."

I breathed a little easier then, but I still felt the tightening noose around my neck. "Look, I appreciate it, but I don't need protection. And this job, like I said, my past is going to come back to haunt us at some point. You don't want me in any position that's going to embarrass you."

"Just think about it. In the interim, I'll do what I can from here, but—" He chewed his bottom lip. "Okay, truth?"

I nodded.

"Tressel. The very same man you just lifted some cufflinks off of. He's on the board. He manages the charity donations. I just—I need someone looking over his shoulder. And I figured..." his voice trailed.

"It takes a thief to catch a thief?" I wasn't sure how I felt about that.

"Not a thief, necessarily. But if anyone can *spot* a thief, it would be you. Besides, the Tressel thing is a sensitive situation. He's on the Council. He voted in favor of you. We still want his final signature once we locate our sister, so it's going to be tricky."

I shook my head. "I want to do this for you. I do." I leaned forward, silently begging him to see the sincerity in my eyes, if he even knew what sincerity was. "I don't want to be the one responsible for bringing embarrassment to you. This whole thing is already uncomfortable. I just want to keep a low profile, finish my classes, and see what happens next."

Sebastian's gaze searched mine. And it was a little like looking in a mirror. From the pictures I'd seen, he looked a lot like our father. He looked like his Mom too, but there was definitely something about us that said we were brothers. He nodded slowly. "All right, I'll put your answer on ice then. Give it some thought. Get back to New York. Get started on school and stuff, and just let me know. We're not in any major rush, but, you know..."

"But you are."

He grinned at me. "There is something else too."

"Oh my God, Sebastian, you keep asking a former con man for favors. Do you realize that this is how you come to owe me? And then I come and ask for the crown jewels or something."

He chuckled low. "This one is right up your alley."

"Fine, lay it on me."

"It's Tressel's daughter, Bryna. She's going to be in New York starting an internship. He knows you live there, and he wants you to look out for her."

I frowned. "Wait, if he sits on the Board, how is he not in New York?"

Sebastian shook his head. "I know they keep a residence there. His wife goes back and forth a lot, but he's based here, mostly. If you ask me, I think he's trying to get another foothold in the palace. For now, I'm willing to let him have it. You don't have to do much, just babysit the girl."

"You're letting me babysit a *female*?"

He shook his head. "You can be cool, right?"

"Seb, I just lifted about two hundred grand in jewels at your wedding. Do you really think I'm the one you want, A, managing money, and B, looking after someone's tempting daughter?"

"You don't know she's tempting."

"Does she have tits?" I was far more discerning than that,

honestly, but, I did have a reputation. And I wanted to make sure he was entirely aware of it.

He chuckled low. "Listen, just try to think all of it over. Can you do that for me?"

After what I'd just done, I owed him. I nodded slowly. When I didn't say anything else, he continued. "Listen, you are not your past. Sooner or later, you're going to realize that."

He had far too much faith in me. "I'll think about it, okay?"

"Okay, that's all I can ask."

I could see the disappointment etched on his brow. But I knew I was doing him a favor by declining. I was a fucking liability. Eventually, he'd see it too. "Can I go now?"

Sebastian shook his head. "I'm going to take that lapel pin you took off of him too."

I sighed and handed over the pin and the cufflinks. "Way to ruin a perfectly good night." I was unaccustomed to feeling a twinge of shame. "I guess you're regretting having me here now."

"On the contrary, if I had half your skill, I would have robbed half the people in there blind by now. None of them deserve their money, but when you're a king, you don't do such things." He chuckled. "Try to stay out of trouble, okay? Don't do something I wouldn't do."

I shrugged. "I'll try. But remember, I'm not a real prince yet, right? So far, I'm just the royal bastard, so I'm not supposed to behave."

Sebastian half grinned at that and said, "Lucas..."

I gave him my best smile. "Okay, okay. I got it."

It was going to be a hell of a fight against my instincts to behave. But for my brother I would certainly give it a shot.

⚜

## *Bryna*

When I arrived at the ferry landing, I found Jinx pacing by her car.

"Where were you?"

I adjusted my corset and tried to set my boobs back into place. "Long story. Sorry. Am I too late?"

"You just missed one ferry, but you're in luck. There is another one leaving at eleven and you can catch a shuttle that will take you to the charter flight."

"Thank fucking God. I jumped out of the wrong window. That's why I'm late. Then there was this guy, and he was with Charity. And I totally lost it. Then I had my dress in my thong. I was a mess."

Jinx barely suppressed a giggle. "We don't have time right now, but I want that story."

I took the duffel she handed over to me and quickly climbed into the backseat of her car as I unzipped it. I unhooked the side of my corset and slipped it right off, sighing with relief as the restrictive material fell away. I was in my bra, long sleeved T-shirt, jeans, and comfortable tennis shoes in no time at all. "Oh my God, I've never felt more like myself than right in this moment."

From the front seat, Jinx laughed. "You're insane. Listen, as your best friend, it is my duty to ask this, so hear it with love."

Before she could even open her mouth, I sighed. "Jinx, I know what you're going to say."

She lifted a brow. "Oh yeah? What am I going to say?"

"What you're going to say is, 'Bryna I'm thrilled that you got the internship, but maybe this is overkill.'"

Jinx's lips twitched. I could tell she wanted to smile, but she didn't. She kept a stern face as I continued. "I must tell you that your plan is foolhardy. It's not like your parents won't know where you went, and they'll not only be pissed, but worried, too. And as your father has connections to the palace, it could be an international manhunt."

This time, she didn't grin, but furrowed her brows. "Fine. Okay, but I would have said, *incident* instead of manhunt."

"Well, can't it be both?"

She sighed. "Look, I'm down to ride or die, but you know they will flip out. Why can't you just talk to them?"

It was my turn to lift my brows.

"Look, all I'm saying is this seems extreme, even for you."

"I'm *not* the extreme one."

"No, I know you're not. And I know that the parental units have gone a little far in the past."

My mouth fell open. "Far? You mean like Braxton and the forced-engagement thing?" I couldn't even think about my ex without the sharp edges of rage closing in.

Jinx winced. "Yeah, okay, that was dirty."

I shook my head. "Sometimes, I swear I'm adopted, you know. I don't even look like them."

"Oh my God, back to this? You're not adopted."

I sighed. It was my favorite fantasy, that somewhere my real parents were looking for me and somehow, I'd been sucked in by these pod people of a family.

Yes, my parents were mostly good people. They just had a different set of values and didn't seem to understand mine.

They would do anything, and I meant *anything* to get and stay on good terms with the royal family.

My grandfather on my father's side had squandered our family fortune and lands. My father had worked tirelessly to get some of that back and to keep his stature. He still had his useless title, but these days, 'Lord' didn't mean much. Not unless you had the money to go with it.

He'd married my mother for her wealth, but my grandparents had been shrewd, securing her money away in trust funds, upon trust funds, upon trust funds, and she still only received a monthly stipend. They even bypassed her entirely and gave me my inheritance independently, as if they knew what my parents would do with that money.

"Jinx, I hear you. I really do. And I appreciate that you're looking out for me, but I need to do this. I will die if I am trapped in this gilded palace of mine. I need out. Either you're with me, or you're not."

Jinx didn't even blink. "You know I'm always with you. Let's get you on that ferry and to the airport. NYC awaits."

# 3

BRYNA

SWEAT TRAILED down the nape of my neck, all the way down my back, barely slowing at my bra, and still I dragged the suit-case up one more step, then another, then another. It was unusually warm for September in New York. Beads of sweat rolled off my temples, under my tank top, and down into my boobs, pooling right there in that catch of the bra right where it clasped in the front. My tank top clung to me, and my hair matted and curled on my exposed skin.

This heatwave in New York was really no joke when you lived in a sixth-floor walk-up.

I'd already dragged my suitcase up three flights of stairs. I had three more to go. How hard could this be? I could do it, right? When I arrived, I was so excited, but the damned elevator was out due to a brown-out or something, and so was the air conditioner. Cue me, sweating my tits off.

'New York,' they said, 'Follow the fun and adventure.' All I wanted to do right then was lie down in an ice box and cool the hell off. But this was my adventure, like it or not, and I was free.

No one would tell me what to do or who I was supposed to be. I was on my own, and it was going to be great. Just as soon as I got into my apartment.

I let myself in the front door, vibrating with excitement despite my sweaty state. My roommate and I had been talking through email and chat for three weeks. Her name was Charlotte. She'd grown up in upstate New York with fairly well-off parents, but she was also looking for freedom and excitement. I was pretty sure the two of us were going to get on like a house on fire.

Unfortunately, when I unlocked the door to my apartment, all I heard was a deep, low, sharp bark. I immediately jumped back and flattened myself against the wall in the hallway.

"Oh, Rufus, stop it."

I peered at the short, pixie-haired girl in the door way. This was *not* Charlotte. Charlotte said she was 5'10". In her picture, she was a blue-eyed blonde. Who the hell was this?

"Who are you?" I squeaked out.

"I'm Dana."

"Where is Charlotte?" Maybe I was a little paranoid, but this was just the kind of stunt my parents would pull.

"Oh, there was some kind of roommate switch-up or something. That girl, Charlotte or whoever, her program tuition wasn't paid for the term, so they shuffled me in here. And considering I almost didn't have student housing, I'm lucky as hell. This is Rufus." There had been a block of residences that had been reserved for intern housing close to campus and my new job. The program was run in conjunction with the NYU graduate program. The flat had cost a pretty penny, but it was totally worth it. Or would be without the killing machine in the doorway.

I stared at the massive Great Dane she held by the collar. "Um, you have a dog."

"Yeah. Look, don't narc me out, okay? He rarely ever barks. He mostly thinks he's a lap dog. I didn't have anyone who could look after him for the next month until my mother can take him. That's it, then he'll be off. I swear."

"It's fine. I just—he's huge." And also, I wasn't really a dog person. Not so much didn't like, but more terrified. I'd been bitten when I was six, and still had the damn mark on my ankle. Yes, the dog was a Chihuahua, but it was *vicious*. The stupid Duke of Essex's daughter, Bridget, had let the dog run amuck. Ever since then, I hadn't really warmed to man's best friend.

Dana waved me in. "It's okay. I have him under control. It's fine, okay? Just don't tell."

*Breathe, relax.* It was fine. Control what you can control. "I —I sent some boxes ahead. Do you know if they arrived?" I was still sweating and needed a cool shower.

She nodded. "Yep. Hope you don't mind, because I have Rufus, I chose the bigger room. But uh, he got into your room. Ate some of the food. And uh, destroyed some of your things."

I blinked at her. "He what?"

She shrugged as if that was the end of the conversation and continued, "It only makes sense. He's so big."

I stared after her. My instinct was to let it happen. After all, that's how I'd always been. But I'd fought for this.

Since the window jumping, I was a new person. You have to fight for what you want. No one is going to hand it to you. I wanted to do what I always did, accept it. Make do. But I took a deep breath. "I'm sorry, but no."

She frowned. "What?"

I swallowed and swiped at some sweat on my brow. Why

was it so hard to stand up for myself? Maybe if I did it more often, I'd deal with things instead of letting them fester and then blow up. *Like your engagement party.* "I said no. I paid for the bigger room, so I'd like to move into it, please. You and Rufus can figure it out. And please keep him out of my things." God, I hated to think of his monster attack teeth tearing through my clothes.

Rufus cocked his head as if he could hear me. And I would have sworn her doggy smiled at me. I shuddered.

Dana's gaze swept over me again, as if reassessing. "Fine. Whatever." She muttered over her shoulder then slammed the door to her room.

I sighed. I missed Charlotte already, but there was no way this setback was going to ruin this experience for me. I was here to find out who I was, and I was going to do that.

❧

## Lucas

'Stay out of trouble,' he'd said. 'Don't do anything I wouldn't do,' he'd said.

The thing about my brother was ever since he'd become king, he'd become a lot less fun. And yes, of course, he had to lead people now. But there was no reason why I couldn't have fun.

*What about the part where he said don't slip your security detail?*

Not that I'd slipped them exactly, but the club was crowded. Not my fault if they couldn't find me.

*That job looks really good now, doesn't it?*

The sounds of dub step pounded off the walls, making my head ache, but I was determined. I was out, and this was great. This was fun, never mind that my stupid drink cost nearly $30. And by fun, I meant I was bored out of my skull.

There was a part of me that was over this scene, bored with the endless flow of alcohol and stream of women, and the constant high of picking out a mark.

I might be a reformed bad boy, but sometimes for fun, I would still do the work of picking out the mark, the best angles, the best way to make his wallet bleed. But I never actually went through with it. Not anymore. Not since I'd walked away from my mother. It didn't mean the temptation wasn't strong, though. It didn't mean that there was no itch to go there. So when I felt the itch, I came to places like this. Places that would pretty much guarantee that I wouldn't scratch the itch. No one in here was rich, and so far, no one had been an asshole. So that meant no scratching this partic-ular itch.

It was fine though, just being out was good enough.

*Why don't you call a friend? Someone to actually kick it with?*

Yeah, that was the next problem. I had no friends. Okay fine, I had a couple, but they were just surface friends. Not a single one of them *knew* me. How was it that my brother and my body guards were the only people who actually knew the truth about me? Sometimes, I just didn't want to fake it.

"Hey, I've never seen you here before."

I turned and found a petite blonde sidled up to me on my left side. She was mostly hair, tits, and a bright white smile. A little too done, a little too obvious, but hey, she was there. And I didn't have to do any work to pick her up, so, bonus. And like I told the brunette at the wedding, there was something a little wild about her.

*She's not brunette.* Funny thing was, since the night of Sebastian's wedding, I'd been more interested in brunettes.

"Well, would you believe it if I said I was a stranger in a strange land?"

"No, of course I wouldn't believe it. You might be new here, but you're a player. I can tell."

Oh okay, I got it. It was time to dance. "Who, me?" I placed my hand on my chest and managed to fake an incredulous look. "I am shocked and insulted you would insinuate such a thing."

She giggled. "You're funny. Come on, take me to the dance floor." She stumbled on her heels, and I steadied her.

I wasn't in the mood. But, she at least kept me somewhat interested to pass the time. There's no way I wanted to go home and face the empty penthouse. Roone was just across the hall, but even he didn't know what lay deep inside. "Don't worry. I practically live in these things. I fuck in them too, just in case you were wondering."

*Jesus.* Okay then, we were doing this. Not my first choice, but I wasn't going to complain. Besides, screwing her would take my mind off of all the other shit that was looming in the distance. I had one class left that I'd missed in my third year taking time off to help my mother. Then I had to figure my shit out. Was I going back to the Winston Isles? I needed to decide. The previous plan of taking a consulting gig and making a lot of money was moot now.

The tune changed to something only slightly more recognizable. At least this song had lyrics to it, a recent pop song. Most of the time, I didn't pay attention to what was on the radio. I would just set it to some iHeart Radio rap-pop nonsense and let it play in the back ground. I didn't care that much for the most part. A lot of it sounded the same to me—some wannabe princess, shaking her ass to some tune that was catchy but not that meaningful.

The blonde shook her ass, turning around in my arms, backing up into me, making sure I could feel every swell of her curves. Yep, it would be almost too easy.

*What, now you want a challenge like the brunette?* I needed to get that girl out of my damn head before I broke and asked Sebastian to pull the security footage and tell me who she was.

We danced some more, and after a few minutes I started tugging her off the dance floor back toward the bar. I really couldn't stand this music. Note to self, no more dub step or electronic. And also, next time, find a partner who can actually dance, because Sexy-and-a-Smile, as hot as she was, couldn't move at all. Or maybe that was just the dub step. I wasn't really looking to figure it out.

"Hey, where are we going?"

"Let's head back to the bar. I'll get you a drink."

She glanced over her shoulder as if waiting for something. "Are you sure you don't want to dance anymore?"

"Yeah, I'm pretty sure. You go ahead though, if you want."

She took one of my hands in both of hers and tried to pull me back. "Please?"

I sighed. "Okay fine. One more, but then I'm probably going to get out of here."

"But the night is young. We haven't even had any fun yet."

"Yeah, tell me about it." I let myself be pulled back. It was fine. But mostly, my attention kept wandering over the crowd. And then I felt it. Like the faintest hint of a brush. But, in that moment, I knew I was light one wallet.

*Son of a bitch.*

My head snapped to the left, and I saw the guy turn and wind his way through the crowd. *Oh no you don't you fucker.* I didn't even let Miss Tits-and-Smile know where I was going. I just headed straight for him. She tried to tug me back, but I shook her off. I was irritated now that I'd slipped Roone and Marcus.

"Hey, where are you going?"

I spotted my babysitters' heads over the crowd. They'd spotted me. Neither looked pleased. I didn't even slow down, but instead I followed the guy through the throng of people toward the back of the club. In one of the darkened hallways, I made a quick move, kicking out my leg and hooking it through his legs onto one of his feet. He immediately stumbled forward, crashing to the ground. "Hey, what the hell are you doing?"

"Hand over my wallet. We don't have to do this." I couldn't even muster actual anger.

"I don't know what the fuck you're talking about. I'm just here looking for the fucking bathroom."

"No, you're not. You lifted my wallet on the dance floor. I have to tell you your pick needs work. I *felt* you. I swear, who's teaching you kids these days? Hand it over." The last thing I needed was my ID out in the wild. Not the brand new one I'd been using for the last year that called me Lucas Newsome. Or the other ID I had, the one that was from the Winston Isles. It's not like it said, 'hey, this guy is a prince,' but it did have the family crest on it, and then an in-case-of-emergency call number. I didn't need any of that shit getting out. "You have three seconds."

The guy pushed himself to his feet. "Or you'll do what?"

Or Roone and Marcus were going to be on him like white on Wonder Bread.

"I really think it's not necessary to elaborate on that. Look man, I'm not in the mood. All I'm telling you is your lifts are weak. If you really want in on the game, I have some people you can train with, but you're not going to make it very far if you keep messing up passes like that. Give my wallet back."

The guy scowled, and I could tell this was going to be a fight. To be honest, I was not looking for one. I swear to God.

The guy made his move, coming at me with a wild, pseudo hook punch. I blocked that easily enough and sent an open palm straight for his nose. He howled and staggered back.

"You broke my nose. You fucking broke my nose."

I sighed. "Plus, you suck at self-defense. Hand over the wallet."

Did he listen? Nope. The world would be a lot easier if he had. But oh no, he came at me again, this time with blood spurting out of his nose and sliding down his chin. He tried to just plain old push me then grabbed me around the waist and lifted.

I delivered a series of elbows over his shoulders and on the back of his neck. He let go quickly and staggered a little bit. *Yeah asshole, I'm not your average lightweight.*

And I wasn't. From the time I was a kid, I'd learned to fight and fight well. I refused to be deadly about it, but I knew how to defend myself. It was one of the few perks of growing up with my mother's boyfriend.

"We don't need to do this. Hand over what's mine, and you get to walk away. No harm, no foul. I won't even call the cops."

He staggered as he came for me again, and I sighed. Why couldn't he fucking listen? He came with another feeble attempt at a punch. I delivered a steady rhythm of combination, basic punches, and he went down like a sack of bricks. He groaned a little as I stepped over him.

"See, this is what happens when you fuck up. I just want you to learn this lesson right now. This was your doing. I had nothing to do with this. Next time, make better life choices."

I reached inside his jacket and found my wallet. Everything was still intact, cash, cards, fucking IDs. It seemed that the guy had been a little busy tonight because I found three other wallets, too. I considered lifting them from him, just to teach him a lesson, but hell, the kid had to eat, right? I turned to find the blonde in the middle of the hallway staring at me.

"Oh my God, what did you do to him?"

I shrugged and rolled my shoulders. "He'll live. Listen, let me take you home or something."

She looked from me to him and back to me again. "Okay, but listen, I kind of find it hot, what you just did. I thought it was really sexy. Where did you learn to fight?"

I frowned at her. Was she insane?

She started rubbing herself all over me, and look, I'm not proud of it, but it was pure adrenaline. It was coursing through my veins. And well, her tits were pretty much out. I could almost see nipple. It wasn't my fault. I swear. But when she pressed into me, basically bringing her nipples across my chest, I responded.

I lifted her up and planted her on the filthy counter nearby. My tongue slid into her mouth, and the adrenaline that led to most bad decisions of my life basically took over. Yes, I was making out with some random chick I would most certainly never be calling again in the back hallway of a club. Yeah, pretty princely, I know. And so much for me worrying about this girl's virtue, because she was basically taking off my shirt, hands all over my skin, cold, a little bit clammy, but part of me didn't care because this at least was familiar. I felt like me, the *old* me. Her thumbs brushed over my nipples, and I shivered before murmuring, "Let's get out of here."

She moaned and nodded her head. "Let me just head to the bathroom. I'll be right back."

I nodded and leaned back against the wall, giving her space to shimmy around me.

*What are you doing?* All in all, a really good question. But right then, I didn't care because I just wanted to drown it all out. It was only after she'd been gone several minutes that I looked at my watch. Hell, she'd been in there ten minutes already. I knew the lines to girls' bathrooms were ridiculous, but come on.

And then it struck me. I patted myself down for my wallet. It was still there, but when I opened it, I cursed.

My IDs were intact, but the cash was gone.

*Son of a bitch, I'd been played.*

By *her?* I started after the petite blonde headed for the front door, but a meaty hand pressed on my chest and forced me backward. Only then did I look up.

*Roone.* At 6'3", the guy was barely an inch taller than me, but he had more muscle. If I wanted, I could evade him, but it was going to cause a ruckus, which despite the contrary, I really didn't want. "Let go."

He shook his head and rolled his eyes. He leaned around me to look at the guy on the ground. "That your handiwork?"

I shrugged. "He started it."

"Mature, mate. Real mature."

## 4

ONE WHOLE DAY in my new life and I was ecstatic, despite the evil roommate and the monstrous attack dog. She hadn't been kidding when she said Rufus had gotten into my things. He'd eaten bags of plantain chips. And the home-made marmalade. He'd torn through my underwear and shredded it. How was I supposed to live with him for a month?

The doorbell rang, and Dana didn't budge. She just sprawled on the bed. She was probably still pissed I'd insisted on taking my room. Rufus though, barked like someone had taken his bone. When I opened the door, I stopped short. The ice box I'd been begging for yesterday was on my doorstep.

"Mom? What are you doing here?"

My mother gave me her best narrowed-gaze, pursed-lip expression. "Did you really think you were going to move to New York for a grand adventure and we wouldn't notice?"

I shifted on my feet, because, yes, sort of.

She waved a hand and rolled her eyes. "My God, darling. You always over exaggerate everything. This is not some nefarious scheme to keep you from living your life. Get your things. Let's go. You're not staying here." My mother slid her gaze over my shoulder to Rufus, who Dana had apparently wrangled. "And is that a dog?"

"Mom—"

"Never in my day would they have allowed a dog in a flat."

My mother had gone to Vassar for two whole years before she married my father. She never let anyone forget it. Vassar was an excellent educational establishment. She was not thrilled that NYU was my choice for post-grad school. Maybe she would actually have let me go to Vassar. "Mom, I'm not going anywhere. This is my choice. Besides, the money grandpa left me pays for housing too, so I don't need to live in the apartment you rented for me."

I should have been used to my mother's best withering glance by now. I called it withering glance number seven. It was cold, direct, not meant to make you cry exactly, but still conveyed her extreme displeasure. It was a full pursed lip and a narrowed gaze, but not too narrow. And then she'd hold it on you, waiting for you to change your mind. Except this time, I didn't change my mind. I just stared right back at her.

"Stop being stubborn, young lady. Get your things."

I folded my arms. "I'm not being stubborn. Mom, you tried to force me into an engagement with the same guy who broke my heart by cheating on me. There he was as my plus one at the king's wedding, and you guys acted like nothing had happened."

She shifted on her feet. "Do you know how embarrassed we were when you didn't return to the table? Braxton was willing to take you back after the unpleasant mess. I mean—"

I cut her off. "Take me back?" Yes, I had taken all his clothes, put them on his parents' lawn, and set them on fire. But

I'd caught him screwing two of my would-be bridesmaids. Charity had been one of them.

Then I'd posted the dick pics he'd sent to Charity's phone on the projector at our rehearsal dinner before dumping him in front of everyone.

I'd blurred out most of them, but it was still apparent who it was in the photo. I'd just started to get over that whole embarrassment. Seeing him at the ball had been the last straw.

"If I leave here without you, you'll be making a big mistake."

I stood my ground. "Then I guess I'm making a mistake. I love you, but I'm not coming with you."

Her lower lip trembled. God help me if she actually cried. I don't think my mother had any teardrops left. But I guess we'd see.

There were no tears though. Perhaps the quivering lip was more wrath than sadness. As in, how dare I defy her? Well, it had just happened, so God help me. The problem was once I started standing up for myself, it was impossible to go back.

⚓

*Lucas...*

"Remember that thing that I said about not giving your security a slip, and keeping a low profile?"

Sebastian's face filled the video screen on my laptop.

He clearly wasn't thrilled. But, I'd kind of figured that with the way Roone looked.

"Yeah, about that... I didn't exactly mean to give Roone the slip. I mean, he just couldn't keep up." That was weak. I knew it. "Like on a scale from 1 to 10, exactly how mad are you?"

He sighed. "Lucas, this isn't one of those times where you

can flash your cheeky smile and get away with it. This is bloody important."

*He was right, but it still chafed.* "Look, no one even knows I'm here. No one knows who I am, it's not that big of a deal."

"So you, little brother, are telling me, the *king*, what is and isn't a big deal?"

I snorted. "Well, look who became a pompous asshole the moment he became king."

"Shut it. I'm trying to keep you alive."

I sighed. "Look, I get it. I'll be more careful."

"More careful won't cut it. You went to a bar and got yourself fooled by a little slip of a thing with some gigantic tits?"

I slid a glance toward Roone, who chuckled to himself and became suddenly very interested in his magazine. I wasn't sure I liked him anymore. "Look that, was unfortunate. I'm pretty sure that she and her boyfriend were in on it together, the one-two punch, so to speak. They were working as a team."

"And do you realize that if the turd had gotten your ID, it could have been really bad? That quiet life *you* wanted wouldn't be possible. It would make your protection difficult."

*So dramatic.* "I mean, it doesn't even say anything. It just has some crest on it."

His eyes narrowed. "Do you care? This is important. I've already lost enough family. I hope you don't mind if maybe I could enjoy my honeymoon and not worry that my brother is trying to kill himself."

*Shit.* "I'm sorry, okay? Won't happen again." He was right, but I was feeling petty.

He sighed. "Lucas, why do you do this?"

Because I was waiting for it all to come to an end. To find out I was in a dream. *You don't deserve this.* Deep down inside, I was terrified this would all disappear. If I didn't stop, my past was going to fuck up my future. I needed to change.

And not just bullshit change, *real* change. Sebastian was right. I swallowed hard. "I'm sorry. I'm committed. All in. The job, the girl, whatever you need. I'll stay with Roone and Marcus. I swear it." It was time to be the guy I wanted to be.

## 5

"So, your brother asked you to babysit a debutante?" Roone's laughter filled the tight space at Prohibition Bar as the happy hour crew rolled in.

"It's not that funny."

"Yes. Yes, it is." He slapped his palm on the ancient wood bar. "It's hilarious. He does recognize that you basically lifted nearly a quarter million dollars from Tressel, right?"

"Yeah, well, the guy was acting like a prick. He deserved it."

Roone lifted his hands. "No argument there. The guy is a full-on twat. I have been on his service more than once when there was some delegation or something. He still acts confused that I should dare to speak to the king. He's a total cunt, and a social-climbing twat at that. But now your *king* demands that you help him, so what are you going to do?"

"I don't like those words, 'demand', and 'king'. I have no king."

He chuckled. "Actually, technically you do."

"Okay fine, *technically*, I do. But more than that, Sebastian is my *brother*, and he changed the course of my life. So if he needs something, I need to figure out how the hell to get it done."

"So, you're going to do it?" He assessed me as if I'd just told him Snuffleupagus was real.

I took a sip of my beer. "I don't think I have much choice. Besides, how bad can it be?"

Roone's chuckle was more than jovial as his shoulders shook. "You have clearly not been around enough debutantes. There are the wild-child debutantes. Those are the ones who make your life miserable. They love to fuck you, fuck up your life, run around, do drugs, drink far more than they should, fuck all men at random, and you're supposed to keep them out of trouble. They are my least favorite kind of job."

My eyes went wide. "Aren't debutantes supposed to be like, boring and have sticks up their asses?"

"You haven't been around enough debutantes."

"Guess not."

"Yeah, those sticks-up-their-asses ones, they're boring mostly, going to museums and those kinds of things. But the way they look at you? Icy as hell. It'll almost make you wish for a wild-child debutante to keep things interesting."

"Oh, fantastic. Maybe I'll hope for that kind. Then I won't have to do much. She'll barely want to leave her house."

Roone shrugged. "Who knows? I've seen their daughter once or twice. I've never been on her service though. She's pretty, but she never looked particularly happy. It's like every time I've seen her, she was staring off into space thinking about something else entirely. Never had a peep or a problem out of her, though, so she's tops in my book."

"I don't know why I agreed to do this. This is stupid." I scrubbed a hand down my face.

Roone stopped with the laughing then. "You did it because Sebastian asked you. And you know he doesn't ask for much, or anything really, so you'll do it... babysit this girl, take her to a couple of bars, show her a good time. Obviously, don't show her how to pickpocket. She'll be easy-peasy."

"I fucking hope so because I—" The hairs at the back of my neck stood at attention. I don't know what it was, but something had me turning around quickly.

Out of the corner of my eyes, I swore I saw someone familiar... Someone I had shaken a long time ago. Someone from the past I'd rather forget.

Roone noticed my silence. "Mate, are you okay?"

I ignored Roone for a moment, forcing my senses to focus. Something was off. There was something or someone that wasn't supposed to be here.

I took my wallet out and slapped some cash on the table. "Let's head out."

"Fuck, I'm barely done with my beer." Roone groaned, but he quickly chugged the rest of what was left of his beer and stood with me. He then went before me and waded through the crowd at Prohibition and pushed open the heavy doors of the exit into the spring night. "All right. Let's head back."

Roone studied me for a long moment and then shrugged. His job was to keep me safe. And I was pretty sure it was also to keep me out of trouble.

Once we reached the apartment again, Roone went in first, checked the rooms, and came back out with Marcus. They had a two-bedroom apartment across the hall. It was sort of ridiculous that we took up a whole penthouse, but it worked. Marcus nodded in greeting. "What's up? I'm on already? I thought you guys would be out later."

Roone angled his thumb toward me. "That one's a light-weight. He wanted to get home and get some rest. Who is this guy?"

I rolled my eyes. "Beats me. Good night, buddy."

Roone headed into the apartment across the hall and flipped me the middle finger.

I just chuckled. Once they were both back in their apartment, I studied the exits. I knew full well they'd know if I left.

*Unless you leave your phone here.*

This might not be the smartest thing, considering I'd already had an earful from Sebastian about the whole 'murder of my father – attempted murder of my brother' thing. But I couldn't shake the feeling. Something was off. I needed to know what the hell it was, and why the hell my past was coming back for me. Two attempted lifts in a night.

That didn't happen.

I waited another hour until things were definitely quiet, and then I knocked on their apartment door and poked my head in.

Marcus was up studying. "You need something?"

"Nah, I'm good. I'm just going to run down to the vending machine. Do you want anything?"

Marcus eyed his gun and pushed to get up, but I waved him off. "Man, I'm going to the vending machine. You can watch me on my phone. I swear."

He sighed and nodded. "Okay. But seriously though, let me know when you're back."

"Sure thing." I knew things would not take very long

because I had a sinking intuition that I knew who was tailing me. Also, I was glad I didn't have to break my promise to Roone. I'd sworn to him I wouldn't make him look bad. But I'd made no such promise to Marcus. *Sorry dude.*

I took the elevator down to the fourth floor from the Penthouse. It took a moment, but then I reached behind the vending machine and left my phone there so Marcus would know that I actually did go to the vending machine. And then I took the back exit with the stairs all the way down to the first door and out the front door. I kept my head down, my focus on, and it didn't take long. There it was, that feeling again.

I rounded the corner at the park and got yanked into the nearest alley just off the street. When I saw who pulled me in, I rolled my eyes. "What the fuck do you want?"

⚜

## *Lucas*

"Oh, it's good to see you too, kid."

*Tony Mendoza.*

I twisted out of my stepfather's grip and then shoved him back hard. Just a little reminder that I was stronger than he was. There was a time it wasn't always so, a time when he'd knock me around if my mother wasn't there to be a punching bag for him.

By the time I hit fourteen, I'd grown several inches and gained some muscle strength. It wasn't so easy to knock me around then. But still, I didn't really fight back because if I did, that meant bad things for my mother. And, as I'd learned pretty early on in the relationship, she was never leaving him, so I stayed to keep her safe, and to do that, I had to behave.

But given all our underworld contacts, I learned to fight along the way. I preferred more peaceful means of getting out of scenarios, but if I had to, I could do it. I had seen enough violence in my life to choose not to inflict it if I didn't need to.

"What do you want? Why are you here?"

"Imagine my surprise when, a year ago, I came back from my little business trip down to Mexico City to find that you'd taken our cut from the Pelaski job and split."

"You're such an asshole. I told you the Pelaski job was my last one. I only came back because Mom begged me. I put my life on hold and helped you pull that off. I took my cut and made a clean break." I'd maybe *also* taken his cut and my mother's.

"Here's the thing kid, you don't seem to realize that there is no break. You are part of this family, and it's one of those life-long membership things. I call, you come."

I leaned back against the brick in the alley, letting the cold seep into my T-shirt. "No, you don't seem to get how this works. I *left*. My mother, she's on her own. I want nothing to do with you. I've been living peacefully on my own for over a year now."

"Yeah, about that. Your digs, they're nice. What con are you running? Rent boy? Down on his luck college kid? Are you shackin' up with some rich co-ed?"

This was what I'd tried to warn Sebastian about, but he'd been insistent. He'd said that Tony wouldn't be able to find me. He'd said he'd worked with the guys at Blake Security to really scrub my cover and my trail. But still, here was a blast from my past, insistent on tainting my future. "That's none of your business. You and I, we're done. We've been done a long time."

"You keep believing that. But let me make it very clear, we are never done. Real soon, I'm going to want part of whatever you got going on here. Let's assume I'm getting my two-thirds cut."

"Over my dead body, because there is no scam. I'm just a college kid."

"A college kid with a penthouse?" He shook his head. "You don't really think I'm that dumb, do you? I know you're a college boy and all. But I got smarts too. Street smarts. Real soon, I'm coming to collect. Either I get a piece of what you've got going on here, or you do a job for me. It's big. Not that penny-ante shit we've been running for years."

I shook my head. "I'm not interested. Whatever you've got going on, it's your gig. I'm not getting pinched on American soil. Are you joking?" Especially not now that I knew who I was. I wasn't bringing the shame down on Sebastian. Not for anything. This was my shit. And I'd deal with him.

Tony stepped in real close. He knew by now not to touch me. If he put his hands on me, it wasn't going to end well for him. Much like the last time.

Last year, when my mother had called me to Mexico, begging me to come because she was ill, I'd discovered that she'd been diagnosed with stage-two breast cancer. The drugs and booze certainly didn't help with her recovery.

When I arrived, she was thin, and ill, the chemo doing a number on her. But the thing was she hadn't called me home because she was sick and wanted to see me or wanted me to take care of her. Oh no. She'd called me because she was too sick to pull a job with Tony. And it was a two-man gig. It was then that I'd realized my mother was long gone.

Somewhere, her life had taken a drastic turn, and she couldn't right the ship. I'd also learned somewhere along the way that it wasn't my job to right it for her, despite the niggling, gnawing urge to do so.

There would always be a part of me that wanted to go back and fix her life for her. Get her off the pills, off the booze, and take her away from Tony. I'd managed it once.

When I was sixteen, I'd earned enough money from a job to get us new names, new identities, and a different place to live. She'd been sober for six whole months, and it had been one of the best times of my life. But then she called him, and that had been the end of that. He made her pay for leaving too. And at that point, I watched my mother start to slip away again. By the time I was eighteen, I knew she was gone. I fought for another couple of years, but eventually, I gave up.

After that last job in Mexico, once I realized why she'd put my life on hold, I vowed to never do it again, even if it meant saving her life.

"I got to tell you man, that breath of yours, it's kicking. Mind backing up?"

"See that's your problem kid. Always so glib, always quick with a joke. Let me put this in terms you'll understand. You do this job, or I kill your mother. You do this job, or I kill you. I don't really care which. But either way, you're doing the job."

I forced myself to lift the corners of my mouth into a nasty grin. "That's where you're wrong. I'm done with you. If you even come near me again, *I'll* kill *you*."

He chuckled low. "You think you could? If you lay a hand on me, it means very bad things for your mother."

I turned my back on him and headed out of the alley. I was

going back to my new life. Nothing was dragging me back into the darkness. I was a prince now. I wasn't the pauper. I wasn't the con artist willing to do anything and anyone just to survive. Not ever again.

I was Lucas Newsome, and I was a goddamn prince of the Winston Isles.

# 6

BRYNA

"She's crazy. I'm convinced she's cooking up some kind of witch's brew in her own room while I sleep."

Jinx chuckled over the line. "I still can't believe that dog. I swear this would only happen to you. How long did she say the dog would be there?"

"She said that he'd only be here for another month, but I'm telling you, I saw her bring a dog bed in here. That dog is staying for a while. What am I going to do?"

"Well, you could report her. But hey, at least you got your room back."

Yeah, there was that. But as much as he terrified me, I couldn't report poor Rufus. "I said I wouldn't. I just want him, you know, not here."

Jinx laughed. "Any hot-guy action?"

"Nope. Rufus's constant crotch sniffing is the closest anyone has come to my snatch. Besides, it's hard to look fresh and sexy with boob sweat. It's ninety degrees in the shade. No one looks good that sweaty."

"Don't go ruining things for me. I will dream of sweaty guys serenading you."

I laughed. "Okay, you do that. I'm going to get a snack. Love you."

"Love you too. I'll call you tomorrow after work."

I really wanted a snack out of the fridge, but I was too terrified to go to the kitchen in case Rufus was waiting for me. *Maybe it'll be fine.* I was a *grown* woman. I was *not* afraid of this dog. I owned the place. Well, not owned it, but I was renting it, so it was fine.

With my shoulders squared, I pulled back the door and marched into the living room. Rufus had taken up his familiar spot on the couch, all laid out and acting like he was some kind of lap dog. Pretty sure the dog outweighed me at this point.

I was pretty sure he was also taller than me. But, whatever. I grabbed a glass of milk and started searching for my comfort cookies. Damn it, I couldn't reach the damn Oreos. I stretched up into the cupboard, standing on my tippy toes and propping myself up on the counter. Just another inch... just another... and then my fingertips grazed the plastic wrapping. *Success!*

But when I turned around, there was Rufus, staring at me, looking at the bag of cookies. "Okay, no, no, no, we're not going to do this. You are not going to jump on me, attack me, sniff me, or take my cookies. You hear me?" I used my firm voice. I was firm, damn it.

But Rufus ran right for me.

I squeaked and jumped back, trying to push myself onto the counter, but oh no, I didn't quite make it. So there we were; Rufus with his nose straight up my crotch and me, with the Oreos above my head, half crouched on the counter, half crouched on Rufus's nose. At that moment, in walked my room-mate and some tattooed guy I'd never seen before.

*Kill me now.* I officially had the roommate and the hound from hell.

Thirty minutes later after a long, hot shower, I tucked my towel around my chest, securing it tightly, and then flipped my head upside down with the other towel, trying to get the thick waves of my hair to cooperate. When I flipped back over, I frowned, swearing I heard something.

"Is anyone there?" There was silence. I turned my music off, but I didn't hear anything, so I went back to my hair. I heard another bark and scratch. I swear to God, that damn dog.

*He is defenseless. You can't put him on the street.*

I grumbled under my breath.

On the way to my room, I heard the sound again and realized it was the door. Someone was knocking. *Shit.* Rufus.

He was barking at the door, standing up to his full height, and throwing his full weight against it. *Hell.* If anyone heard him, we were toast. *I* was toast. Damn it.

"Rufus, down. Down." The overgrown dog was hard to wrangle. "Sit. Quiet. Goddamn it. I hate you." I flipped open the lock on the door and yanked it open. It was only when the man on the other side stumbled back, that I grabbed Rufus by the collar and finally glanced up.

"Oh, fuck me. Rufus, down!" This couldn't be happening. Not him. *Jesus Lord.*

"I'd love to sweetheart, but I prefer my women less prickly."

Rufus wiggled out of my grasp then jumped up. Almost as if in slow motion, my feet slipped, and the towel disengaged. My ass hit the ground with a thud as I glared up at none other than Lucas Newsome. "What the hell are you doing here?"

He grinned. "Getting another eyeful."

With a shriek, I grasped for my towel to cover what I could. "I hate you."

That grin stayed on his face. "Oh, you'll get used to me. We'll be spending a lot of time together it seems."

"Over my dead body."

Rufus was still barking, and Lucas grabbed him by the collar. His voice went extra low as he said, "Rufus, sit." There was no yelling or frantic shouting that included demands and pleas for the dog to shut the fuck up and sit down. Just a very low, calm, command. Rufus sat as if nothing happened. I stared at him. "How did you do that?"

He shrugged. "My mother's husband used to keep these mean-ass dogs around. He insisted the only way those dogs didn't tear me apart was that he had them completely well trained, so I learned a thing or two, despite myself."

Rufus now settled, I stood awkwardly, keeping the towel over my cooch. "I'm uh, just going to get dressed."

"Oh, don't run off on my account. I figure one of these days we're just going to see each other naked anyway."

I snorted a laugh. "I wouldn't count on it. You're never gonna get it."

The idiot grinned. "Sweetheart, that sounds like a dare."

※ ※

*Lucas*

*This* was Bryna Tressel? *Oh hell no.* Nope, absolutely not.

Sebastian's words clanged around in my head. But when I'd agreed, I didn't know it would be Little Miss Window Jumper and her sharp tongue with her serious set of amazing—nope, never mind all that.

*You can't touch her.*

And it was fine. There were a million girls I couldn't have or wouldn't have for whatever reason. She was no different. I was a good guy now and I was not ruled by my dick.

Well, not usually.

The problem was as I watched Bryna Tressel scoot down the hall with a towel barely covering her naked ass and the massive Great Dane chasing her, I had a feeling that not touching her was going to be easier said than done.

When I glanced down the hall and saw her shuffle into one of the rooms, I pulled out my phone and called out my brother.

Sebastian answered on the first ring. "Listen, before you flip out on me—"

"You could have mentioned she was fucking *hot*. Roone said she was cute. That was *hardly* accurate." I ranted before he could even finish.

"Yeah, I could have mentioned, but then you really wouldn't have done it, especially if you *can't* touch her."

"Dude, this is some bullshit. You didn't give me all the information."

"Well, I gave you the information you needed. At the end of the day, you still can't touch her, so that doesn't change anything. The only thing that changed in this equation is that now you know what she looks like."

To be fair, I knew what she looked like before. I just didn't know her name. "A heads-up would have been great. Like, 'hey, go get laid before you meet the totally hot brunette with a really ridiculous set of tits.'"

"Look, it's fine. You don't even have to spend that much

time with her. Just take her out for coffee even. Keep it brief if you can't keep it in your pants. And why do you know what her tits look like?"

Okay, he was being a shit. "Look, I'm a fucking adult. I can handle it. But I just would've appreciated a fucking heads-up. A little 'hey, she's totally cute' warning. Anything, you know? Act like you're my brother?"

"Okay, sorry. Next time, I swear I'll warn you about the hot girl you're about to meet that you can't have."

"That's all I'm asking for, a little warning so I could, like, gird my loins or something."

Sebastian sighed. "Keep your loins away from her. Dealing with Tressel will be hard enough."

"Yeah, I hear you." I hung up with him and said a little Hail Mary prayer. How hard could this be?

When Bryna emerged from around the corner, she was wearing leggings, a T-shirt, and some sandals. Her hair was wet and wavy around her shoulders. Thick long ropes of it clung to her, leaving wet streaks on her T-shirt. And of course, I kept picturing her half naked, because once I had seen her tits, I couldn't *unsee* them. *Way to torture yourself. Look, don't touch.*

"So, it looks like you and I are going to be hanging out." I gave her a winning smile.

She lifted a brow. "Like I said before, since I gather my parents sent you, thanks, but no thanks."

I frowned. "You were serious about that?"

She nodded. "I appreciate the gesture, but given your *last* helping hand, I'm going to go it alone."

What the hell? Had I just been shut down? "I don't understand."

She grinned, her smile full of vinegar. "I know, it's shocking.

A woman just opted not to spend time with you. Whatever will you do with yourself? You seem resilient. I doubt your ego will be down for that long, Tin Man. You'd need a heart for that."

Despite her taking pot shots at me, I smiled at the used of my nick name. "So, does that mean we're on for tomorrow?"

"That's a first, huh? Strikeout?"

I slid a glance over at Roone as we walked out. "I don't know what you're talking about." We headed out of Greble Tower toward the car. God, I almost missed the strum and hum of the student housing life. Ever since Sebastian moved me to the penthouse in the tower next to Blake Security, I felt a little detached from everything, from my old life.

"Obviously, I didn't hear everything that was going on, but something tells me that Bryna Tressel was not too interested in your offer to play tour guide."

I rolled my eyes. "Whatever. She was interested. What I don't understand is what other thing could possibly be more exciting than having me to show her around the city?"

Roone shrugged. "You know, maybe it's time to realize you might *not* be that irresistible."

"Whatever. I'm pretty irresistible." I grinned. "Dude, I have dimples. I'm hot."

He snorted in response. When we reached the parking

garage, I tried to get ahead of Roone and he shoved me gently, letting me know that that was still off limits. "Jesus man, I just want to get to the car. Since when does everything have to be so dramatic?"

Then he gave me his *serious* Roone face. That look I have come to know well; mouth set in a firm line, eyes narrowed in a deadly glare, brows slightly raised. "Yes, Your Highness, it is necessary."

I also hated how he tried to call me 'Your Highness' whenever he was pissed-off at me. "Don't get your panties in a twist."

"Knickers." He corrected.

"Fine, knickers, whatever you call them. I'm just giving you shit. I understand that it's very important. I'm not to walk into any potentially dangerous situations first. I get it."

He rounded on me. "*Do* you get it? Because you're traipsing around here like you don't. This is my job. You really don't get that I'm supposed to take a bullet for your sorry ass."

I hadn't exactly been thinking about it like that. "Sorry, Roone. I'm just not used to it. It's an adjustment."

Roone ran a hand through his thick red hair. "Look, I get it. You and Sebastian have to deal with things, and I get that, for you especially. It's a huge adjustment to your life, and it's not something you were looking for or sought after. But it is what it is. So I'm begging you, just make everyone's lives a little bit easier. If this doesn't work out, Sebastian will call you home. One simple call to the paparazzi, and they will make your life so miserable here you'll never want to leave home. And that will mean far more guards than you have ever seen."

The noose tightened even more around my neck. "Yeah, I hear you. Sorry. I didn't mean to make your job more difficult."

"You guys never do."

"What's that supposed to mean?"

Roone laughed as he led the way to the stairwell in the 3$^{rd}$ floor of the building. "Look mate, Sebastian isn't a fool. Nor is he a wanker. He just doesn't always think it through in terms of what may or may not be more difficult for the people guarding him. His whole life, he's had people watching him, and I get that he doesn't want that. But, it is what it is. You, I get that you are not used to it, so you think it's cute to run off and ditch your detail, but if something happens to you, that's my nuts in a sling."

I frowned. I hadn't really ever considered that. Not that I was that insensitive, I just hadn't given it much thought. "Sorry, I didn't know."

"At the very least, I'd get fired. But it could get far worse than that if I was found negligent or at fault, so stop being so selfish for once. I know you don't even mean to be, but by virtue of you thinking about yourself first, that's called selfish."

"Thanks for that little definition there. I understand. Like I said, I'm sorry. I didn't think about it. It just—it's a lot. On the one hand, it's like, 'Oh boy, my whole life changes.' On the other hand, it's like, 'Oh boy, my *whole* life changes.' I don't think anyone can be quite ready for that."

"Tell me about it." Roone mumbled. "Just try not to die on my watch. Marcus's, sure. Just not mine."

THE FIRST FEW days in New York were maybe off to a shaky start, but my first day at work had been bustling, and challenging, and a little scary. But I was excited. I already had an assignment. I was to go check out a busker in central park. Some teenager. Right up my alley.

I was on my own and I couldn't wait. Now all I had to do was figure out my living situation and everything would be fine. Dana was a less-than-ideal roommate, and as it turned out, she spent a lot of time at her boyfriend's place, which left me to care for Rufus.

But I wasn't going to dwell on that. Today had, so far, been a great day.

I was feeling so good that I stopped to look up. Like a total cliché. But the thrum of the city made me vibrate, like I was totally alive for the first time.

The smell of the exhaust and the food carts, the constant thrum of people, and the sunlight glistening off of skyscrapers were all dazzling to me.

Of course, I forgot that this was New York and not the Winston Isles. I was jostled and shoved aside, and someone muttered, "Tourist."

I shouted after him. "Hey, that was rude."

A voice from behind me chuckled low before saying, "Yeah well, that's what you get for standing in the middle of the sidewalk, face tilted up, staring at skyscrapers like some kind of noob."

I whirled around. *Lucas.* "Oh my God, are you following me?"

"Nope, but if you keep doing things like that, I might need to follow you to make sure that you stay out of trouble."

"What do you want?"

"Well, I was asked to look out for you. I would like to do the favor and see it through. You're making it really difficult to do that. So, you and I are going to work out the differences we have, so that we can both pull this off."

"Have you considered that maybe I don't *want* to spend time with you?"

He shook his head. "Impossible. You just don't know me yet. *Everybody* likes me."

I snorted. "I don't think I do."

"Trust me," he flashed me a brilliant smile and my knees nearly buckled like a fool. "Just give me time. Like I said, everybody loves me."

I glared at him as he pulled out his phone, and he handed it over.

"Now, put your phone number in here. I'm tired of having to track you down."

＊ ＊

## *Lucas*

"All right, now that that's done, let's go. I'll walk you home."

I grinned as Bryna slid her glance around. "Listen, I get it. The king asked you to look out for me because my parents pressured him. You don't actually have to *do* that. Why don't we just say that we met, we had coffee, you took me around sight-seeing at Lady Liberty, all the good things."

It was disconcerting. My success as a con man was predicated on people liking me, or at least believing the 'me' I presented.

"Listen, we could actually *do* all those things. Why can't we do that?"

She blinked up at me with wide dark eyes, shook her head, and tucked the loose strands of hair behind her ear. "It's not that I don't like you. You seem fine. Nice even, or whatever. I just have things I want to do, and you're not really the kind of guy I want to have help me."

I frowned. "What kind of guy is that?"

"Look, in case you didn't know, my mother is doing the whole 'time to find Bryna a husband thing,' and you're just the latest in the long line of guys she's shoved at me. So it's not about you *personally*. It's just about that whole scenario. I kind of just want to be left alone, you know, because you're exactly the type to be too good looking for your own good. You seem very nice, but there's probably some kind of a douche-bag part of you that knows how attractive you are and will eventually make me quite well aware of it. We could just pretend that we did the whole you-show-me-around thing, and we can both be on our way."

I didn't like how she'd summed me up. She'd gotten the lay

of the land, or what she thought was the lay of the land, anyway. It irritated me. I was even more irritated that there was a part of what she said that was valid. Yeah, I knew what I looked like. I have used it to my advantage more than once. And yes, perhaps I've spent half of my life being some asshole fuck-boy. So she might be right, and that ticked me off.

Roone followed at a discreet distance, but I knew he was there as I jogged to catch up with her. "Look, maybe we could actually try to explore together. Just coffee even. At least let me walk you home. I'm not used to—"

"Women telling you no? So, now you're going to insist?" she finished for me.

I didn't like that tone. "No. I just—I'm trying here. As far as I know, you're still new to a strange city." Damn, I was fucking this up. The one thing Sebastian asked me to do. The one thing. I needed to get this shit right. She rounded the corner, and I recognized her dorm.

"Look, I'll call my mother. Even though she's pissed off right now, I'll tell her you were lovely. Then we can be done with this."

I threw my hands up. This girl was infuriating. I was offering to help her, but she wouldn't even give me a shot.

I got it. She didn't need to be saved or what not, but for some reason she'd taken an immediate dislike of me? Not possible. *Or maybe she sees who you really are.* "Just tell me why? I'll leave you be. I'll walk you to your door, and then you never have to see me again. I'm just curious."

"Why? Because…" she sighed. Several students exited the front door and she shuffled into the opening before it closed. I followed her straight into the elevator and she frowned. "Look, I knew someone like you once. Very good looking, charming, sweet even, but it turned out that he wasn't really. And I didn't recognize those signs until it was too late. So right now, this whole charm offensive thing that you're doing, I'm done with it. I get it, my parents are bothering you to do this, but it's unnecessary."

"I'm sorry some guy dicked you over, but I'm not *that* guy. Let's just do this. It's important to me. Please."

She tipped her chin up at me. "You realize that's the first time you've said please to me?"

I frowned. I had said please before, hadn't I? "That's not true." I was sure of it.

"Oh yeah it is. You showed up at my doorstep, then you flirted with me outrageously and stared at my boobs and my crotch."

I coughed a laugh. Jesus Christ she was direct. I wasn't sure if it was intentional or a product of verbal diarrhea. "Yeah, well you have spectacular breasts, so... But to be fair, it's not like I made the towel fall off of you." I shook my head. "And I only briefly glanced at your crotch. Staring would have been rude."

Her lips twitched as she fought the smile. "No, it was not your fault. It was that crazy dog."

"If you don't like the dog, why did you get one?"

She sighed. "He's my roommate's. Look, we're almost there. We can pretend this whole thing never happened."

The elevator chimed, and the doors slowly slid open. My mind racked itself for ways to change everything, just somehow make it better, and somehow not get screwed up.

"We're here. I'll tell my mother that, you know, you walked me from class, we talked, we had conversation, and then you're done, okay? You don't need to do this."

"I don't know what you're talking about."

She sighed. "No, of course you don't." And then she stepped into the apartment and closed the door in my face.

*That's strike two.*

‍ ‍ ‍ ‍ ‍ ‍ ‍ ‍ ‍ ‍ ‍ ‍ ‍ ‍ ✢

*Lucas...*

*Now you're free.* I could tell my brother I'd done my best and that I'd even walked her from her classes once and asked her if there was anything she needed, so now I wasn't a disappointment. *Yay, me!* The problem was as I rode down in the elevator, something lingered at the back of my mind. Why was she so uptight about me even helping her? Why did she keep saying 'someone like me?' Why wouldn't she even so much as have a coffee with me? It's not like I was asking her to marry me.

*Let it go. This is not a challenge to be solved. This isn't the one last mark. Let it go.*

I recognized the impulse immediately. It was as if someone was telling me I couldn't do something, thereby forcing my curiosity. Tony had used that tactic over the years to force me into doing things that I didn't necessarily want to do. All he had to do was tell me that he didn't think I had the balls or that I wasn't capable. He told me I was too stupid to do it. And sure enough, I would be proving him wrong, getting larger and larger scores.

*Those days are over now. You don't have to do that anymore.*

No, I didn't, but I had to resist the urge to scratch that scab.

Once downstairs, I bypassed the front desk with a smile to the attendant who beamed back at me. *See?* She wasn't immune. But somehow, I only wanted to go back upstairs to figure out what the hell was wrong with Bryna Tressel.

*Leave it.*

When I got outside, I jogged down the stairs and found Roone talking to a bohemian-looking grad student. Or rather, *she* was talking to him, leaning forward, hand on his forearm, giggling at whatever it was he said. I could only laugh because he was completely at ease. But I knew the moment I came outside he knew exactly where I was. I nodded toward a hotdog cart and inclined my head. He nodded in return. "You want one?"

He shrugged. "Sure, why not."

When I walked over to pay for the hotdogs, I was surprised by the line. Then I realized this wasn't your average dirty-wild hotdog stand. This was some kind of permanent food truck. The line was long enough that I had to wait for my specialty dogs to get made. I pulled out my phone to check it and told myself I wasn't looking up at Bryna Tressel's apartment. *Yeah right, how's that working out for you?*

I knew it from the curtains, because she had a purple unicorn plant that she hooked out on the railing. I'd seen it the last time I was in her place.

*Let it go. She's not the right challenge.* I forced myself to look back at my phone as I waited, but something had my hair standing up at the back of my neck, and immediately I looked around. Then I saw him.

Tony... again.

"We got to stop meeting like this kid. By now, you really shouldn't be surprised. Did you think about what I said?"

"Nope."

"You're really so cold you don't care about your mother? After she was so sick?" Tony rubbed his jaw. "Time is running out. You really want to go out like a pussy?"

"There is nothing you can do to me now."

"Oh yeah? Does your new friend, the one from the papers, know about you?"

Fuck he knew about Sebastian. What did he know? "I don't know what the fuck you're talking about."

Tony grinned. "Oh man, your poker face is still outstanding. It's a shame you don't use your talents for good. You were photographed with the prince. You know how your mother is. Anything about royalty, she's there for it, especially if it's about the Winston Isle folks. She was obsessed with them. Like she would get everything she could lay her hands on. I could swear she cried when she heard that king died."

My heart squeezed. My mother and I had a conversation last year about King Cassius. She was forced to confess the truth when I asked her if he was my father. But I hadn't even thought that she cared about him anymore. *Looks like you're wrong.* "Is this story going somewhere? Because I'm waiting for my hotdogs, and I've got to get to class."

"Yeah, class. Fancy NYU. I got to ask though kid, is that real? Or did you hack in? You never seemed that smart to me."

And there we were... the first insult lobbed over the wall. "Does it actually matter?"

"Come to your senses kid. Don't jeopardize your life on principle. Besides, you owe me. I want part of your take and all of what you owe me. This kind of mark looks good for it, *or* you can do the job *I* want."

"I don't know what you're talking about. I met that guy at a party." Tony stuck real close behind me, and something poked in my back. My sweat turned suddenly icy. I knew it was a gun. I'd seen Tony pull this very same move on countless other people to force them to play into his hand. "You and I aren't done kid."

With the pressure at my lower back, the bile swirled in my gut. I told myself I was not going to puke. No way, no how. And then my fucking number was called. Oddly, the smell of onions and ketchup actually helped settle my stomach. What the fuck was I going to do? If Tony was in town, then my mother was too. It meant every move I made was one that could hurt her.

I heard the now distinct-to-me bite in Bryna's voice from above as I grabbed my dogs. "Don't touch me!"

Instinctively, I sought her out and my gaze honed in on her on the balcony of her apartment. I couldn't see clearly, but there was a guy out on the balcony with her. *Shit.*

I didn't even stop to think. I dropped the dogs and ran.

I HADN'T RUN that fast in ages. Hell, I'd probably only run that fast once, when Tony was going after my mother. I'd been determined to protect her with my life at that point. I ran like that now. Sweat on my brow, legs pumping, heart racing in a not-so-steady gallop. Roone all but forgotten.

When I reached her room, I knocked on her door. Pounded really. I could hear the dog inside barking. "Bryna, open up."

I heard things crashing to the floor inside the apartment.

"Fuck it." I stepped back and kicked my foot to the door jamb where the lock would be.

All that happened was me falling back and landing flat on my ass. *Motherfucker*.

That shit looked easy on *Law and Order SVU*. What the fuck? I heard more thrashing around inside.

I reached into my back pocket and pulled out my lock pick set. This was a simple door. I could do this in seconds.

*If you don't fuck up. Stay calm, open the door.*

I pulled out the slim tools, and hearing the metal clang

together was almost reassuring in a way. All of a sudden, calmness washed over me, and I took a deep breath. This was my wheel house. *This*, I knew how to do. Slide in one, slide in the second, bend the apparatus, and turn.

The door opened without any fuss. I found the asshole pressing his body into Bryna's against the rail of the balcony.

I didn't even think. I grabbed the nearest weapon I could find, which was a wine bottle, raised it over my head, and *whack...* right across the face. No glass shattering, but he did swear as he fell away from her. I didn't give him any time to recover. I grabbed him and dragged him back inside the apartment. Thn I was on him, fists flying. I picked him up and shoved him against the wall. His head made a satisfying cracking sound as it dented dry wall. "You have two choices, get lost or spend the next several nights in jail. I swear to God, I will make your life a living hell."

His eyes went wide, and he tried to struggle out of my grip, but I applied pressure across his throat and he wheezed then coughed.

Very calmly, I lowered my voice so Bryna couldn't hear me. "I will find you, and I will end you if you come anywhere near her again. Do you understand me?"

I knew there was something in my voice, something in my eyes, something that said that I was dangerous. And I was. Those lessons I'd gotten long ago from Tony had included how to get my hands dirty. But no one needed to know that. I let the piece of shit go, and he stumbled away, glaring at Bryna as he went. It wasn't my first choice to let him go, and if I had been thinking straight, I would have called Roone and given him the guy's description to detain him and take him to jail. But I was worried about her. She was shell-shocked in the corner, just staring at the door, her tiny body pressed against the wall.

"Bryna, are you okay?"

She stood there still staring, unmoving.

I snapped my fingers in front of her. I didn't want to touch her without her being fully okay with it. "Hey, are you okay?"

Suddenly, she blinked, shook her head, frowned and then squared her shoulders. "Yeah, I think so. I just—I didn't know what to do."

"Yeah, we'll fix that. In the meantime, get your shit. We're going."

She blinked rapidly. "Going where? This is my apartment."

I pointed at the door. "That guy has access to your apartment. That's the very definition of not safe. Do you understand?"

She nodded.

"Good. Pack. You're never coming back." I didn't know what the hell I was doing. All I knew was that she couldn't stay there. I'd figure the rest out once we got to the penthouse. I dragged my phone out of my back pocket and shot a text to Roone.

He came running through the door no less than thirty seconds after I sent the text.

"Dude, you cannot just take off like that."

I put my finger to my lips and inclined my head toward Bryna's room where she was rushing and throwing things into her bag, whilst trying to step over the Great Dane. "She's coming with us."

His eyes went wide. "Your Highness," I gave him a sharp shake of my head. "No. None of that. Tell Marcus too. As far as she's concerned, you're just two friends of mine across the hall.

She clearly needs help, but I don't trust her father. So, we just won't say anything about anything. For now, she can't stay here. I'll explain later."

Roone narrowed his gaze at me but gave me a sharp nod. "I'll wait outside the door."

"Thanks." Now all I had to do was figure out what the hell I was going to do with her.

⚓

*Bryna*

I didn't know what the hell happened with my life. Two weeks ago, I was escaping a ball. All so I could come to New York on my own. Make my own way in life.

It felt good.

Then Murphy and his damn law happened. First, I ran into a too-good-looking-for-his-own-good guy, and he was a friend of the king's. The last thing I wanted. And apparently, I had a shitty sense of direction, so I had been going the wrong way and missed my ferry.

Then, I moved to the city. My roommate was crazy, and her Great Dane regularly attacked me. Then her boyfriend *actually* assaulted me. And now, said gorgeous guy, who I never thought I'd see again, ended up saving me from crazy roommate's asshole boyfriend.

That pretty much summed up my life in a nutshell. I had no apartment anymore. Not one that was safe anyway. I was stuck with the one guy who would probably cause me more trouble than happiness.

*Way to go Bryna. Way to go.*

He handed me a mug of tea and leaned back against the counter. "I'll ask you again, are you okay?"

I shook my head. "You don't have to worry. I'm fine. He didn't actually hurt me."

"Whether he actually hurt you or not isn't the point. The point is his intent. And he terrorized you. So, I could kill him for that."

Heat crawled at my neck in little licks as I flushed. "Thank you. I'm not sure I said it before, but I appreciate it."

He shrugged. "I would have done it for anyone. You just have to be careful."

He was right. "I know, and I will be. I'll be getting out of your hair soon. I'm just waiting for my best friend to call me back, and I'll grab a hotel maybe. I'll try to find somewhere else to stay. It was hard enough to find graduate student housing when I did it ahead of time, but now I have to find an apartment."

He shook his head. "No, you're staying here. No hunting for apartments will be necessary."

I widened my eyes. Was he insane? I couldn't stay here. "Uh, while I appreciate it, there's no way I'd do that. I don't even know you."

"Honey, I have basically seen your uh, lady parts." He shrugged even as a slow grin spread over his lips. "Okay if I just call you Spanks from now on?"

I shook my head. "Oh my God, this is exactly why I can't stay here."

"Why, because I'm awesome and hilarious? And I'll try not to be hurt about you calling me Tin Man before. I promise, I have a heart... a big one." He winked.

"You have a high opinion of yourself."

"When you're awesome *and* hilarious, you should. I don't understand what the problem is."

"The problem is, I don't know you. And while you promised my parents you'd look out for me, this, I think, is above and beyond. So, I'll be getting out of your hair."

"See, that's just the thing. When I'm asked for a favor by my friend, I do as I am told. So, you're not shaking me. You can't go back to that apartment; it's not safe. I have more than enough room here."

He wasn't lying. The guy lived in a penthouse. Well, half a Penthouse. He must have come from money or something because there was no way an average student lived like this, even if the place was rent controlled, and *even* if he had some killer side gig.

*Of course, he comes from money.* He was friends with the king. No doubt he was some kind of trust-fund kid. "I appreciate it, but I don't want to be in the way."

"Why don't you let me determine if you're in the way or not? Spend the night. You'll be able to figure things out in the morning, at the very least."

I sighed. He had a point. I checked my watch again. It was getting late. I might as well stay here and wait until I could get ahold of Jinx. Her cousin lived in New York, and she might be able to help me out. "Okay, I'll stay the night. *One* night."

He nodded. "Fantastic. I'm so glad I didn't have to twist your arm on that."

♔ ♚

*Bryna*

At 7:30, Jinx finally called me back. "Hey, I have a break from class. What's wrong?"

"It's a long story, but something happened at my apartment. I can't stay there. Any chance your cousin might be able to lend me a couch for a few nights?

She cursed under her breath. "For you, almost always, but she *just* sublet her place to go to Europe."

*Shit*. That meant I really was staying with arrogant, pain-in-the-ass Lucas. *Fantastic*. Just what I needed. "It's okay. I'll figure it out."

"What do you mean, you'll figure it out? What happened to your apartment?"

"It's a long story. My roommate's boyfriend is a total dick-head. I basically can't go back there. Call me when you're done with class and we'll talk about it."

Jinx was silent for a beat. "Are you okay?"

"Not particularly, but I will be. Call me later."

"All right. Stay safe and make sure you answer when I call, okay?"

"You got it." When I finished with her, Lucas was leaning against the sink with a cocky smirk on his lips. "So, did I tell you so, or did I tell you so?"

"This already feels like a mistake."

He grinned. "It should feel awesome."

I swallowed hard. He wanted me to say he was right, but I wasn't going to. "Again, I'm grateful for your hospitality, But it's only temporary."

He chuckled low, and the sound made butterfly wings flap against the insides of my belly. "Okay, whatever you need to tell yourself. But, as I'm in charge of keeping you safe and making sure you have fun and all that jazz, let me put it plainly for you.

You're staying here. It's either that, or I'll call some friends at Blake Security, and they'll follow you around everywhere you go. They'd basically hang outside at whatever apartment you get. That could get uncomfortable."

I scowled at him. "You know, I have a father. He's older, balding, and has a slight paunch."

"Thank fuck I'm not him." He lifted up his T-shirt in a hint of tease and looked down. "If I ever lose this six pack, please, shoot me in the head."

Jesus Christ. I wanted to lick it. *Look away.* "Oh my God, you don't suffer from ego problems at all, do you?"

There it was again. That cheeky grin. "Nope. So, now that we have that settled, come on down here. I've got two master bedrooms. Each has its own bathroom."

I sighed. He was annoying, but he'd just saved my ass. "Seriously, thank you. I appreciate it."

He nodded. "Sure. Let's not go around telling anyone that, you know, I'm a secret softie and shit. Besides, this won't be complicated. You've made it clear you barely like me. Though I have no idea why. And you're not even my type." *Liar.* "So we can be roommates."

I pursed my lips. "Don't worry, your secret is safe with me. As a matter of fact, I'll just go ahead and call you a dick. You know, to keep up appearances."

His crack of laughter filled the cavernous space, ricocheting off the walls in the hallway by the bedroom. "I'm glad I can keep my secret with you. Way to do me a solid. I'd have more women knocking down my door." Then he continued. "You're going to be fine. I promise. We'll get you all settled."

He led the way to the bedroom and left me to settle in, the scent of him swirling around me.

There went those damn butterflies again. The moment I sat on the bed, trying to get my bearings, something about Lucas lingered, and I could really smell him.

It was a crisp and clean scent, mixed with a little musk, and all Lucas. No way was I going to examine why I knew exactly what he smelled like. Completely divine. This was going to be a lot tougher than it seemed.

# 10

BRYNA

I slept like a baby. It was pretty fantastic. I didn't know anything about Lucas, or who he was. He was basically stranger to me, but yet somehow, I felt entirely safe in his home, in his bed, which, by the way smelled amazing. Why was that?

*News flash, it's called hormones.*

Hormones I didn't plan on doing anything about.

In the morning, I had a quick shower, tossed on my jeans and a T-shirt, and headed for the door. After class, I was going to track down the kid in Central Park. I knew he played in one of two subway stations, so I hoped it wouldn't be too hard to locate him.

I stopped when I heard grunting and a low, throaty moan. Something deep in my belly clenched like that moan was a call to my long-buried lady parts in an attempt to raise them from the dead. Oh Jesus, what is going on out there?

I heard another thump and then what sounded like a curse muttered through clenched teeth. More moaning. Groaning.

Holy shit, that wasn't—he wasn't... Was he actually doing

the do in the common areas? He'd said I was welcome to stay, but what the hell? He wouldn't, would he?

There was only one way to find out.

I put my hand on the door. I couldn't help myself. I had to know.

*This is your problem. You're too damn curious for your own good.*

Yes, that was a problem of mine, but that was fine because maybe I had it wrong. Maybe...

I twisted the door handle and yanked it. And yes, there was a very sweaty Lucas looking gorgeous and delicious, and wow... *No, we are not going to ogle our new temporary roommate.*

But he wasn't naked, much to my disappointment. Instead, he was in a sweaty tank, grappling with the other guy from the wedding, the other friend of the king's. That guy looked a little older, mid-twenties, maybe a little older.

He had his arm around Lucas's neck in a head lock, and then Lucas twisted an arm up over his head and got the other guy under the nose. The next thing I knew, the other guy was flat on his back, groaning on the ground. Then I was worried that Lucas may have hurt him. Had Lucas hurt him?

But no, within a second and a half, the other guy jumped to his feet, and the two of them were trading fists. I didn't know what else to do, so I grabbed the nearest heavy object, a glass vase of some sort, decorative, but nice and heavy. Yes, I knew I shouldn't have butted in because, hey, for all I knew, Lucas had stolen the guy's girlfriend or something, and this was payback. Sweaty, gorgeous, hot payback, but still payback, nonetheless. But Lucas had done me a favor, so there was no way I was letting any guy kick his ass.

Although, I had to admit that Lucas was holding his own.

Bracing my hands and raising the vase like a baseball bat, I charged into the fray. "Let him go, you asshole."

Both of their heads whipped around. And quicker than a flash, the bigger, older guy charged right toward me, arm raised. Behind him, Lucas yelled out, "Roone, no."

Every instinct in my body told me to run, but it was already too late because my body was charging in that direction, and I had a weapon raised. I had no idea how to stop myself. But it seemed that the guy called Roone, knew exactly what to do.

He was coming for me, and there was no way to stop either of us. Even as I squeezed my eyes shut, prepared to deliver some sort of fatal blow, or if not, at least a maiming blow, he easily gripped my wrist with one hand and grabbed the vase out of my grasp with the other. Then he gently turned me around and wrapped an arm around me. In a heavy British accent, he whispered, "Easy does it. Put it down. I don't know what he promised you, but clubbing him in the head isn't going to get him to deliver."

I frowned. "Him? What?" He thought I was going for Lucas? "I wasn't going to club Lucas in the head. I was going to club *you* over the head."

I could feel the guy turning around and chuckling. "You've got this one trained well, Lucas."

"Shut up, you asshat."

I struggled in his grip. But there was no way I was breaking free. He certainly wasn't letting me go, so I did the only thing I knew how to do. I raised my foot and stomped my heel hard into his instep. He grunted and released me immediately. I shuffled out of his reach, frantically searching for another weapon.

Lucas put his hands up. "Easy does it Bryna. This is Roone.

He's a friend of mine. He lives across the hall. We're just getting our work out done."

I grabbed what looked like a heavy wood of some sort and clasped it in my hands. "I recognize him from the wedding reception. But are you sure he's a friend? It looked like you were getting your ass kicked."

Roone placed his hands on his hips and chuckled. "I like her."

Lucas rolled his eyes. "I was not getting my ass kicked. Besides, you missed it. I just put him on his ass a second ago."

"Oh, I saw that. But he looked like he was ready to kick your ass again."

Lucas tossed his hands up. "I can't win in my own house."

Roone inched closer with his hand out. "Sorry about that. I thought you were aiming for Lucas."

I gave him a narrow-eyed gaze. When he smiled, he seemed harmless enough. And, well, he had a British accent, which I know doesn't preclude anyone being a dangerous asshole, but he was cute too. "So, you're not hurting him? He didn't steal your girlfriend or anything, so you were forced to kick his ass?"

Roone laughed hard, the full grin morphing his face into one that was easy going and open. There was something honest about his eyes. "I see you know him well. But no, nothing like that. Just a work out."

I took a deep breath and glanced over to Lucas who nodded in confirmation.

"Yup, just a work out." His gaze raked over me. "You look ready to go already. It's early."

"Yeah, I was going to grab breakfast and go over my notes about the professor. I'm pretty excited about class."

Lucas nodded. "Wow, okay. You're really eager. Do you feel

okay about walking to class and stuff? Do you want me to walk you or something?"

I blinked. Was he serious? "No, God no. I'm fine. Besides, you're in the middle of getting your ass beat, so..." I let my voice trail.

There was that chuckle again from Roone. "That's all right. I'm done kicking his ass for the day anyway."

Lucas just grumbled. "You did not kick my ass the last time."

Roone just shook his head and headed for the front door. "Not according to her. If you're keeping this one, I'm going to hang out here a lot more often."

Lucas shut the door firmly behind Roone. "You're no longer invited." When he turned to face me, his grin was wide. "A vase? Really?"

"Yes. It looked heavy, and I really did think you were in danger."

"And instead of running the other way and hiding and calling the police, you ran right *toward* the danger?"

"Yes, of course. Honestly, he looked like he was going to kill you."

Lucas just rolled his eyes. "Why do I have the feeling you're going to be a handful?"

"You know what? You are not the first person to say that."

"Admit it, you thought I was in here tuning up some girl." He was close. I took a step back. "You can tell me. Don't worry; I won't tell anyone."

My eyes flared, and I diverted my gaze from him. That's exactly what I'd thought.

He took another testing step forward. "Please tell me. It will be our little secret."

Too bad for him, I wasn't a runner. Instead, I squared my shoulders and tilted my head toward him. "Does it matter?"

He grinned down at me. "Only that you opened the door to see what was going on." He leaned closer, and I hoped he could smell my perfume.

The thought stupidly made me salivate. Was he wondering if I smelled like that everywhere? *Stop it. You know what happens with a guy like this.* Guys like Lucas were born to seduce. And he was so damn good at it.

"My God, you really think you are God's gift to women. I mean, I could see it that night of the wedding, but in the clear light of day... Wow, it's staggering. Do these lines actually work on anyone?"

His smirk deepened and out popped that delicious dimple. "Well you know. Once or twice." He leaned closer, his heat wrapping around me and making my mind foggy. "So tell me, Bryna. Are you disappointed or relieved that you were wrong?"

*Relieved.* "I couldn't care less either way."

"You're not a very good liar Bryna." He chuckled low. "That's okay. I'm going to go with relieved then."

⚜

### Lucas

Oh, she wanted to act like she wasn't into me? Fair enough. But I was sure as hell was going to test that theory. I took another step into her space, and she backed up into the counter top. Then I bracketed one arm next to her left hip and watched her closely. Her pupils dilated, her lips parted slightly, and I could almost see the pulse at her neck quicken. Yeah, she felt it too, the pull of attraction. I bracketed my other hand next to her other hip, effectively trapping her. "Are you mad that I saw your ass in the ball gown? Is that what this is about?"

That broke the spell. She was all spitfire and hellcat again. "Oh my God, you are impossible. It was an accident. I clearly wouldn't have flashed you on purpose."

"Well, I don't know that. For all I know, you were literally dropped from heaven to torture me."

"Oh my God, please stop. You're just making a fool of yourself."

"I will have you know that many women find me charming and hilarious."

"Clearly, they don't have eyes."

I chuckled softly and felt, rather than heard, her short intake of breath. That one soft, whispered sound had my blood thickening and my pulse raised.

Feeling her want me was one hell of a turn on. Now there was just something to be done about her attitude. "You can act like you don't like me all you want. I know you do."

That just earned me a tilted chin. "I don't. And while I appreciate you giving me a place to stay, I don't particularly care for *you* very much. I'll be finding my own place soon enough."

"Yeah, you're welcome to do that just as long as everyone approves the arrangement."

Her mouth fell open. "You said you wouldn't say a word to my parents."

"Well, as long as you're doing something safe, I'll keep my words to myself. The moment you step out of the safety zone, I will call in the big guns."

Her dark eyes narrowed. "I swear to God, I will make your life hell."

I grinned down at her, the charge of electricity between us sparking, crackling, singeing my skin. "You're welcome to try, sweetheart."

I should have known those words were the equivalent of throwing down the gauntlet because her eyes sparked fire, and she smiled beatifically at me, like the Cheshire cat.

Oh yeah, I was in a hell of a lot of trouble.

*Bryna*

So, it turned out that living with Lucas was going to be a problem. I wasn't sure why, but just being in his presence had me all itchy and agitated and made me want to throw things. Okay fine, I was already prone to throwing things on occasion, but with Lucas, everything was just worse. I think it was that smirk he always had on his face. That cocky one, the one that said he knew exactly what I was thinking when I looked at him. Gorgeous, sexy, confident.

The thing was, guys like Lucas depended on their looks and expected girls to fall at their feet. Well, not this girl. *Are you sure about that? You've been thinking about him since you left the apartment.*

Whatever. *From now on, no extraneous thoughts about Lucas. And find a new apartment.* It would be fine. I'd just have to petition the school to get my housing funds back, which would mean ratting out Dana. But her boyfriend was dangerous. He could harm someone else. I knew it could take a while to get that money back.

But it was fine because I would be getting a stipend, though miniscule, for my internship. Plus, I had managed to save some money while working for a fundraising organization.

My mother had thought she was so slick volunteering me for her charity functions. Well, the joke was on her. I'd parlayed that into a job, and I had a few thousand dollars saved, so I could make do until I figured things out.

But the money wouldn't last forever. Transportation back and forth to campus was costing me more money than I'd planned for. I stopped at the ATM, inserted my card, and tapped my foot impatiently while busy students buzzed around me with their back packs on, jabbering on their phones, clutching their Starbucks lattes. I tapped in my PIN number and then waited. A loud beeping alerted me, and I stared at my balance. I'd tried to withdraw $200, but the fucking message said, *insufficient funds*. That had to be a mistake.

The machine beeped at me again, and I frowned and tapped the monitor. Maybe that would help. The message appeared again. I was sure that I wasn't seeing correctly, but there it was, *insufficient funds*.

What the hell?

I took my other card out and tried again. Nope. *Insufficient funds*. Fuck me. I panicked and tried another card, the one tied to my parents' account. I typed in my PIN, and then the machine started beeping at me again. Not just *insufficient-funds* kind of beeping, but loud, honking beeps. I cancelled immediately and yanked out my card.

What the hell had happened to all of my money?

A small line had started to form. Just three people, but they all stared at me curiously. The woman at the end gave me that sad-eyed, oh-you-poor-dear look, as if to say, 'Yes, we've all been there before, honey.'

This was not my life. I actually had money. Not my parents' money, either. It was money I had worked hard for. So what the hell had happened to it?

I hated to do it, but I needed to call my parents, or at least call the bank.

When I checked my watch, I groaned. I had ten minutes to get to class, call the bank, and call my Dad. Despite all of their nonsense, I was worried about my parents. If my money was gone, that meant theirs could be too. And I knew that there was nothing that made my mother worry more than a lack of funds.

I made the first call as I hustled down the street, narrowly missing being struck by a yellow taxi.

"Shit. Watch where you're going."

His response was less than friendly. It involved middle fingers and several four-letter words.

When my father answered, his voice was a lazy drawl. "Yes, what seems to be the problem?"

"Dad, have you checked your accounts lately? All my money is gone."

And then he did something that chilled my blood to ice. He laughed. "Yes, well, that's what happens when I drain your account."

I stopped.

Right there in the middle of the sidewalk, never minding that I was hit, and struck, and jostled by the rushing pedestrians around me. "You did what?"

"I drained it. You forgot that your account still linked to our main accounts, so I simply went in and took the money. Not to worry; your mother and I won't touch it. After all, what's your measly $5,000 going to do for us? But, this will teach you that you really do have to listen to us."

"You took the money that I worked for? You took it from me. In other words, you *stole* it?"

His voice dropped an octave and went cold and flat. "Watch your mouth, young lady. You did this to yourself, running off to New York. Your mother said you wouldn't even talk to her. You insisted on living in some student dorm. What kind of nonsense is that? If you'd have just followed our instructions, you could be living in the lap of luxury right now."

"Doing what you wanted involved marrying my ex who *cheated* on me."

His sigh was heavy. "I swear to God, whose child are you? Your concerns are so pedestrian. You know how this game is played. He could have made sure you had an easy life. But now, you have no money."

"I have no money because you *took* it."

"Yes, well, it's for your own good. It'll teach you a lesson. As soon as you call your mother and go stay in the apartment on the Upper West Side, all of this ends. You'll get your money back, and you'll have access to ours again. Until then, I have cancelled your credit cards as well, just in case you're wondering."

"What is wrong with you two? I'm your child. I'm not a pawn for you to control."

"That's where you're wrong, and it's where your fundamental view of life is going to get you hurt. The sooner you realize life is all about having power and control, the sooner you'll be happier. Until then, things are going to get very difficult. Let me know when you've called your mother and when you're ready to have your things moved. I'll be in the city next week. I love you. I'll talk to you later."

Then my father hung up on me. The man had robbed me,

made me destitute, and he thought I was going to just do as he said. Well, he had another think coming.

Still shell-shocked, heart beating too rapidly, brain a complete blur and fuzz of *what the fuck am I going to do and how the fuck did this happen,* I charged to my class, Principles of International Marketing Management. I blindly took a seat, not even seeing the other students jostling around me. To me they were just bodies, a sea of them, all acting as some obstacle in my way. I was numbed, unable to move, unable to perform. My life was over.

One guy stopped in front of me and smiled down. I barely even registered what he looked like. "Hi there, are you okay?"

I only gave him a curt glance and nod. I was not looking for connections with strangers today.

*All you have to do to get it back, is do as they say. What's the worst that could happen?*

That was it. That was just the thought I needed to snap me out of it. The worst that could happen *had,* several times at their hands. They had literally taken my passport from me, kept me from leaving Europe, and kept me beholden to them.

They had practically insisted that I marry someone I didn't love and when I found out he had cheated on me, they not only blamed me, but insisted it had been my fault and I should take the turd-monkey back.

Well, not again. It was just not going to happen. I would do what everybody else had to do. I'd get a job and figure it out. I didn't need them. Never mind that they'd stolen from me; that was a different matter altogether. I wasn't caving. Never again.

"So, were you even going to say hi?"

My head whipped around at the familiar voice that sent a flair of heat spiking through my body. "Lucas?"

He lifted a brow, and there was that signature smirk. The right corner of his lips tipped up, hint of dimple, mischief dancing in his green eyes, full lips looking ridiculously soft and absolutely kissable, face smoothly shaven, dark hair curling slightly and falling over his brow. While he was sitting there looking gorgeous and at ease, my life was falling apart. And he had the nerve to smirk at me? "If you know what's good for you, I wouldn't say anything."

"Oh boy, looks like you're in a fantastic mood, roomie. That makes two of us. Tell me, are you as sexually frustrated as I am? Honestly, we could just bone and get it over with. I mean, I'm offering this one, you know, free of charge."

I rolled my eyes at him. I had bigger fish to fry. Lucas Newsome was the least of my problems.

## 11

WHAT THE HELL was wrong with me? Bryna Tressel was very firmly on the list of things you do not touch. Things you do not look at. Things you do not covet. But since that morning, the way she charged to the living room as if expecting to find me naked, just thinking about her made me twitchy.

*Who are you kidding? You've been twitchy about her since you realized she was the one you need to look out for.*

The moment Sebastian had asked me to do this thing, I hadn't wanted to do it. But the second I had seen it was her, the girl from the wedding with her canary yellow dress tucked under her thong, I was very onboard.

I wanted to touch her. I don't know what it was, but I remembered the exact smell of her on the island. Ocean breezes, the scent of hibiscus and gardenia mixed with her sweet and spicy scent. I didn't know what it was, but I remembered it curling around me, holding me trapped while that raging buttercup read me the riot act, insisting I tell her why men were pigs.

Back then she had been some random hot girl. But now she had a name, and I was tied to her whether I wanted to be or not.

*Who are you kidding? You're the idiot who invited her to move in.*

Yeah, well, it seemed like a good idea at the time. Besides, I needed to prove my worth, that I deserved the faith Sebastian was putting in me, so I could do this. I could keep my hands to myself. How hard was that?

*You mean besides the fact that you have impulse control issues?* As if to punctuate the point, my dick twitched. Asshole.

Sitting next to her all day in Principles of International Marketing Management had been torture. Whatever her perfume or shampoo was, it was driving me mad. And I just kept picturing her perfect ass as it marched ahead in her yellow dress, giving a nice jiggle with each step. God, there was something wrong with me. And then it never just stayed at the ass. Of course, in my best fantasies, somehow the whole dress had just ripped right off. *Like the towel.*

Marcus snapped his fingers in front of my face. "Are you okay?"

I shook my head and frowned at him. "What?"

"Dude, you've been staring at your coffee for the last twenty minutes. Don't you have French or something right now?"

"Oh shit." I put the lid on my coffee, irritated that it was now cold. I grabbed my bag and notebook. I'd been sitting at the corner of Tenth at a bistro that I loved.

While I'd meant to be going over my schedule, instead, I'd spent the last fucking twenty minutes daydreaming about Bryna Tressel, the one girl I had no business dreaming about.

*You know you can't do it, so find another solution.*

That was actually a good point. The girl clearly didn't like me, and I didn't like her.

The damn dick twitched again, as if to say, 'You cannot like her all you want, but I like her plenty.' But anyway, she'd come storming out to the living room earlier in the day, assuming that I was with someone. So maybe I *needed* to be with someone. That would certainly take the edge off. It might even serve to piss off Bryna.

*Why do you care that you're pissing her off?*

I didn't.

*Liar.*

Perfect point. All I have to do is call any number of girls. It would be easy. Then I could stop thinking about and focusing on Bryna Tressel.

⚜

## Bryna

This was the day from hell. And it looked like it was never going to end.

I made it through class, despite the fact that I'd somehow managed to find a spot right next to Lucas. Like, legitimately *right* next to him. During class, I could feel him *breathing*. Not going to lie, it drove me absolutely insane. With the events of the morning still fresh in my mind, sitting next to him was just adding insult to injury.

After class, I'd called the bank too. Only to be told that nothing could be done as my account was, in fact, linked to my parents' and because they were the original owners of the account, they had full legal access to any and all money in there.

*Shit.*

I was so desperate, I half considered going up to the apartment on the Upper West Side and giving my mother what she wanted for the time being. But if I did that, they'd control me for the rest of my life.

The cost was too high. I'd have to figure something else out and quickly. The stipend was barely enough to cover my transportation.

*You're going to keep it together.*

It didn't matter that my life was falling apart. I still had a job to do. I'd just have to deal with my personal crisis on the go. I headed to Central Park to find an elusive beatboxing teen who played the spoons. Word was he could really move too.

But so far, when the slick A&R guys had tried to talk to him, he'd bolted. So they were sending me in to see if fresh, young, and passionate worked. I was no idiot, they were clearly hoping that, being female, I could dazzle the kid or something.

But I'd been standing on his supposed block for over three hours, and he'd never shown. With a sigh, I packed up my bag and headed back for the subway. Defeated.

Nope. Just a setback. Tomorrow will be better. But right now, I couldn't see my way clear to that.

I made a left toward Columbus Circle then headed down toward the East side. It was then that I heard it, across the street, the sounds of a flute. At least I thought it was a flute. A piccolo maybe. My eyes scanned the crowded streets, but I couldn't see it. And then the tunes were wrong. It was hip-hop... I thought. Obviously, it was missing all the drums and the bass sounds, but in essence, I would honestly have sworn that that artist was playing Biggie songs.

I forced my brain to focus and locate the sound. It was

coming from under the tree across the street, by the subway station. There was a girl with a flute and a hat out in front of her. And she was playing hip hop, which I thought was just astonishing.

Without much care for the traffic or the busy taxis, I dashed out in the middle of the street, skipping, hopping around the cars, and nearly lunging to my death in front of a yellow cab. Happily, I was able to step aside, unscathed and unscratched, and then I ran down to her. "Oh my God," I took deep breaths. "Holy cow, I love your sound."

Still more breathing. Wheezing really. And then she said, "Do I know you?"

I shook my head. "No. But you play beautifully. And that flute, with a hip-hop beat? That's amazing."

"Uh. Thanks, I guess." She stared pointedly at her hat.

Still panting I mustered up a sigh and dropped the two dollars I could not afford into her hat. Then I pulled out my card. "I'm with Turntable Records. I'd love to talk to you sometime about what you're doing with your music."

Her brows furrowed. "Are you for real?"

"You better believe I am. I wouldn't have attempted death by cabbie if I wasn't. Listen, I was looking for someone else today, but then I heard you playing and it stopped everything for me. Honestly, your music is like a beacon of light in a dark tunnel. You were just what I needed to hear right now. Can you play something else?"

As a show of good faith, I put my last five dollar bill in her hat and nodded at her. "Play me something else, please."

She did. She played some Fugees and a little Lauren Hill, all on the flute. I could almost hear Wyclef Jean with his distinctive patois. "Oh Mona Lisa, can I have a date on Friday..."

When she was done, I stepped back. "You are astounding. Are you represented by anyone?"

She laughed, her afro wiggling in the wind. "No. I just play for little extra cash for me and my sister. Not much to go on at home."

"Well, I would like to tell you that I think you should be dreaming bigger."

"You're the real deal?"

"Pretty much. I'm basically a glorified intern. And my whole job is to find fresh new talents doing new, innovative things. You were just to incredible to walk away from."

A flush crept up her neck, showing pink on her café au lait skin. "But this was just me playing for fun."

"It doesn't matter. Every great artist comes from somewhere, and I think that you can be terrific."

She fingered my card, folding it back and forth. "Can I think about it?"

"Of course. Just call my number on the back."

And then I left her. It killed me to walk away. I wanted the win. But I had her in my sights; I just needed to bide my time. No use rushing it. This was a good thing to happen today. I didn't want to wreck it by pushing too hard.

Besides, I had a train to catch. Maybe if I let her think it through, process the opportunity. But for the first time all day, at least I'd started to feel good. I was doing what I was supposed to be doing. The problem was my whole world outside of this. I needed to get everything back on an even kilter, or I wasn't going to last three more days.

Let alone three more months.

## 12

LUCAS

*W*AS THIS REALLY HAPPENING? *Was Tressel late?*

It certainly looked that way.

I still couldn't get used to my brand-new digs. Sebastian had put me in the charitable trust headquarters which occupied one of the towering skyscrapers just uptown from Broadway.

The whole place was kitted-out with all the latest tech. Glass and steel was the overall décor, with some pops of color added in priceless photos and art prints on the walls. So far most of my job had consisted of meeting with the directors and finding out about their teams, getting to know them.

I had only been here a week, so I was still getting my bearings. Most of the people there wanted to do a good job and not fuck up, which I respected. And no one had balked at my position or even asked any questions.

One thing I had noted was that Tressel wasn't in the city. His whole team lived and worked remotely, so that old reach-out-and-touch-someone thing was far more difficult. And his entire team was stonewalling when I asked for data.

I was seated in my fancy new Herman Miller chair for a video conference with all the directors, including Lord Tressel. Everyone was on the line, tapping away.

My assistant came in, and I asked, "He's really late. Are you sure he saw this?"

She nodded as she deposited a stack of folders on my desk. "Yes. I sent you his confirmation just now. He should be there."

*But he wasn't.*

So far, what I'd been going through for Sebastian was a lot of paperwork. There were all kinds of regulations that needed to be met when dealing with charities and donations. And I could see it. His concerns were founded. There was money missing.

Not a lot. I couldn't, so far, tell how far back it went, but I could certainly see it. A few thousand here, a few hundred there. And it wasn't just the Artistic Trust either. Once I'd started looking at that, I could see discrepancies in the other foundations since the very beginning.

So, Tressel was dicking with me. Did he want to see if he could just disrespect me and not show?

So far, what I'd done for Sebastian had been pretty basic. Just a lot of paperwork, exploring down the rabbit hole on the various trails. Where the money started, where it came from, how it was classified; None of it was particularly rocket science. What was interesting was I could *see* it, whether it was misfiled donations or inaccurate paper work. There was always some step along the way where the wrong dollar amount was put in. And it wasn't a lot from any particular place. It was just little. A few thousand here, several hundred there, nothing much really to raise alarm. That's what had sent me digging into the other arm of the Winston Isles's charities. The Artistic Trust was just one of the many where I had started seeing the worrisome trend.

This activity went back for years, at least seven that I could see. It was time to put everyone on notice. I want air-tight documentation. I didn't want any questions, and I had a feeling that Lord Tressel was not going to like that.

Ryan Cox, the director of the charity arm in our London offices, spoke up. "Do you think we should reschedule?"

I glanced at the clock again. "No. We're not rescheduling. This meeting was on the books. We'll wait. If he still doesn't show up, I'll dismiss you guys and just talk to him myself."

Ryan's brows lifted. It was pretty clear I was not impressed with what was happening. I hadn't been here long enough for them to form an opinion probably, but I was going for tough but fair. I'd been friendly, accommodating when asking for information, and fair about giving them time to do it, but I'd made it clear that when I said I wanted something, I most definitely wanted it. And they had all been instructed to give me everything I needed. So far, we hadn't had any problems.

The only person I had a problem with was Lord Tressel. His office often gave me the run around, making it clear that he was oh-so-busy. He couldn't always give me what I needed, when needed it. The kicker of it was, I couldn't come right out and accuse him of anything untoward, because I didn't have enough proof. I didn't have enough information. I didn't have enough documentation. And to boot, I wasn't sure how things went on the back end or how much access he had, but something was definitely fishy. He was the only one who hadn't given me all his financials.

Then the alert button on the monitor told us that he was coming online. Finally, Tressel appeared, looking not at all hurried or concerned that he was late. "Yes, yes. Is everyone here?"

I took a deep breath. "Yes, we've all been here, Lord Tressel, for the last twenty-five minutes."

He only shrugged. "You know, I got tied up. What's all this about?"

I forced calm into my voice that I didn't feel. "Well, Lord Tressel, we're meeting because you have discrepancies in the charity funding. Incorrect amounts filed, inaccurate paperwork..."

"Yes, well, everyone is using the old antiquated system that the Winston Isles Charity Trust has always used. There is so much paperwork, every department has to bring different information. It's no wonder."

"I'm glad you pointed that out, Lord Tressel. I seem to find the most discrepancies come from your department."

I pointed out the accounts, small amounts, discrepancies, and things that people could easily overlook. "We need to be able to account for every cent. I want every discrepancy found and accounted for, and documentation of where in the process we've made mistakes."

They were all busy taking notes when I glanced up. All except Tressel, who looked like he might have swallowed his tongue. "Do you have any idea how much time it will take to unravel years of bad data?"

I gave him a brusque nod. "Yes, I do. Forensic accounting is a field I happen to excel in." I turned my attention to Bill Wexler. He ran the most active charities division. "Mr. Wexler, your paperwork is outstanding."

The guy pushed up his glasses and nodded vigorously. "We pride ourselves with getting things right sir." Wexler looked like he was an actual IRS accountant... glasses, hair parted just so, nothing out of place.

"Mr. Wexler, if you could so kindly remind me of when you joined the Winston Isles's trust?"

"Four years ago, sir."

"You've done a remarkable job. I could find nothing wrong with your files."

The man practically beamed. I'd have said he was about thirty. And he certainly loved a bow tie. "Thank you, sir. When I started, I made some notes about things that were sloppy, and I tightened the ship, changed the processes."

"That's exactly what I'm looking for. If you don't mind sharing the processed documents with the other directors, that would be fantastic and would at least help us plug the holes. Then we can do a deep dive on any discrepancies."

Tressel was having none of this. "You think I will just bow to what you say? Who died and made you king?"

No one else on the video conference knew that was a direct jibe intended for me. "King? No one. But the president of this trust, the actual King of the Winston Isles, directed me specifically to do this work. If you have a problem with it, you can take it up with him. Until then, I expect your report at the end of the week."

I was done fucking with him. If it was going to be war, I was ready. Guys like Tressel had been looking down their noses at me my whole life. For once, I was on the right side of things. If he wasn't, I was going to give him hell.

*Aren't you complicating things since his daughter lives with you?*

Yeah well, my life was made slightly easier by the fact that he didn't know Bryna was my roommate. And she didn't want me to tell him, so I wasn't going to. But yeah, my life was just about to get all kinds of complicated.

It looked like instead of an ally, I'd made an enemy.

⁂

## *Lucas*

After a day like I'd had, I needed a break. I didn't need the guys giving me shit. We'd braved the happy hour crowds at Prohibition, one of the city's oldest speakeasies. It had been modernized and upgraded, but the place was an institution. It had original oak wood with modern steel accents. It was my favorite spot in the city. But that night, even the familiar atmosphere felt uncomfortable, given the line of thinking I was having.

"So, let me get this right," Roone leaned in across the table, chuckling. "You have the hots for Lady Bryna Tressel?"

"Not the hots. I just said she *was* hot. There's a difference."

So what if Bryna was exactly my type? Dark hair, eyes the color of malt whiskey. A voice like the sweetest vanilla but with the bite of cayenne. It didn't matter, because Roone knew as well as I did, given who her father was, she was way the hell off-limits.

Marcus shook his head. "And the hot girl you're not supposed to go near at all, you've invited to live with you?"

"It's not like that." *Yes, yes, it is like that.* "But while we're at it, neither one of you tell Sebastian. She's not a threat to my safety." She wasn't, but he'd likely be pissed.

I sat back on my bar stool and ran my hands through my hair. "She needed a place to stay. She couldn't stay there."

Marcus slid Roone a smile. "This is the same chick that he broke protocol for, went running after, and left you, his Royal Guard, behind?"

Roone chuckled, picked up his longneck and took a long sip. "The very same."

Marcus was usually a lot more reserved than Roone was. He didn't laugh easily. He was all about the job, but he actually started to chuckle. No, that wasn't a chuckle. That was a full-fledged laugh. As a matter of fact, it was a guffaw. I didn't think I'd ever seen him guffaw before. And I wasn't a fan that it was at my expense.

"Shut up. It's not like that."

Both Marcus and Roone shook their heads, but it was Roone who said, "I can't wait to tell Sebastian."

"You aren't telling Sebastian shit."

"So, when Sebastian asked you to look out for her, you realized he meant you weren't to sleep with her, right?" Roone asked.

I scowled at the both of them. "Oh, ye of little faith. It's easy. Yeah, sure, she's hot, and okay, she's living with me, and we apparently have a class together. But it's fine, because I'm not some idiot kid who's just getting his dick wet. I have self-control."

That caused another guffaw from Marcus, who then mischievously hooked a thumb in my direction. "This guy knows control?"

Roone threw up his hands. "I know, right? Isn't it the tits? This is going to be a bloody train wreck. I can't wait."

"I thought you two were supposed to be my friends?"

Marcus grinned then. "Define friend exactly. We're your guards. And I like taking your money at poker, but that doesn't mean I'm *not* going to give you shit."

It was Roone's turn to grin then. "And I actually would call you my friend, which means I will be giving you all the shit in the world. You're the one who insisted she stay..."

"Yeah, but come on, she's hot. You didn't for one second think that this was going to be a problem?" Marcus asked.

"The thing is, I sort of agreed to do this for Sebastian before I'd seen her. I figured she'd just be some average girl I'd show around the city, point out the coffee shops, and my obligation would be done. How was I supposed to know it would be her?"

Marcus frowned then. "You said that like you know her from before."

I rolled my eyes and then quickly recounted my first meeting with Bryna. The more I talked though, the more Marcus started to shed that stern, serious exterior, and the more he laughed.

He actually laughed so hard he almost fell off his stool. Roone had given up the ghost and had jumped off the stool and laughed so hard he had to move around to walk off the stitch in his side.

Marcus held up a hand. "Wait, wait. So you've seen her bare ass?"

"Yeah." I left out what else I'd seen. "Look, that's not the point. The point *is* I'm not going to do anything stupid."

Roone held out his hand. "Want to make a bet on it?"

Marcus reached for his wallet. "I'll take that bet."

Roone nodded. "Okay, we'll both put fifty in. You keep your hands off her, you get a hundred. If you don't keep your hands off of her, you pay us each a hundred."

Jesus Christ. Steep betting odds. But I knew one thing that they didn't. Bryna was prickly, a pain in the ass who went off on wild bouts of cussing me out. She was basically a porcupine.

One should not fuck a porcupine. "I'll take that bet. Besides, how hard can it be? All I have to do is keep my hands off her."

She was hot though. The safest thing to do would be to find someone else to start fucking immediately. *Stay the hell away from Bryna Tressel.*

I could do that. Easy money. Besides, I'd promised my brother. *A hell of a time to start being the good guy.*

# 13

Never taunt the gods. Why?

Because when you taunt the gods, they fuck with you.

There was no way in hell I was ever admitting to Roone or Marcus that they might be right, but I was a little out of my depth.

That night after I got home from Prohibition, I walked in on Bryna doing yoga in the living room in those tight little yoga pants. As if she didn't know she was torturing me. I mean, she was actually trying to kill me. *Or maybe she has no idea.*

She mumbled some kind of *sorry I'm in your way* and then packed up her little yoga mat. The problem was I'd already *seen* her. Tight pants, sports bra, midriff showing, smooth, tanned skin... It was hard not to imagine her in that canary yellow dress tucked into her thong with her nearly bare ass on display.

*No, never mind that. You will be good. Your brother asked you not to be a dick, so try not to be a dick.* I could do that. It was fine. Easy even.

But the next morning, she was sitting at the dining room table in the shortest pair of shorts I have ever seen in my life.

I told myself to look away.

Apparently, my brain did not send the message to my eyes, because I *couldn't* look away. Then of course, once my eyes got in on the action, my dick... well, he was never one for listening anyway. Thanks to her, I was suddenly prone to hard-ons in my own house, just by walking around. It was like I was thirteen again.

When I walked out of my room, she looked up, eyes wide and brows lifted. She started to gather her things. "Sorry, I spread out a little."

*You're a dick.* "You're fine. I told you to stay here as long as you need to. I meant it."

I felt like the big bad wolf. *Oh Lucas, what big eyes you have. The better to see you with, my dear.*

"Sorry. I'll be looking for an apartment soon."

Now, I really felt like a dick. For some reason, the pit in my stomach bottomed out. "Come on. I didn't say you need to leave or anything."

Her brows lifted. "I'm in your space. You have generously given me a place to crash. I got the impression last night that you weren't too thrilled to find me doing yoga in the middle of the living room. It's probably time for me to go. You've given me a place to stay for a couple of days, and I appreciate it, but I don't want to overstay my welcome."

See, that part where my brother asked me to be a good guy, I needed to remember that. "Stop." I joined her at the dining room table, trying to ignore the long span of legs that I could see through the glass. "When I said stay as long as you need, I meant it. And like I promised, I haven't said a word to your parents. So, there's no rush."

She sighed. "Thank you. It's just that I'm struggling with the internship thing, and the funds I had saved all vanished in a bonfire basically, so everything is shitty." She spoke in that rapid-fire way of hers, all the words clamoring to spill out over each other. "I'm trying to find a job and an apartment, but I haven't had any luck. My internship only pays a small stipend. Everything else is asking for lots of experience. All I really have as experience was doing this charity work, and that extra commitment is sort of going to take a bite out of my actual college work, and I just—"

I held up my hand. "Relax. One problem at a time. What's the priority?"

"A job, I suppose." She frowned. She looked so cute with that little furrow between her brows and her floppy ponytail.

Cute was certainly better than sexy as hell. The big crease on her brow made me want to run my thumb over it and ease the worry. What the hell was that?

In my old life, that frown was exactly what I was looking for. I would take advantage of it, manipulate it, and make it work in my favor. *But you're not that guy anymore.*

Her eyes narrowed. "Why are you being so nice to me? Where's the smug smirk?"

I didn't focus on the last part there. "Because you look like, wait—I'm always nice."

She shook her head. "Something tells me that you're not always nice."

"I am *always* nice. I'm nice in all kinds of ways." I used being nice to work in my favor.

Bryna rolled her eyes, but I could see the hint of a smile tugging on the corners of her lips.

"Okay, so you said the priority is a job. Well, my brother happens to own a bar."

Her brows lifted. "You have a brother? There are *two* of you?"

Shit. I hadn't even realized that slip. Old Lucas never would have made that kind of slip. You lived a con; you were the con. But somehow after a year with Sebastian, I was making all kinds of mistakes. I was living this open kind of life where I didn't have to lie all the time. It made me rusty. "Yeah, there's another one of me. Not nearly as good looking though."

"Oh Lord. I bet you there are dropped panties and angry boyfriends from coast to coast."

I couldn't help a chuckle. "Is that what you think of me? That I cause dropped panties and angry boyfriends?"

She shrugged. "I don't really know you, but from what I do know, I'd say that's probably pretty accurate."

I opened my mouth to argue with her, but then I remembered how I'd met her. About to hook up with some chick at my brother's wedding. So that was really all she knew of me. *Except that time when you saved her.* Yes, there was that. So, hey, there was a good guy in there somewhere. I was not a Tin Man. I did have a heart.

God, there were days when I would have hated being considered a good guy.

"That might be fair in some instances, but not in this one."

She shook her head. "Whatever you say."

I cleared my throat and then, I couldn't help it, honestly, my gaze dipped to her chest. And Jesus, Lord, was that thing she was wearing see-through?

*Look away. Look away now.* Okay, on the count of three. One, two, nope. Still looking. Her fucking T-shirt was see-through. Her nipples were dark. I clearly remember the dusky rose color.

I licked my lips and then forced my eyes to do one thing that they did not want to do. *Close.* Then I hit the reset button and forced them open to look at her again.

She wasn't even paying attention to me. Her gaze was back on her computer, and then it flickered to mine. "You were serious? You can help?"

Fuck, I was going to need to say something. Not 'Can I lick your tits?' *Please do not say can I lick your tits. Do not say can I lick your —*

She cocked her head. "Lucas?"

I cleared my throat. "Yeah, I was serious. I can help you with an apartment, I mean, a job. My brother, like I said, owns a bar in the city. It's not too far from here. Well lit, lots of tourists. It's busy and safe and close enough that if you need anyone to walk you home, I'm right here, so I can do it."

She shook her head. "That's too much to ask. I'll take the job if it's open and you can get me an interview. I'll be super happy to have it. But you don't have to do any of the other stuff."

"Look, I take my job seriously. King Sebastian asked me to do him the favor. It's no big deal." The way she was looking at me, wide eyes, tucked chin, and slight smile, made my dick twitch. "I'll have to check in on you, so that's what I'm going to do, which means that if you need me to walk you home, I can manage that."

A flush crept up her neck, dusting her cheeks a pretty pink. And, oh hell, it sent more blood straight to my dick. Roone and Marcus were right. I was in trouble.

She frowned a little when she caught my gaze directed on her nipples.

"Lucas?"

"Huh?" I dragged my gaze back to hers.

"What the hell is your problem?"

I couldn't help it, my mind was drinking in her nipples and the first thing out of my mouth was, "I can see your tits."

She squealed and then immediately crossed her arms. "Oh my God. Are you just now saying something? Ugh, forget what I said about you being a nice guy."

"It's not my fault. Your goddamned shirt is see-through."

"It is not." And then she glanced down and looked at her shirt. The thing was threadbare and white. And her nipples, God, her nipples...

"See, I told you."

Her face flamed. "Oh my God, why do I keep mortifying myself in front of you? First my ass, then my bare tits, now my tits again."

I dragged my eyes away from her again and forced myself to look up at the ceiling. "I don't know. Maybe I shouldn't have said anything because... well, then you would have kept sitting here and I could look at your tits some more. By now I figure you should just walk around naked. I've already seen all of the good bits."

"Oh my God, you're a pig."

I shrugged. "Well yeah, kind of. I could have told you that. But I'm a nice pig. Remember, I'm helping you get a job."

"I'm grateful, but I'm going to change now."

I sighed. "Yeah, probably a good idea."

She just scampered off. I told myself not to stare at her ass and picture the first time I met her. But apparently, my eyes were *still* not taking commands from my brain, because my gaze was glued to her ass with the added booster of still seeing her nipples in my head. Yeah, that little don't-touch-your-new-room-mate bet with Roone and Marcus was going down in flames. I was so screwed.

# 14

LUCAS

"You don't have to say it. I know this is a bad idea." I was pacing my new office when Matthias Weller walked in through the adjoining office. He wasn't even fazed when I asked if we could speak privately. Marcus and Roone had kept Bryna out of their weekly reports back to Sebastian, but me meeting with Blake Security would have raised a lot of questions I wasn't ready to answer.

The Blake Security resident tech-master shrugged and watched me with shrewd eyes. "What's the big secret, mate?"

I had met him once before. He was mostly quiet, and there was something about him that made my hair stand on end, but he seemed like a decent dude. He and the rest of the Blake Security team had been at Sebastian's wedding. At that time, his attention had been focused on his date, a pretty red head I'd eventually realized was also connected with Blake Security.

"Sorry, but this requires discretion."

He gave me a brisk nod and then rolled his shoulders. "What do you need?"

Wow, that was easy. Just like that, and what do you need? No questions, no recriminations, just a what-do-you-need, and a how-the-hell-do-I-get-it-done. I couldn't lie. Having Blake Security on royal retainer was pretty flipping awesome. I just hoped I could get the information without Sebastian being alerted right away. What I was asking for wasn't a security risk or issue, so it shouldn't raise any kind of alerts... I hoped. "I just need you to look into someone for me. Adele Joninski."

He nodded, but his brows furrowed for a moment. "Anything in particular I need to look for?"

"No. Just the usual warrants, any trouble she might be in. And also Tony Rush."

It felt like a betrayal, giving him my mother's name. But I had to know, because if Tony was here in New York, that probably meant she was too, which also meant they were likely in real trouble. And if they were coming to me, trying to pull me back in with them, it meant *big* trouble.

I made it clear when I left last time that I was getting out. I'd also made it clear that she should join me. I'd begged, but I'd been left standing at the airport with a spare ticket in my hand, and she never showed. She'd chosen him. So, she was on her own.

*Sure, she is. That's why you're standing here with a renowned hacker, trying to see how much trouble she's in.* Okay, so my relationship with my mother was complicated.

You can't want for someone what they don't want for themselves.

Matthias checked his phone, tapped something, and then gave me a nod. "Anything else?"

I frowned. "Ah, no, that's it." But I had to ask. I had to know. "So, I just ask you to do shit, and you do it?"

Matthias's lips tipped in a smirk. "Basically. As long as it's not illegal, and even then, that's a gray area. Anything *you* need done? We work for the crown, so if you need it, we'll do it."

"Where were you two years ago? I could have used you then."

His gaze clouded over then. "We're here now. Anything else?"

I shook my head. "If you can just give me that information, that'll be good."

He opened his mouth and then shut it again, seeming to hesitate. And then he shrugged and decided to go ahead and speak. "None of my business mate, but from the cloak and dagger, it looks like you're trying to unearth some shit."

"I guess you know my history."

He nodded. "Of course. I probably know more about you than you think is even possible."

Yeah, that did not give me the warm fuzzies. "I'm just checking on my Mom. She never made good choices, so I'm just trying to look out for her."

He gave me a nod. "Piece of free advice; You can't save everyone. Some people don't want to be saved."

The problem was I knew that. I knew it well. But she was still my mother, so down the rabbit hole I went.

⚜

## Lucas

After my meeting with Weller, I went to class and tried to ignore Bryna. Everything was fine. I was managing. Not that my new roommate wasn't hot or that I couldn't seem to get her and her tight ass out of my head. Nope, not a problem at all. As a matter of fact, everything was *fine*.

One row down, Marcus glanced back at me and winked.

*Turd.*

Next to me, Bryna took her notes, her glasses sitting perched on the end of her nose. I resisted the urge to reach over and push them up her nose for her because that was too familiar. Too close. *Don't forget creepy.*

And leaning closer would not help at all with the whole scent thing. Everything about her reminded me of the islands. Her hair smelled like lemon and gardenias with just a hint of hibiscus mixed in. Technically, I wasn't even *from* the islands, but all of those scents called to me as if they were beckoning me home.

Every time she got close enough for a whiff, I swear to God, my brain shorted out. It was torture. But, there was no way I was telling that to Roone and Marcus.

They didn't think I could do this. And honestly, they might be right. But I had to try, because the guy I'd been before would have been all *I'm gonna do what I want and fuck the consequences*, and I was not that guy anymore. I couldn't afford to be, honestly. So I clenched my hands around the edge of the desk and prayed for sanity, because how hard could that be? It wasn't like she was *deliberately* torturing me to death.

*Can you be so sure about that?*

Okay, for the most part, she had seemed completely disinterested. Either that, or she was straight up diabolical.

*Either way, you can't touch her.* And I wasn't going to. I could keep my word.

After the professor reminded us that we needed to each

present our own draft outlines and highlight what portions we focused on for our project, she stood.

Out of the corner of my eye, I saw the guy that had been sniffing around her the other day, hovering on the edges. I'd watched when he'd walked up to her that first day, but she'd been so out of it she'd barely noticed him.

What was his name again? Jase, Jason, something like that.

As soon as the people in front of us filed out and she started to scoot, Jase blocked her path. "Bryna, hey."

She craned her head up to blink at him and then inexplicably turned to me.

I gave her my best *I don't know what the fuck he wants with you* look. I shifted on my feet uncomfortably. I didn't want to watch this. It was going to be a shit show.

"Hi, James?"

I cringed for the guy. *Harsh.*

Granted, outwardly I just smirked because I was an asshole.

"Jase, actually. Um, I was thinking, you know, maybe we should grab a coffee. I thought maybe we could run through project ideas. I read some of your work on International Marketing and the Effects of Other Cultures."

Bryna glanced back at me again. Her eyes were wide, and her brows were lifted. She looked like a deer in the headlights. What was wrong with her? I kept waiting for her to tell him off, like she'd done to me, but it never happened. What the hell?

"Um, yeah, you know, sometime."

Poor Jase. His face fell, frown sliding into place as Bryna scooted around him and gave him a small wave.

And then he was left to stare after her.

I couldn't help it. I chuckled. I'm not proud of laughing at another man's heartbreak, but that shit was hilarious. He needed to work on his game.

He turned his gaze sharply on me. "Something funny?"

I shrugged. "No. It would be easier if you had game though."

"I knew it. You want her."

I assessed him again. Was he a threat? "Bryna? Nope." I lied smoothly. "But if I did, you know you wouldn't stand a chance, right?"

"Well, considering you've been sitting next to her for a couple of weeks and you still haven't made that happen, you'll forgive me if I'm not taking love advice from you, right?"

"Hey man, whatever floats your boat. Bryna's a handful. If you think you're up for the challenge, hey, go ahead. Give it a go. It should be fun watching the show."

"Are you always a dick?"

I gave him my trademark-Lucas smile. "Yup. Ask anyone. Good luck with that."

"Oh, don't worry. I don't give up that easily. May the best man win?"

I shook my head. "You don't get it man. If I was interested, I'd have her by now."

*Bullshit.* Yeah okay, mini-bullshit, but he didn't know that. Besides, he was giving off serious twat-vibes and I was not interested in any of that. But I couldn't believe that Bryna was so dumbfounded and tongue-tied around him. It pissed me off.

He had basically just made it my mission in life to keep him from going out with her.

*You still want to believe that you're not interested?*

It was all about the little lies we told ourselves.

# 15

BRYNA

I THINK it was apparent to my trainer, Ellie, that I had never mixed a drink in my life.

Ellie looked like she could be in a music video. She was the kind of girl that rock gods sang about, with her sexy curves.

She had that pouty-lip look that made her a little too sexy to be a model, and she was drop dead gorgeous. There was something innocent about her wide green eyes, but there was also something inherently sexy about the way she laughed. I saw the tip jar getting filled up every single time she walked by the men *and* the women. She had an ease about her that people loved.

So far, all I'd managed to do was mess up orders, break a few glasses, and oh yeah, spill drinks all over myself. I hadn't gotten a single tip.

Luckily, we were all paid a salary on top of whatever we got in tips. When I started, the manager told me that on good nights, once the tips were split, we could all easily walk away with two hundred bucks a night.

If the tips were shared, I wanted to earn my keep and not be a strain on everyone else.

Ellie bounded over. "Let me guess, you've never worked in a bar before?"

I shook my head and wiped off the beer I'd spilled on my hand. "No. Is it that apparent?"

She laughed and nodded. "Yes, absolutely. For starters, when you pour a pint, you're letting in too much foam. Tilt the glass."

"Oh, is that what you do? Mine have all been foam."

"You'll get the hang of it. It's fine. And stop apologizing so much about not getting all the drinks right. You'll get it. Besides, everyone can tell you're a newbie."

I glanced down at my shirt. It said, 'Be patient with me, I'm a noob.'

I laughed. "Yeah, I guess so."

She chuckled and then walked me through how to make a blow job drink.

"Now if only you were giving lessons on real blow jobs."

Ellie cracked a laugh so hard, throaty, and low that every male head in the bar turned to stare at her. She completely ignored them though. "Oh my God, you're hilarious."

"If only I was kidding."

Her jaw dropped open. "What? How does a pretty thing like you run around single and not giving blow jobs?"

My face flamed. "Oh my God. Is that how it sounded?"

Laughing, she nodded. "Yes, that's exactly how it sounded."

I covered my face with my hands.

"No, no, don't cover your face. Pay attention to what I'm doing. You're going to have to do this yourself, so flirt a little. There's no rule that says we can't date customers. And some of the guys that come in here are loaded. Not that you'd necessarily want to date a loaded guy. Sometimes they're just selfish assholes. But sometimes you can get the best date experiences you'll tell all your friends about later. I once got taken to the Hamptons. The guy was a douche though, and the Hamptons? Honestly, I didn't see what all the fuss was about. I'd rather stay in the city and go clubbing with my friends, you know?"

I liked her. "Why did you go out with him then?" There was something refreshingly honest and direct about her.

"Honestly, he was really nice when we met. And I thought he was being sweet when he was like, 'Let me take you to the Hamptons.' But I think he just wanted to show me off. The second we got there, he ditched me for his rich friends. And the girls, they weren't particularly nice." I shuddered. Her story sounded familiar. "Yeah, I know that type." They'd been my friends most of my life.

Slowly through the night, things got better. I finally started delivering the right drinks, and every time Ellie caught me concentrating too hard, she'd force me to smile. The moment I did, I got tips. Decent tips too. Eventually, I started to relax into it.

I wasn't going to start rocking it like I was Coyote Ugly all of a sudden, of course. It wasn't that. Besides, no one would want to see me shake my ass, but I was getting better.

Earlier that day, I had also opened a brand new bank account that was my own and couldn't be accessed by my parents. So whatever money I made, would go into that. Then maybe I wouldn't get robbed by my own family again. Bonus.

As soon as our breaks hit and the two other bartenders, Marie and Alex, took over, we both hit the back room and moaned as we slid onto the bench to sit and rest for a few minutes. "Oh my God, my feet," I complained. "I had no idea."

Ellie eyed my ballet flats. "Yeah, those are cute, but get yourself some nice slip-on tennis shoes, those will do you better. They'll go with anything. With the skirts we wear, they're perfect." I massaged my heels and nodded my thanks. My phone buzzed in my pocket, and I pulled it out, frowning.

**UNKNOWN NUMBER**: *Hey, it's Jase. I hope you don't mind I grabbed your number from the class roster. Earlier, I wasn't that smooth. I was trying to ask you out on a date. No pressure, but I figured I probably should make myself clear.*

I stared at the text. Oh, holy hell. Jase. He was cute, and I'd gotten his name wrong like an idiot. He was very cute.

Not cute like Lucas.

*No, we are not doing Lucas.*

"What are you staring at?"

I held up my phone. "I've got a date dilemma. A guy from one of my classes asked me out. I have no idea how to respond."

Ellie giggled. "Well, is he cute? Do you potentially want to bone him?"

My face flamed. "I don't know. I just... Ugh, I'm so bad at this kind of stuff. I mean, I've had boyfriends, but it's always been kind of a setup situation." I left out the part where my parents set me up, because life was humiliating enough.

"Come on, just reply to him. Say yes. What's the worst that could happen?"

I frowned. "What do I say?"

"Oh my God, just type back, 'Yes, I'd love to. I have plans with a friend from work. Why don't we all meet up?'"

I frowned. "I don't have plans."

Ellie laughed. "We do now." She grinned. "Let's double date. I have this guy I'm sort of seeing. It'll be fun. We'll go to one of those adventure things, you know, like when we were kids, play arcade games and all that stuff. That way he can win you a big plush teddy of some sort. And you can get to see how he is during competition, and under stress, under pressure. It'll be fun."

"I think he wants to spend time *alone* with me, and I don't know..."

"Which is exactly why this is going to be great to see how well he thinks on the fly."

It wasn't a bad idea. And it took pressure off me to perform. "Actually, you know what? That sounds like a much better idea than me going out with him on like a high-pressure date or something."

"Text him back." She leaned back.

**BRYNA**: *Hey, sounds like a great idea. I have plans with a friend on Friday.*

I looked up at Ellie to confirm. She nodded her consent, and I continued.

**BRYNA**: *We should all do something. Maybe at The Spot. Does that work?*

He replied right away.

**JASE** : *Yeah, sounds perfect. Do you want me to pick you up or meet you there?*

I turned the phone to Ellie so she could give me the appropriate response.

"Have him meet us there. That way, you can determine if he's a creeper. If he's not, he gets to take you home. If he is, you and I will just get in the cab together."

I replied back, and suddenly, I felt more at ease. I had a new friend, which was helpful, considering I'd been feeling alone and adrift since I got here. *And* I had a new job. That was thanks to Lucas, so I did need to actually say thank you properly to him. I felt like was on even footing again, like everything was going to work out. And now, I even had a date.

*What are you going to tell Lucas?*

Not a damn thing, because I am not interested in him.

*Liar.*

## 16

WHERE THE HELL was she going?

On Friday, Bryna came home from class frazzled, running in with barely a hello to me on the couch. I was ready for a night of basketball with Roone, but clearly, Bryna had plans.

Thirty minutes later when she came running out of her room, lips looking all glossy and soft, dark hair curling softly and shining, wearing jeans and a semi-clingy top with a low back, I sat up and took attention. So, it *was* a date.

I felt rather than heard the growl. *Down boy.* "Are you going on a date?"

She stopped in her tracks as she was hopping on one foot trying to put a bootie on. "Um, what makes you say that?"

I lifted a brow. "Oh, I don't know. You're running out of here in a rush. You have makeup on." I took a whiff. Yes, I was a glutton for punishment. "You have on perfume. If you don't have a hot date, is this all for me? I told you sweetheart, you're not my style."

She narrowed her gaze at me. Yes, I knew I was irritating

her. I just didn't care at the moment. "If you must know, yes, I have a date."

I lifted a brow. I was going for nonchalance, but I probably looked pissed the fuck off. "Oh yeah? With who?"

"Jase. You were there when he asked me out."

I narrowed my gaze. Just hearing that douche bag's name had my hackles up. "That guy is a twat. Why do you want to go out with him?"

She laughed as she fixed her shiny shades to her ears. "What? You don't even know him."

"Yeah, but I know guys *like* him. Hell, according to you, I *am* a guy like him." I hadn't thought she'd go out with him. In retrospect, I was digging myself into a much deeper hole. And that was probably a bad idea. But the way I figured, I was too far gone now.

"You know what? I don't have time to argue with you. I'll be late."

"You wouldn't want to keep him waiting now, would you?"

She rolled her eyes at me. "You don't even know what that's like, do you?"

I grinned at her. "That's because I'm a sexy motherfucker and girls clamor to go out with me." *All except her.*

She eyed me up and down. "Frankly, I don't see the appeal, but if you say so."

What the hell? Somehow, I always ended up on uneven footing with her.

"Where is he taking you anyway? I doubt anywhere he takes you will be good enough for Lady Bryna Tressel." I regretted it the moment the words were out of my mouth.

That frown between her brows was back, and somehow, I felt bad. There was something about the sadness in her eyes, as if I'd disturbed a nest I wasn't supposed to know about. "I don't use my title. It's meaningless anyway."

"All right. No need to get all prickly. Listen, I'm just trying to look out for you. It's my job, remember?"

She rolled her eyes and just slipped her other shoe on and grabbed her purse.

"Aren't you going to need a jacket? You're showing a lot of skin there."

The glare she shot me said it all. "You know, I don't like my father very much, but I do have one. I don't need another."

*Okay then. So, I overstepped.*

"Fine, where are you headed anyway?" I put out my hand before she could throw darts at me. "I'm just saying it's a safety thing, being your roommate and all. I should have an idea when the cops come knocking."

She sighed. "We're headed to The Spot. It should be fine."

I refrained from saying anything about their date location because secretly, I was thrilled. There was nothing intimate about it. It would be loud and impersonal. There would be people everywhere, throngs of people, and she would hate it. It was just fine by me.

"Great, have fun. Make good choices. Don't do anything I wouldn't do."

"Don't worry, you won't enter into my mind at all during this whole date." With that parting shot, she was out the door.

After she left, I waited a whole five seconds before I had my phone out, calling Marcus and Roone. Roone answered on the first ring. "Mate, where's your girl going? She's all tarted-up."

"I know. Get dressed up boys. We're headed for drinks." There was no way I was telling them that we were headed to Prohibition, which was, coincidentally, right across the street from where she was going. Not that I was being a dick or anything. I was just looking out for her.

*Yeah, yeah, all the lies you can tell yourself.*

⚜

### Lucas

"So, explain to me how you were the one who wanted to go out when we had plans to watch the Knicks game, and now you're the one who's barely touched your beer. And you're glaring outside."

I dragged my gaze back to Roone. "I'm not glaring outside."

Marcus chaffed. "Yeah mate, you are. What's the matter?" He chuckled low. "Are you mad that Bryna had a date?"

"Nope." I lied unconvincingly to myself and to them. The problem was, I could see the front of The Spot. The place looked busy, like it was hopping. They'd done a whole take on the adult game thing, offering everything from dodge ball and that sort of thing to adult arcade games turned into drinking games and such.

Roone spoke up then. "Look mate, we won't give you any shit if you claim you're not into the girl. You can tell us. Of course, you're into her."

"I'm not. She's going out with this guy who's a complete douche-waffle."

Roone grinned at me. "Oh, he's a douche-waffle, is he?"

"Yeah, he is. He clearly sees me as some kind of competition or something."

Marcus guffawed. I didn't like this new side of him, the one that laughed all the time at my expense. I like the one who was serious with a stick up his ass. "He sees you as competition huh? Bet you didn't tell him that Bryna can't stand you."

"She can stand me. She's my roommate, isn't she?"

Marcus shook his head. "Do you have any idea how much apartments in the city cost? You're the cheap option."

I rolled my eyes. "Of course I have an idea. I didn't become a prince until about six months ago, remember?" It was times like this that I missed Sebastian. Well, he'd give me shit. Probably endless amounts of it, but he'd likely cut me a little slack too. There had been a time when he'd been my hang-out buddy. We'd torn the city up. Like Roone and Marcus, he would give me shit, but I think a part of him would have helped me out. He would be my wingman. There was none of that anymore. Rightfully so, because he'd married Penny and she is freaking fantastic.

Marcus leaned forward. "Mate, enough with the charade. We know something is up. Why are we here?"

I glanced at the both of them. "Can you both keep your snark to yourself for a minute?"

Marcus gave me a brief nod. Roone just rolled his eyes and shrugged. "Jury is still out, tell me what it is."

I sighed. "You're such a twat. Bryna's across the street. I don't want her, but there's no way that jackwagon is going to date her."

Roone grinned at me. Marcus just shook his head.

I can lie to myself, right? It wasn't about how I wasn't able to get her out of my head. It was more about not wanting that guy to date her. She deserved better.

*Right. Whatever you need to tell yourself.*

"Drink up boys. We're crashing her date."

## 17

Is THERE *a reason you're hiding in the bathroom?*

I wasn't hiding. I was merely resting, taking a breather from my oh-so-exciting date.

Ellie knocked on my stall door, and I had no choice but to open it. She stood on the other side, all sass and brass. "You have a perfectly cute guy on the other side of those doors, waiting to show you a good old time, and you're in here hiding?"

"I mean, Jase is nice and all, but I just don't feel it, you know?"

Ellie laughed. "Then what are you doing on a date with him?"

This was her idea. "You told me I should open myself up to new experiences. Remember that?"

She chewed her bottom lip. "I did say that, but you said he was cute, so I thought you liked him."

"He is cute. I just—" I sighed. "You're right. I should at least go out there and make an effort."

She shrugged. "Don't make an effort on my part. As far as I'm concerned, we can both climb out the window."

"Wait, what about poor Brian? I thought you guys were a thing?"

"No. He *thinks* we're a thing. He'd been trying to lock me in for months now. I keep telling him I want something casual. I tried to break it off because he clearly wants more. But he says he can do casual, and then he forgets. So, I think I need to just cut him loose."

"So, what do we do? Climb out the window for real?" I glanced down at my top. The front was held down with stickies and a prayer, so I was not confident about my ability to jump out of the window without flashing my tits to the world. *You've done it before.* "I don't think I'm wearing the right outfit for this adventure."

"No, we'll go finish our dates, but then we'll beg off. We're tired, girl time, that time of the month, that should do it."

I laughed. "Oh my God. Actually, Jase might offer to go to the drug store for us or something."

Ellie threw her head back and cracked out a laugh. "Oh my God, he does seem like the type. Overly eager. Almost like he's trying to prove how awesome he can be."

"What's wrong with me? He's a perfectly nice guy, and I can't even get into it."

"Maybe you don't want a nice guy."

I sighed. "Actually, I do. But mostly, I want someone who's different than someone my parents would have picked. Jase is nice, and he's cute. But he's within that realm of someone who would have been picked for me. I need someone different. Someone nobody would ever pick for me. Someone I can get a little lost in, you know? Someone who's not going to fall in line and do what he's told."

Her lips tipped up on a knowing smile. "You sound like you have someone in mind."

*Lucas.*

"I do not."

*Liar.*

"Okay, if you say so. But if you did have someone like that in mind, and you don't want him, toss him my way. I could use a guy like that too."

I laughed. "I don't know. I've always done exactly what I was supposed to do, so I'm trying to do something different. I don't think Jase is it."

"No harm, no foul. At least it will be a fun night still. Did you see the giant beer pong they had? I say we go out there and kick their asses. Then we can just hang out together. At the end of the night, we'll send them packing. Jase might cry, but that's his problem."

"You're right. There's no reason that we can't get our great night."

"One day at work, you're going to have to tell me about your opposite of Jase, because he sounds delicious."

I scowled automatically. "He's not. He's a pain in the ass. He more's more charm than brains." All true statements, except for more charm than brains. As much as I hated to admit it, Lucas was really smart. His responses in class were thorough and in-depth. From what I'd seen, he might be brash, but he made calculated decisions. His mind was always working. Watching him work in class was like watching a completely different human being. It was illuminating and also strangely hot.

After we washed our hands and freshened our makeup, we marched out of the bathroom, determined to still salvage our night by going all-in on the girls-versus-guys scenario. But we were pre-empted.

Not by a couple of girls but by the hottest trio of men. Lucas, his friend Marcus, and his other friend Roone, the one I'd seen him fighting with the other day. They were talking to Brian and Jase. Well, Lucas was mostly just kicking ass, and Jase was glowering at him.

When we marched up, introductions were made all around. Marcus took the drink orders and headed to the bar. Meanwhile, I glared at my roommate. "Fancy seeing you here. I thought you were staying home and watching basketball."

He grinned at me. "I mean, that's the thing. The boys called, so we had to make a night of it. Imagine running into you here."

"Yeah, *imagine.*" *Was he here on purpose? No way this was coincidence.* "Well, Ellie and I are on a date, so we'll see you guys around."

Lucas groaned. "Oh, come on, at least let us finish the game."

Roone flashed me a grin, and even I was momentarily stunned. They made a stunning trio along with their boy Marcus, and every girl in the joint had started staring over at our group. Ellie was no help because every time Roone opened his mouth, she would stare at him like he was a lollipop she wanted to lick.

"Well, we're on a date."

Jase nodded. "Yeah. Sorry, Newsome. I guess you're shit out of luck."

But Brian was having none of it. "Oh, come on Jase, at least let me win my money back."

Jase didn't look like he wanted to. But then Lucas gave him a grin that made me want to slap him and said, "Oh no worries, we'll just take the W. No big deal. Enjoy your date."

I could feel the change in Jase then. The inability to walk away from a fight. But it was a dumb fight and with Lucas, no less. Still, Jase's arm fell away from my shoulder, a fact that somewhat relieved me. He'd rather fight with Lucas.

And then it was on. Marcus returned with drinks for us, but the guys were already locked in the game of beer pong. The problem was, apparently, Lucas was a ringer. Before Jase and Brian even knew what was happening, Lucas and Roone had won... again. And Jase and Brian had consumed copious amounts of alcohol.

It was Jase who suggested another game after that. Lucas grinned. "Pool? Oh, come on guys. Aren't you supposed to be on a date?"

Jase didn't even look at me. "It's cool. We'll just finish a quick game."

And just like that, my date was now on a date with my roommate.

At the pool table, Ellie and I were left mostly standing around. We soon found the giant Jenga next to the pool table and occupied ourselves with it, having a blast. Hell, who needed dates anyway? Or annoying roommates?

At some point, Lucas came over and was watching our game intently. "Aren't you supposed to be over there, playing pool?" I asked him.

"It's taking your boyfriend forever to set up a shot."

"He's not my boyfriend."

Lucas grinned. "I know. I just wanted to hear you say it."

"Why are you such an asshole?"

"What are you doing having a date with that guy anyway? I thought you had better taste."

"Oh yeah? And who should I be on a date with? Someone like you?"

I hadn't quite meant to make it sound like a suggestion, but the *'you'* came out on a hushed tone that even to my ears sounded like a come-on.

Lucas's gaze dipped to my lips for just a second, but I saw it. His pupils dilated, and something low in my belly pulled. *Oh God. Why this one?* He licked his bottom lip, and, swear to God, my lady parts clenched. Lucas shook his head. "Nah, I like my girls less uptight. Besides, my charm doesn't work on you. It would make it a lot easier if it did." His voice was low, hypnotic, lulling me into compliance, pulling me into falling under his spell. But then I remembered the first time I met him and got the cold shower I needed.

"Oh, or you could just be an honest guy. No charm, no pretense, just a guy."

He laughed. "What's the fun in that?"

Ellie came over with her beer. "Your turn."

While I went over to ponder my move, I could hear her jabbering to Lucas. "So, your friend, the red head, like what's his deal?"

Lucas laughed. The low rumble of it had a velvety quality that made me want to wrap it around myself, and roll all over it, which was obviously a problem.

"Roone's single. Why?"

Ellie grinned up at him. "You know, just curious. I might need to take a ride on that fire crotch."

Lucas cracked-up so hard he snorted beer up his nose and then started coughing.

Jase called over. "Newsome, your shot."

Lucas nodded, but he was still coughing until I smacked his back and rubbed. Was it me, or did he start to purr? His gaze lifted to mine, his hazel eyes looking green in the light. "Looks like you know how to rub me."

"Right." I snapped my hand back and scoffed at him. I wanted him to run back to his game. "Ellie, what did you say to him?"

She shrugged and laughed. "I don't know. Something about fire crotch. The poor thing almost wasted a perfectly good beer."

I laughed too. "You are impossible."

She grinned. "Yep, I know. So, are you going to tell me what your deal is with your roommate there? Is he the *not* Jase? Because the way he looks at you makes me want to bust out my battery-operated boyfriend."

"No deal. He's just my roommate. He's someone my parents asked to look out for me. Hence, why I want nothing to do with him."

"Why? He's cute, super charming, and he's totally into you."

"Are you insane? Him? First of all, he's *not* into me. He just acts like that to annoy me." But somewhere in the deep, dark recesses of my mind, my inner diva sat at attention. Just the idea that Lucas might be interested in me made the butterflies in my stomach dance yet again. *Stay strong.* "Second of all, he will sleep with anything or anyone at any time. That's his deal. I don't need some long relationship, but I need to not be one of many. It's just a thing I have."

Ellie nodded. "I can see that. As it stands, he's very popular here."

The waitresses had all been over several times to offer any assistance he might need. He'd even gotten us a free pitcher, just from that pretty mug of his and his never-ending charm. I don't know what it was, but to me it just came across as insincere. I liked him better when he was being real.

"Are you sure you don't like him?" she asked.

*Not really.* "No. I promise, he's a pain in the ass."

Ellie held up her hands. "Okay, fair enough. I'm just saying you're mighty defensive for someone who doesn't like the guy. And he keeps staring at you like you are the last ice-cream cone on earth."

I shifted my gaze to the muscles of his back as he leaned over the pool table for his next shot. "I mean, I'm not blind, okay? He's, uh, cute."

She laughed. "Honey, he's more than cute. That man is hot enough to make you ruin your life."

"Yeah well, I have no intention of ruining mine for Lucas Newsome."

🍂

## Bryna

It turned out Lucas, Roone, and Marcus won that round of pool too, and the giant Jenga, and giant Connect Four, and what do you know, the giant poker as well. By the end of the night, Jase and Brian were feeling thoroughly like losers. *Drunken* losers. I don't know what possessed me to throw Jase a bone when he offered to take me home. Lucas, as usual, was being a dick and said, "Well, considering she lives with me, I might as well just take her home."

I glanced between the two of them and finally threw out a tie breaker. "Oh my God, we can just all share a cab."

Except, I didn't really *want* Jase to take me home, but because Lucas didn't want him there, I absolutely did. It was childish, I know.

Marcus and Roone took a different car back to the building, with me, Jase, and Lucas crowding into the back of a taxi, but we arrived at the same time. The five of us took the elevator in silence. As soon as we hit our floor, Marcus and Roone vanished into their apartment. Then Lucas unlocked our door and went in first. He didn't even look back but left the door wide open.

I rolled my eyes. Way to give me privacy. I'm surprised he didn't stay to watch. "I'm so sorry. I didn't realize he would try to screw with me and mess with our date."

Jase shifted on his feet. "It's fine. It was actually kind of fun. Who knew you would be so competitive?"

"It's a little-known fact, but I hate to lose. As a matter of fact, I'm not even allowed to play Monopoly in my house. I get a little crazy."

He laughed. "Yeah, I can see that."

And then I could see it coming. That look in his eye told me he was going to kiss me good night. He'd started to sober up, but I still wasn't that into it. If I didn't want that, now was the time to stop him.

My gaze darted toward the door. Lucas hadn't turned on any of the lights inside, and all I could see was darkness. I didn't know if he was right inside the door, waiting, or watching, or anything. This was how it was going to go down.

*Fantastic.*

*Asshole.* What right did he have to make judgments on who I decided to date? If he wanted to stand there and watch, hell, so be it. He was going to get a show. I could practically feel his gaze on me. My skin was tight and itchy. It was like a low, trembling pulse between us, and if I followed the feeling, I'd know exactly where he was in the darkened room.

When Jase slid a hand to my waist and pulled me close, I could feel Lucas's gaze on the back of my neck, watching me, *daring* me.

*Okay, you want to play that game?* Fine. I gave Jase my warmest smile and tipped my head up, and he planted his lips over mine.

His lips were soft, sliding over mine, his tongue persistent, but not intrusive. All in all, it was a nice kiss. Great. *Fine.*

Except, I felt nothing. No heat, no interest, just pleasantly surprised. Just knowing Lucas was there changed everything.

I didn't mean to do it, but I started pretending that it was Lucas I was kissing, wondering what it would feel like, his tongue sliding against mine, his hands clenched on my hips. Would he pull me closer? Would his hands slide over my ass, pulling me against him, making me feel every pulse of him?

Because Jase's hands certainly didn't wander.

When I pulled back, he gave me a wide smile. "So, I'm going to call you tomorrow, okay?"

I nodded but said nothing. Because I knew tomorrow when he called, I would either avoid his call, or have to tell him that while it was a very nice date, I wouldn't be going on another.

As soon as I stepped into the apartment and closed the door, I sighed and leaned against it. I spoke into the darkness because I could still feel him. "Did you enjoy the show?"

He chuckled softly from his spot against the window. "Oh immensely. He looked oh so engaged. But there was something at the end there, it was almost as if he got good all of a sudden." In the moonlight, I could see his gaze directed at me. I could feel him. "So tell me, who were you thinking about those last few seconds? You certainly weren't thinking about him." His chuckle was low. "Matter of fact, if I had to wager, you were thinking about me, maybe?"

"You wish. Good night." I deliberately marched by him down to my room and closed the door. The second I was on my own, I sighed against the frame and slunk down to the floor.

He could completely tell. He knew I'd been thinking about him in those last seconds of that kiss. And I couldn't help but wonder, if that had been Lucas kissing me, would I have been able to even think of anything else?

JINX WAS MY FIRST CALL. I hit one on the speed dial, and she answered on the second ring. "What's up, buttercup?"

"I have the worst roommate in the history of roommates."

She just laughed on the other end of the line. Behind her, I could hear the distant sound of calypso. Was she outside? Was she on her balcony just soaking up the smell of hibiscus? Hell, I missed home.

"What did he do this time?"

"Why are you so calm about this? You should be mounting attacks or coming to rescue me from his shenanigans. He is a pain in the ass, an asshole, all the things with ass in them."

"He's a twat-cake, but he's a totally hot twat-cake, if that helps."

Not good enough. "It does not help. Thank you very much."

"What did he do?"

I crawled over to the closet and put her on speaker as I toed off my booties and changed into my comfy pajamas. "I had a date tonight. A perfectly nice date."

I could practically hear Jinx perking up on the other end as her voice went just a little bit chirpier. "Ooh, a date?"

"Okay, it wasn't like a date, *date*. I mean, he was nice. Cute. Eager, I guess. I just wasn't, I don't know, super into him."

She sighed. "Oh, well that sucks. What happened to operation live life to the fullest, your best life and all that?"

"Well, I was trying to do that, which is why I said yes to the date."

"Okay, well that's good. It gets you out there to see what's happening on the market."

"That was my thought too. We were having fun, I guess. We went on double date with my new friend Ellie and this guy she's seeing."

"Okay, double date still sounds fine. What was the problem?"

"I don't know." I was trying to say it out loud, but it didn't sound very convincing. "I just wasn't feeling him, I guess. He felt like the safe choice. No chemistry, no challenge."

"Ah, so no fun. I can see how you'd go safe."

"But the whole point of leaving home was to live my life. Like really live. And the first thing I do is go out with the kind of guy that my parents want me to date, which just sucks. So, left to my own devices, I have no idea how to pick the right kind of guy. I mean, basically, you dress this guy up in a nice suit, send him to the Hamptons or St. Kitts for the summer, and he is basically every single guy my parents have forced on to me."

"Okay, so we need to just edge up your choice making a little bit. A great guy who's different and unique. That should be easy."

I sighed. "Easier said than done. Besides, the date with Jase wasn't really the problem anyway."

"Oh God, his name is Jase? It's like straight out of the standard rich-frat-boy playbook."

I groaned. "I know. Jase. He sounds like he belongs in a soap opera. I don't know. He was fine. He wasn't the problem."

"For the record, I'm going to let you finish your story. But just so you know, your date should never be *fine*. It should be 'That was really fun' or 'I'm not going to see that guy again.' Those are the only two acceptable options."

"Hmph, I guess you're right. But anyway... So there I am with Jase and Ellie and the guy she was dating, Brian, and in walks freaking Lucas."

There was a pause on the line.

"I swear, what is it with you two?"

I was so angry, I didn't realize I had been squeezing my hands into fists until the slight sting of pain in my palms alerted me. "It's like he's deliberately trying to make me insane, like that was what my parents asked him to do. 'While you're at it, drive her crazy.'"

"I know. He showed up? To what, drive you home?"

"No. To just hang out, like he and his friends had just chosen to go to the same place." I was clenching my jaw too. "When I told him where I was going, I didn't expect him to follow me."

Jinx laughed. "Honey, you know I'm your girl. Ride or die till the end. But is there maybe a chance you *wanted* him to show up? Is there a chance you were hoping something like that would happen?"

"No!"

Another pause.

"Okay, okay. I'm just asking."

"Did you miss the memo where I can't stand him?"

"No, I got the memo. It's just that you keep saying you can't stand him, but half of our conversations are about Lucas."

I opened my mouth to argue with her and then snapped it shut. She had a point there. I needed to stop talking about him. It didn't matter that one look from him and my insides were a melted pool of goo and hormones. Nope. No more. The quickest way to get Lucas Newsome out of my mind was to not think about him. Easy-peasy. I could do that.

"You know what? You're right. No more Lucas. It doesn't matter that he crashed my date. It doesn't matter that I laid a spectacular kiss on Jase and he saw the whole thing and then told me that I have feelings for him."

There was a bark of laughter on the other end of the line. "Say what?"

"It was just, you know, Jase brought me home, and Lucas, of course, had to ride with us in the cab. When we arrived, Lucas went in first, and then there he was, just in the doorway. And I had it in my head that if he was going to crash my date, then he was going to have to watch the whole thing."

"In other words, you wanted to make him jealous."

I sighed. "Yes, I wanted to make him jealous."

She tsked. "I swear, it's like you two are just circling each other like caged tigers."

"I'm not the one being crazy. I'll stop when I finally find my own place. But for now, the fight is on." I needed to stop talking about him, or I really was going to admit to thinking about him. "Tell me about home. I don't want to talk about Lucas anymore."

"Um, you know, the usual. Classes are good. Mom drives me bonkers, of course. I think I'm going to have to move from home and get a small apartment near campus. You know how it is, you're studying oceanography, but you can't be near the ocean. Apartments by the ocean don't come cheap. So, I need to figure that out."

"You know, I should have just stayed home, and we could have had a place together."

"As much fun as I know that would have been, under no circumstances would I have held you back from your dream. You couldn't stay here. Your parents will control you too much. You had a great opportunity. I miss you though."

"Well, my parents are trying to control me now, so nothing has changed."

"Yeah, but it's harder in New York City. Here, it would be easy. It would have been *Lady Bryna this, Lady Bryna that.* You would have hated it."

"You're right. So, Aunt Willow is making you insane, huh?"

"Yes. She answered my phone and was chatting with the guy I started seeing. She's crazy. The other day she loaded my clutch with condoms and lube. I think there is such a thing as too progressive."

"Man, I miss your Mom."

Jinx's mother was one of the circuit judges in the islands. She was brash, unfailingly honest, and one of my most favorite people on the planet.

We chatted for another moment or two, and I could feel my blood pressure lowering. I missed my bestie. I missed all of the things we would've been up to, but I mostly missed talking to her. And then she dropped the next bomb.

"And then, there's this guy, he's been going around the island insisting he's the long-lost prince. I mean, there have been lots of people like that since it was announced that there was a lost prince and princess, but this guy is apparently getting traction. There's like a petition to get his blood tested. He's working this to the end. Apparently, he even got a bank to loan him some money on his claim that he's the next prince. It was a whole hoopla because the bank apparently wanted the king and queen to back the loan. Obviously, they refused. They asked what proof he had that he was a prince, and basically, it was just his word that the bank had gone on. It was awesome. News reports have been going off on him since."

"Jesus, that guy is a con man."

"Yep, plain and simple. And a pretty decent one, I'm guessing, if he managed to convince a bank to give him a loan."

"I swear, people are insane with the things they will do to be close to the royal family. It probably isn't even that great being a royal. The restrictions, God, I ran away from those restrictions. Hell, I'm not even royal. My parents were members of the court, but that has nothing to do with me. I can't even imagine all the people coming out of the woodwork to get a piece. I don't envy the king and queen right now."

"Neither do I. Then, if you remember, the treason trial is about to begin in a month or so. The whole thing has been crazy. But, other than that, it's just, you know, the islands."

An hour later, I felt more like myself. But when I climbed into bed, my brain slipped into dreamland.

Lucas was right. The second my head hit the pillow, it was him I thought about. What if he'd been the one I'd kissed instead of Jase? Instantly, my body went flush, my thighs parted slightly, and my breathing shallowed. Despite myself, I wanted him. Good thing he was never going to find out.

## Lucas

This called for a cold shower. An ice bath even. Jesus. I'd wanted to rip that guy's head off his goddamn shoulders. And his name, Jase. What kind of fucking name was that?

All night I'd kept the low-key aggression and the urge to club Bryna over the head and drag her home under wraps. But seeing her plant one on that douchebag had been my undoing.

Had she been thinking about me? I couldn't explain how I'd known she wasn't thinking about that dude. But there was something about the way she'd turned her body, as if she'd known exactly where I was and knew I was watching her. Knew that I was wishing I was Jase.

*You're an idiot.*

Yes, yes, I was. I needed to get this shit under control or living with her was going to be a problem.

My dick throbbed again, as if to notify me that he was lonely, and I'd blown his shot at getting someone other than me to touch him. "Yeah, man, I know. I fucked up. But she was never gonna happen.

I turned on the shower and hissed a curse as ice water sluiced my arm. As I sent up a silent prayer that the water would warm, I ducked my head under the chilly spray.

This was fine. I could do this. I just had to remember I was in control here. Control the mark. It was something Tony had always said. And I'd thought it was bullshit. But the basics were stay ahead of your mark, and never be caught unaware.

Twice tonight, she'd surprised me; First when she'd announced she had a date, then when she'd kissed the guy in front of me. *You could have looked away.*

As if. I'd been picturing myself kissing her.

Through the window in the bathroom, I could see that stars illuminated the sky and winked at me as the water ran through my hair. My dick still throbbed despite the temperature.

As if on cue, my mind went to the one place I didn't want it to go. The vision of her kissing me, throwing herself into it. I'd imagined how many different ways that she would taste. I could almost hear the hitch I'd hear in her voice, the way her pupils would dilate.

Shit. I'd never get any sleep this way. Wrapping my fist around my erection, I pumped the soap-slickened flesh in a slow, deliberate motion. As blood surged to my groin, I pictured Bryna on her knees before me, all that glorious hair slicked back with water as she wrapped those luscious lips around me.

I could almost feel her tongue lap the length of me before circling the tip in a deliberate motion. I could feel her delicate hands, wrapped around my girth as she stroked in time to her suckling mouth.

Blood roared through my head. I slapped a hand against the shower stall to steady myself against my release. "Fuck, Jesus, Damn," I bit out as I dragged in gulps of air.

This was it. No more fantasizing about my roommate. It stopped here. It had to if I was going to keep my word.

## 19

LUCAS

I STILL COULDN'T GET the sight of her kissing that douche bag out of my head. It had been a long, sleepless night. Did she actually like him? Hey, maybe that was her type... total, complete dickheads. I could believe it.

I returned from the coffee shop to find her gearing up with her to-go mug, jacket, keys, and a map. "Where are you off to?"

The smirk she gave me was all sass and brass. "None of your business."

"Another hot date with Jase?"

She put her hands on her hips, drawing my attention to her curves, which honestly wasn't going to help the situation. "What part of none of your business did you not quite get?"

I held up my hands. "Truce." I held up the second latte I'd brought. "This is for you."

She stared at it for a moment and then narrowed her gaze up at me, and I sighed. "It's not poisoned or anything. It's a peace offering."

"For what?"

I shrugged. I should have known she'd make it hard. "I realized I probably shouldn't have crashed your date last night."

"Probably shouldn't have? Where's the part where you get to apologizing?"

I gritted my teeth. "Okay, I shouldn't have done that. It was wrong. Please accept this coffee as an apology."

She took the coffee, sipped it and moaned. God, that sound. I would never be able to get it out of my mind.

Her tongue flicked out to lap up a drop of latte, and my gaze pinned on it. Oh Jesus. This is a problem, because I wanted to be the one to lick that drop off her lip. I tore my gaze away and poised myself to smile at her. She wasn't even looking at me. She was just merely enjoying the simple pleasures of her coffee. "I take it that's better than the coffee you have?"

She nodded. "Mine was just instant. But I need the fortification if I'm going to find an apartment today."

My brows snapped down. "What?"

"Yeah, I mean, this is temporary. I can't just stay in your place free of rent. You need your space back."

"Yeah, of course. I just—" What the hell was I going to say? That I don't want her to go? We'd been snapping at each other for days. The last three weeks had been this delicate game of cat-and-mouse torture. She had a point. We probably needed some space, and also, that would help me not sleep with her, because I had the propensity to be a dick. "Yeah, I guess I just didn't really think about it."

"How can you not? My shit is everywhere. Don't you want your place back?"

I hadn't even thought about it. This penthouse I'd been given by my brother was at least ten times bigger than most of the places I'd ever lived in. It was nice to live with someone else.

Being on my own with all the luxury made me feel like a fraud. It only seemed to remind me of the guy I'd been before. Even the closets had been stacked.

The suits, the ties, the need to play the part, play a role. I liked to be just plain old Lucas. That way, when the shit hit the fan, I could run. It was easy to run when you didn't have much to carry.

I shook that thought off and focused on her. She'd worn her hair off to the side in some kind of messy-braid situation. Several strands had escaped, curling around her face. She was adorable standing there in her pink T-shirt and white scarf thingy.

She looked young. Carefree. Innocent. I couldn't very well let her go apartment hunting looking like that. Some lecherous landlord would take full advantage of her. Assholes.

*Or you just want to spend time with her.*

No, that wasn't it. I was just doing my job. Like a good prince. Like those commercials. I could almost hear the jingle, 'Like a good prince, Lucas is there.'

"Let me come with you. Some of these places could be shady. They see a young girl looking for an apartment or studio, and they can get weird. I'll help you find something."

What was wrong with me? I was the boogeyman I was warning her against. I had done cons upon cons since I was seven. Saying things like, 'Yes sir, of course I've been hit by that car.'

The early cons we'd started with were personal injury. It worked a lot in stores. When we tapped out of a market, we moved on quickly. I was an expert at packing up in the middle of the night. The older I got, the less I carried, or rather, the less I gave a shit about anything.

As it was now, all I mostly carried around was my passport.

Well, my two new passports, thanks to Sebastian and Blake Security. Lucas Newsome had a brand spanking new passport. And it was clean. I could go anywhere at any time. I had dual citizenship to the US and the Winston Isles. For the Winston Isles, I also had diplomatic status, so I could pretty much do whatever the fuck I wanted, get away with it, and leave the country. Not that I would, because I'm a good guy now.

Bryna's voice brought me back from my reverie. "Anyway, you don't have to come with me. I got this. I know exactly what I am looking for. I got a whole bunch of places to look at that seem cozy and really cute. Maybe kind of a commute, but I can afford them, so that's what matters."

I shook my head. "No, anything that says cozy means it's tiny. If it's cute, they're showing you the wrong apartment. And a bit of a commute, that means you're going to be living in Long Island. Come on, I'll walk you through it."

She eyed me warily. With a hand on her hip, she crossed her legs and cocked her hip. "What's going on?"

I sighed. "Like I said, I was a dick last night. I know it, and you know it. Neither one of us has to talk about it." And then because I couldn't help myself, I added, "Unless you want to talk about when you went to your room last night. Were you thinking about me?"

She just rolled her eyes. No flush. No embarrassment. No nothing. Completely immune to me. What the hell?

"No, I don't want to talk about it. Are you sure you want to come with me?"

"Yeah, this will be fun. I'll show you the city. Like I was supposed to in the first place."

"Don't you have anything better to do today?"

"I have a paper, but it's mostly done. It's not due for another week. We have our project. I figure we can discuss some of it on our little jaunt. Most of my work is just reading. It's my last semester. I took it easy with the load."

"Oh, I didn't realize that." She frowned. "Do you have a job yet?"

"I—" How the hell should I say this? *Lie.* "I'm still looking. My majors were international relations, political science, and economics. So, I've got a couple of feelers out, contacts I'm working. You know how it is. All it takes is one thing, and then everything falls into place."

She nodded and chewed her bottom lip. "Wow three majors. I don't know how you do it. I'd be a disaster. I like planning. I like to know that things are all settled. Which is why all of this has been such... well, you know how it's been going."

"Yeah. Pretty shitty of your parents to shut off your accounts. That's stupid. But you have a place to stay as long as you need it. There's no rush for you to find a place, but I get it. More privacy."

She nodded. "I want to give you yours back too. Never overstay your welcome. It's one of my grandmother's rules. She has many, many rules."

"I'm not sure I'd like your grandmother very much."

She laughed. "Actually, you'd probably love her. While she had rules, the old lady knows how to cut loose. Although, she never really stands up for me. She always just says, 'You'll find your way.'"

"I believe you."

"You're serious?"

"Sure am. Come on, let's go."

As I followed her to the first apartment, I wondered if I was making a huge mistake. That much time with Bryna, in close proximity, that couldn't be good for me.

I pulled out my phone and sent a quick text to Roone and Marcus. Marcus was already waiting for me downstairs. Roone had gone to get the car, but now there was a slight change of plan. I wouldn't be headed to the Young Artists Association meeting like planned. I'd be apartment hunting with Bryna in the city. They were going to kill me, but somehow in my head, it all made sense.

**#worthit**

I HATED THIS. Lucas was right. Cozy, for all intents and purposes, meant miniscule. We saw a place that was smaller than the bedroom Lucas had given me. It had a murphy bed, which was a bonus I suppose. But the kitchenette, which consisted of a sink and a hot plate, was meager. And there was only room in the place for a chair.

But hey, at least *that* place had been clean. Place number two on my list was a decent size. I didn't need much in terms of space. But the landlord neglected to mention that it was legitimately in the back of a warehouse. It was a storage room or something. It had a bathroom with the most disgusting sink I'd ever seen in my life.

The moment we walked in apartment number three, Lucas took my hand and dragged me back out. And for once, I didn't fight him. I had no intention of spending any amount of time in there. The place had zero natural light, one skylight, and one very small egress window that would actually qualify for an apartment. I didn't even see the bathroom. And hell, I didn't want to.

The landlord had seemed insulted that we hadn't wanted to walk in his dingy little hellhole. It was dank and dark, and there was no way I could walk back from class at night in that neighborhood.

We went to Alphabet City next. That one was much better. There was a room for rent in a two-bedroom apartment. The apartment was bright and airy and decorated nicely. Unfortunately, the girl renting the room made it very clear that everything in the common area was hers and hers alone. The only space I was getting was the very tiny, cramped bedroom, which was formerly a closet. I had no access to the living area, and I was expected to buy my own meals elsewhere.

We were walking back to the subway, and out of the corner of my eye I could have sworn I saw someone familiar. "Hey, is that—" I didn't get to finish because Lucas dragged me into the car just in the nick of time before the door closed.

"Everything okay?"

He nodded. "Yeah, just wanted to catch the train."

I leaned my head on his shoulder because, damn it, I was exhausted. My feet hurt. Actually, they full-on throbbed. And part of me wanted to cry. I hated my parents, actually hated them. I hated my stupid old roommate Dana. I hated all of this.

"Buck up. You didn't think you'd go on one apartment hunt in New York City and find the perfect cozy place to accommodate you, did you? I mean honestly, you haven't even seen any roaches yet. How will you ever complete your New York City apartment hunting experience?"

"No, please. I can't. After everything today, please do not show me roaches."

He chuckled softly. I could feel his shoulders moving as I sat with him. The gentle rocking of the train made me sleepy. "Hey, these are the places you picked out. I would have picked out completely different places."

"I mean my set priorities were clear. I wanted a female roommate, a clean bathroom, and a kitchen. Not even a big kitchen. Just, you know, an actual full stove and a sink. How hard is that?"

"Well, in apartment number three, apparently the guy didn't know you wanted a female roommate. So his thoughts of locking you in his tiny little dungeon and keeping you as a sex slave were completely dashed. Did you see the look on his face when he saw me come in with you?"

I shuddered. He legitimately looked upset. And then he looked pissed-off. When he'd said, 'I thought you were coming alone,' it was the biggest clue to get the hell out.

"Oh my God, this is so hard."

"Yeah, it is. People will do all kinds of things for a decent apartment in the city. I once had this great rent-controlled place, not far from where I live now."

"How in the world did you ever get that?"

"Long story."

I wasn't even sure if he noticed, but he started to frown when I asked him questions that were too personal, as if remembering something he didn't want to remember. But every time that shadow crossed his gaze, he looked like he was, I don't know, hurting maybe? But then it was gone all of a sudden. "Why did you do that?"

He blinked and glanced down at me. "Do what?"

"Sometimes it's like you've gone somewhere, remembering something."

He shrugged. "No, I'm right here."

"You looked sad. What could you have to be sad about?"

He licked his lower lip and shook his head. "You're right. Nothing. I've lived a charmed life. Much like you."

There was no malice when he said, "Come on. Let's go find your dream palace."

The train stopped, and he stood and extended his hand to mine. I took it, letting my hand slide into the warmth of his. He made me feel safe and protected. Who the hell was Lucas Newsome, really? Because that persona he put on for the rest of the world, that wasn't really him. I'd seen it today in flashes. Bits and pieces. The Lucas I saw on a daily basis, the one that was too charming for his own good, that wasn't the real one.

⚜

*Lucas*

Was it bad that there was a part of me that was secretly happy she hadn't found anything decent? It was probably worse that I didn't mention that my former place was currently sublet, and I was looking for a new renter. That place had hardly been palatial, but, anything clean, nice, rent controlled, and probably a lot closer to her budget than a couple of places we had seen would be awesome. But I wasn't offering the information just yet. What she didn't know wouldn't hurt her. Besides, I liked having her around. She gave me someone to fight with. That was entertaining as hell.

"Yeah, easy for you to say. You live in a penthouse. How the hell do you live in a penthouse again?"

I shrugged. Let her imagine all the possibilities. "Let's just go with a generous benefactor."

She slanted me a look. "How come you're never serious?"

"Okay, but if I tell you, you won't believe me."

"Try me."

"Bitcoin."

She frowned. "Are you serious?"

I laughed. "No. I have a job as Director of Charitable Contributions." That was true. She didn't need to know when I got the job. She also didn't need to know about the money I'd stolen and used as seed money before Sebastian had popped into my life. "It's a non-profit, but it pays decent."

"I'm curious. I know nothing about you. How is that? You've been my roommate for weeks. All I know is that you annoy me and you have a tendency to walk around shirtless."

I winked at her to annoy her. "Oh, so you noticed."

She rolled her eyes. "You think you're charming, but you're not. You act like you think you're God's gift, but really, while you have a certain appeal, you'd probably do better if you were just yourself."

"Ouch."

"It's like this guy I see is just a shell, like you're putting on a show. There is this part of you sometimes that seems sad."

My heart hammered against my chest. Why did she see so much?

I laughed then. "What about me says I'm sad? I've got it good, and I know it. Women dig me, present company excluded. But hey, the odds are in my favor. I'm good looking as hell. Smart. I make money, and I'm fun."

She slanted me another glance that said she didn't agree. I

continued, "Okay, fine. Most people think I'm funny. You are the only person who doesn't. So why would I be sad?"

As we walked down through Little Havana, she took another tiny bite of her gelato. Her sandals shuffled on the concrete. The cacophony of vendors shouting, taxis beeping, and cars driving surrounded us as she seemed to ponder the question. "Like I said, there's something about your eyes. Every now and then you go somewhere far away, and it seems to make you really sad."

"As if I'd share my secrets with you. What about you, Bryna Tressel? Why did I find you jumping out of a window at a ball? That's the real question."

"My parents had me engaged to my boyfriend on my twentieth birthday. Instead of presents, they got me a ring I didn't want." I sighed. "Later, I caught him cheating with Charity and dumped him. I might have also played their sex tape at the engagement party."

He whistled low. "Wow."

"Yeah, they acted like I was being ungrateful. He cheated, and they wanted me to marry him *still*. Anyway, fast forward two years, and they orchestrated a sit-down at the wedding to resolve our differences and see if things could start again."

"You're kidding."

"I wish I was."

She shook her head then. Most of her hair had escaped the braid by now and was a wild mess of curls. "Let's just say I don't have the best of luck in dating. Actually, I've never really dated on my own."

I frowned. "What the hell does that mean?"

"Well, I've had two boyfriends. Both of them were sort of

arranged by my parents. You know how the last one worked out."

I blinked down at her. "What the hell are you talking about?"

"You heard me. Both times, I ended up dating people that my parents just kind of shoved me toward. And you know, it's like proximity. Like, oh okay, you've been around them. You know the same people. Your parents are friends. There's always a dinner, or a function or something. You're always sitting with that person. You're basically dating them. And so then, you just sort of start *really* dating them. Next thing you know, they're walking you home or you're getting into some chauffeured car together, and someone kisses you good night." She shrugged. "That's how it worked in my case. I have zero idea how to do things the normal way."

I stared at her. "You seem so blasé about it."

"Not really. I wanted a chance at normal, you know? I stayed in the islands for university, but with my father's influence and everything else, it's hard to be me. You can't be normal if your presence is demanded at balls. You can't be normal and get asked out by normal people if your father is chummy with the king. So you see, I endured seeing the same kind of people over and over again. And that was not living the kind of life I wanted. So yes, my methods of escape were slightly unconventional, and I feel like I owe that gardenia bush an apology, but I had to leave. I was suffocating. My parents showed no signs of letting up, and I was at my breaking point, you know?" I chuckled.

"I still can't believe it. You're telling me you've never met a guy at a bar and had him take you home and had random sex that you regretted in the morning?"

She shook her head. "Nope. I feel like I haven't even lived at all. I've been stuck living everyone else's life according to their plans for me, so I started to live a little."

"I feel obligated to fix this."

She shook her head. "I don't need your help. I've got it under control. You already helped me. Because of you, I got a job. Not my first, but my first *normal*-person job. And I will have you know, I have learned how to give blow jobs now."

I choked. "What?"

She frowned then shook her head. "No, no. Oh my God." She clapped her hands over her mouth. "I mean, make blow jobs, the drink. Shit."

I fell out laughing. I laughed so hard tears ran from the corners of my eyes. I couldn't hold it in. I had to stop and hand her my gelato so I could clutch my sides. "Oh my God, that was the funniest shit I've heard all week. That was outstanding."

"I'm so embarrassed."

"You don't get to be embarrassed about this. After you called me a 'little-dicked twat monkey' the first time we met, you don't get to be embarrassed. You get to own it and laugh appropriately."

"Anyway, I've learned how to make drinks." She giggled. "Okay, yeah, it's funny."

"See, I told you it was funny."

"Yeah, you're right. So, what's your dating situation? Leaving dropped panties all over Manhattan?"

"I will have you know that I am selective about where I leave my dropped panties. I mean, I have favorite pairs, after all."

She giggled. I could tell, despite herself, she was starting to like me. "God, are you never serious?"

"Nope, why should I be? Life is hard enough. I'm going to joke my way through it, for the most part."

"It just makes it hard to get a straight answer out of you. Are you telling me you've never had a girlfriend?"

I frowned then. Like a real girlfriend? For some reason, the lie that easily sat on the tip of my tongue didn't come. Instead, I shook my head. "No. Not really."

She stared at me. "How old are you?"

"Twenty-three."

"And you've never had a girlfriend? You know, someone you hold hands with, take to movies, that kind of thing?"

I wanted to lie. I itched to lie, but somehow this felt more important, like I couldn't. Like at this moment, I should opt to tell the truth. "No."

"How is that possible? Even when you were like a teenager or something?"

In my head, I pictured guys going to the movies, parties with girls, and all that shit.

"No, never. I moved around a lot when I was a kid." The truth was that by the average dating of age of say, fifteen or sixteen, I was already running long cons. And Tony already had me working the angles with the trust fund girls. Girls like Bryna, who I had no business being near. But I looked older than my age and it worked, so he'd used it.

"No, but we're not talking about me. We're talking about *you*. One thing I have experience with is dating, actual dating. You know, where you meet a guy who takes you out, you have fun, you have normal conversation, and then he takes you home for a wild night of sex."

She smacked me on the arm. "We will not be having a wild night of sex."

"Just why the hell not?" It was worth a shot.

"I don't like players."

"You made it very clear that I'm not your type. You don't like hot."

She snort-laughed then. And fuck me, it was the cutest thing I'd ever seen. "So, what, you're going to teach me how to date normal people?"

"Why not? I think it's a fantastic idea."

"It's a terrible idea." Then she scrunched up her nose, inhaled deep, and acquiesced. "Okay. Give me all the pointers."

I shook my head. "That's not how this works, Kemosabe. How it works is that we're going to mock-date. I take you out, show you how you're supposed to be treated, and you will give me real reactions. Then I'll guide you on the right and normal way to do it."

*Fire.* I was playing with it and I didn't care.

She stopped and lifted a brow, eyeing me up and down. "Oh really? I'm supposed to trust you?"

"Yes. I won't ever lie to you."

Her gaze searched mine. "Are you capable of such a promise?"

"I am. If you promise to be open and unfailingly honest."

"You mean with my verbal vomit? Who wants that?"

I grinned down at her. "Tell me, what do you have to lose?"

She considered this for a moment and bit her lip. "Okay, fine. You're right. I've got nothing to lose. Let's do it."

"All righty then, let's go. Your first date experience is tonight."

# 21

I ONLY GAVE her an hour to get ready. While she hopped in the shower, I ran across the hall to see Marcus and Roone. When Marcus opened the door, he didn't look pleased. "Are you nuts?"

From inside, I heard Roone call out. "Is that the nutter?"

"Yeah, it's me."

Roone came out wearing sweats like he was about to work out. "Are you mad?"

"Look, Roone—" I held up my hands. They had a right to be pissed. I hadn't given them much time to scramble to get security together, and then I'd slipped the noose. "I know I made your job harder today, and I'm sorry."

Roone glared at me. "You made my job harder? Are you insane?"

"Look, it was fine. We were fine."

He glared at me once more, punctuating every word with a pointing finger in my direction. "Fine? You were in Battery City, Alphabet City, then you went to Harlem, Spanish

Harlem, and Little Havana. What the fuck were you thinking? We had no protocols. Marcus and I were scrambling with Dylan and Ryan from Blake Security, trying to keep your ass covered. And for the two of us, staying unseen. You promised me, you wouldn't make my life hell. You swore up and down you wouldn't be like Sebastian, ignoring his security detail. Have you forgotten? Someone actually tried to kill your brother and your sister-in-law. We don't know who else Robert was working with. We don't know what else is planned. Unlike my idiot best friend, you actually need protection right now. Do you understand?"

I winced. I've never seen Roone get pissed. He's mostly calm in these kinds of situations. He never really got that rattled. I felt bad. *Do you?* I just wanted to give Bryna all of my attention. And now I had another favor to ask. "So, is now a bad time to tell you that we're going out tonight?"

Roone took a step toward me and Marcus got between us with a hand on Roone's chest. "Roone, back down."

"I will not back down. I'm going to kill him."

I eased my hands down and backed up. "I'm sorry. Look, I couldn't let her go around the city by herself. Some of those places were dangerous, one of which, I'm pretty sure she would not have returned from. The guy looked like he was ready to chain her in his basement and never let her out. Sebastian told me to look after her, so I'm looking out for her, okay?"

"Nah, mate, you're looking to get your dick wet. And it's making you stupid. We have no time, and you're fucking around. Security protocols dictate—"

I lifted my chin and cut him off. "I'm sorry. It sucks. I should give you more time, but I'm still going out. You can come with me, or not. It's up to you." Then I turned and walked out.

Yeah, I was kind of being a dick, but Bryna had looked so happy when I said I'd take her out. There was no way I was backing down on this one. Roone and Marcus would just have to deal with it.

I grabbed a five-minute shower. When I came out, my phone was ringing.

*Sebastian.* "Yeah?"

"What the fuck did you do to Roone? He called me cursing. Did you invite a bunch of random strangers back to the flat?"

"One time I'd did that, and no one lets me forget."

"He won't go into detail, but he wants you benched."

I sighed. "Nothing man. I just may not have made his security detail easy today, and I'm going out tonight. I'm taking Bryna out, actually. I'm going to show her the town."

There was a beat of silence. "Bryna, huh?"

"Ugh, I can hear it in your voice, big brother. Not like that. You asked me for a favor, and I'm not screwing it up." *Yes. Yes, you are.*

"Chill. I'm just giving you shit. I know you understand that this is important. Any updates on Tressel?"

"I'm still digging. I've found the trail of bread crumbs. I'm tracking it down."

Another pause. "So, Bryna... you're keeping your dick to yourself, right? I know she's cute."

"Yes, asshole. I thought you couldn't find girls cute anymore."

"Oh, I can still find them cute. Not nearly as cute as Penny, but still."

I laughed. "And how is my sister-in-law? I'm surprised she doesn't have you chained."

"Currently, she's a pain in the ass. She wants to return to

duty. I told her we'd discuss it after the wedding, but I didn't think she was serious. She wants to be in the field."

I frowned. "In the field? But she's the queen. That's insane."

"Yes, please come and tell her that because she won't listen. And especially now, it's so dangerous. I mean, I know that she was a Royal Guard, but still."

My first instinct was to protect her. But she was more than capable, and certainly better trained, than me or Sebastian. "Oh, that is a unique situation, because after all, she did save your ass more than once."

"Tell me about it. She never lets me forget."

"Are you guys all right though?"

"Yeah, why do you ask?"

"I don't know. You seem preoccupied. I really don't need to hear the blow-by-blow, if you get my meaning, but normal life is good? I love you. If anyone deserves a happily-ever-after, it's you."

I could hear my brother chuckling on the other end of the line. "You realize you never say that, right?"

I frowned. "Say what?"

"I love you."

Heat crept on my neck, and I shifted uncomfortably, even though he couldn't see me. "Sure, I do."

He chuckled low. "No, you don't. I know less than two years ago we were basically strangers, and now we're family. I didn't anticipate any of that or the way any of this went down, but for the record, I love you, too."

Shit, too many feelings. "If we're done here, I need to go on my date. I mean..." *Shit, shit, shit.* "You know what I mean."

My brother chuckled, but then he added, "Are you two getting along? What's her place like?"

*Shit.* "I mean, yeah, it's a dorm, you know. She seems happy enough. She's cool. I'm just showing her around. I was going to take her to Little Havana. We're meeting there with some friends. She's pretty independent. She doesn't really need babysitting or hand-holding." Lies mixed with truth. The marks of a good con man.

"Okay, if you say so. All right, I'll let you get going, but give me a call, okay?"

"You got it." I couldn't put my finger on it, but he sounded like he missed me.

"Oh, and Lucas?"

"Yeah?"

"Just be careful. You know the trial is about to start soon. Penny says I'm being dramatic, but I'd like you to be careful anyway."

"You got it." I hung up with my brother, knowing I'd lied to him. Or, omitted. Either way, it wasn't a good feeling. He'd just have to understand. Besides, if anyone *should* understand, it should be him. He and Penny had a whole forbidden-romance thing too. Not that this was in any way a romance thing, but whatever. I needed to haul ass, or I'd be the one who was late.

I HATED TO ADMIT IT, but Lucas was fun. Really fun. He hadn't told me a thing about what we'd be doing. Instead, he told me to dress in something fun and flirty. The second I was ready, his gaze scanned over me for the briefest moment, and then he nodded and said, "Good. Let's go."

So for over an hour, I was obsessed with what the hell he meant by 'good.' Was it good-good, bad-good, just fine, good for a date, or he thought I looked good? It was a mine field.

*Why do you care? This isn't a real date.* No, it wasn't, and I needed to remember that.

The cab took us back to Little Havana. Seeing Lucas in date mode, it was hard to not see the charm. He was naturally charismatic. People wanted to please him. He took us into a little spot called Dom's, where old men were playing dominoes.

He slipped into easy, fluent Spanish with the old Dominican guys, translating for me when necessary.

We didn't win. Actually, I think I got our asses kicked. But it was still fun. There was laughing and joking, and with every laugh, Lucas brushed up against me, took my hand, or wrapped an arm around my shoulders. That feeling I'd been searching for, the elusive one, the one where I felt wanted and actually like my company was cherished, all that stuff I had said to Jinx when I ran away from home—I got that with Lucas. And I knew he was just showing me what it was supposed to be like. But now there was this part of me that wished it could be real. That Lucas could want me.

*Bad idea. You live with him. He's connected to your parents. He's absolutely smoking hot, and he clearly can't stay with one woman. Just look at him.*

All those things were true. Plus, it would just get awkward because we were roommates.

After we left Dom's, Lucas took my hand in his, the early fall evening cooling off my too-warm skin. I couldn't believe how casually he just held my hand. As if we'd been doing it for decades.

When he stood, he barely even looked back at me. He just waited for me to take his hand, as if it was the expectation. The moment I slid my hand into his, that was it, we walked out together.

How was he supposed to know that my heart raced as if the finest thoroughbreds were dragging me behind a chariot.

He couldn't know any of that. As far as he was concerned, he was being a nice guy, showing the noob how to date.

And this noob needed to get her shit under control. Lucas Newsome was not someone I could date. He wasn't someone I could have. He wasn't someone I wanted. Oh yeah, he had some of the edge I wanted, but he was too charming, too slick, too much like the man that I dated before. Too likely to hurt me.

Yeah, there was that too.

"Are you having fun?"

He pulled me into an over-packed restaurant where hordes of people waited outside. The moment we stepped in, my nostrils flared. I could smell the spices and everything delicious mixed together, combined with an elegant and cozy ambiance. "This is amazing. Where are we?"

"Casa Cuba. A friend of mine's parents own it."

An older woman, maybe about sixty or so, came from around the counter. "Lucas. Where have you been? Since Pedro left for his master's, we haven't seen you."

"Yes Maria, I'm so sorry. I've been busy, you know, with school and work. It's my last semester."

"You, this boy, you make me start to love you and then you don't call your mama."

Lucas chuckled low, his grin showing off a slight dimple. Oh boy. He even had this old woman charmed.

She swatted him on the arm, and then she smiled at me. "Oh, we have a guest."

"Yes. Maria, this is a friend of mine, Bryna. Bryna, this is Maria Cruz. She's the mother of Pedro, my freshman year roommate, and the sole reason that I stayed fed my freshman year. She would send these care packages to UCLA, so when I transferred, I looked her up. Pedro, smarty pants that he is, graduated a year early. He went to grad school up in Boston."

Maria beamed at me like a proud mother. "That's my boy. Always too bright for his own good. And Bryna, it's lovely to meet you. Come with me, I'll give you our special table."

She took us to the back, past the kitchens and then to this lovely courtyard. There were two other couples back there, but it was so much quieter. Private. Once we were seated, I turned to him. "You wouldn't even know this was out here."

He nodded with a grin. "Yep. One of the hidden secrets of the city. But when you're back here, you don't get a menu. They just bring out whatever they want. I hope you're hungry, because now that Maria has met you, there's no way you're leaving here without stuffing your face. And the best part—"

He didn't get to finish because out came a young waiter, holding a tray of two drinks with something sticking out of them, green mint I assumed, and then something else. "What are these?"

The waiter grinned. "These, are Casa Cuba's signature mojitos, on the house."

I grinned at Lucas, and he nodded. "Yeah, that line we saw outside, half of them are here just for the drinks, trying to pre-game before they go out. Go easy on these and make sure you sip some water too because they're strong, and their good old Havana rum will knock you on your ass."

I shook my head at him. "You act like I'm not an island girl and I don't know how to drink my rum."

"Oh, I stand corrected. In that case, show me the way."

He was right though. Those mojitos were strong. But God, they were delicious and reminded me of home.

The food that was brought out, oxtail stew, braised and excellent, a decadent desert cake with rum drizzled over, it was all amazing. Lucas kept the conversation flowing well. He was charming and sweet, and it was easy to forget exactly who he was or the fact that we weren't on a real date.

My dinner wasn't even the real treat. The real treat was when dinner was over. The tables were moved out of the way, and the music began. Salsa. Jinx and I had taken lessons a few years ago as a way to meet guys. Surprisingly, there were only about two men in the class, and not enough to go around, so I'd learned to do both the guy's and the girl's parts.

It was one of my few hidden skills. My parents, of course, hadn't approved. But when I heard the music, I couldn't help but switch my hips. Lucas's gaze slid over me. I knew that he didn't intend for me to feel hot and flushed at a glance, but I couldn't help it.

"Oh, you can salsa?"

I nodded happily. "Yeah. I haven't done it in years, so I might be rusty, but I can salsa. And if you want I can lead."

He chuckled low, the sound doing melty things to my knees. "Maybe next time. I'll do the leading for now. Let's see what you got."

"Are you sure? I can even dip you?"

That earned me a wide grin with full dimple. "Come here." Then just like that, he did that hand thing again where he reached out for me as if I would automatically follow. And there was a part of me in that moment that did. It was easy to trust him, easy to believe him, easy to want the warmth to seep in to my bones.

He twirled me quickly and then pulled me to him. My breasts were pressed up against his chest, his thigh was between mine, and oh my God, he smelled incredible. A musky scent mixed with the rum on his breath made my head spin, and I was lucky he was holding me upright. Why did Lucas Newsome smell so damn good?

He could move too. The sexy salsa didn't faze him in the least. He kept his gaze on me. His dark eyes never left mine as our hips swayed in time with the music, and he guided me in the steps, never missing a single one. Not even when he pushed me away from him and brought me back, on beat, on time. He spun the web around me, crowding out everything else but him.

When the song changed again to something a little prettier, a little dirtier, with a heavier bass beat in it, that's when I felt it. The air shifted. Suddenly his direct gaze was slightly hooded, his pupils dilated, and more often than not, I could feel his gaze on my lips. Instinctively, I parted them. Almost immediately, I could feel the hot, hard length of him oh so close to my—oh God. Liquid heat pooled in my center, and my body gave an involuntary clinch. Jesus Christ, Lucas was huge.

I would have thought that he'd let me go then. But he didn't. We just kept dancing. It wasn't until more and more people were allowed into the back area and it became so crowded it was nearly impossible to move that he finally separated from me.

He cleared his throat and wrapped my hand in his. "Come on, it's too crowded. Let's get out of here."

His voice was pitched on a lower octave. More intimate, kind of throaty.

Oh God, I should be concerned. I should be worried. I should be running for the hills. But I wasn't, because whatever his voice promised, I wanted some of that.

He was mostly silent as we left the restaurant and meandered through the neighborhood. There were several similar restaurants with music pouring out of them. We finally hailed a cab, and he held the door open for me. I slid over, allowing him space. When he climbed in, he pulled me close to him, arm wrapped around my shoulder, and instinctively, I laid my head on his shoulder.

This was easy. So damn easy.

The rock of the taxi lulled me into a half-pulsing-with-need state, but that was just the proximity of Lucas.

Lucas exited the taxi first and then held out a hand for me. He walked me inside. In the elevator, he was silent. But he didn't let go of my hand. As we approached our door, my heart started hammering out of control. Something was going to happen, I could feel it. Somewhere along the way, something had changed at that restaurant. I felt it. He wanted me too. And not in just the kind of way where I was a warm body. He wanted *me*. So what now? What the hell was going to happen? Should we do this? *No, you cannot do this. Stop thinking about it. Take a mental cold shower or something because it's not happening.*

Once in the apartment, I turned to face him and nervously brushed the hair off my face. "Lucas, I—"

He stepped toward me, and I attempted to swallow but all I came up with was sawdust. "Tonight was fun. This is exactly how you should feel when you're on a date with someone. That anticipation, the heat, the curiosity, the question."

I tried to swallow again, but it didn't work, so I croaked out, "Question?"

He nodded slowly. "Yeah."

"About what?" Why was my voice so damn squeaky?

As he stepped toward me, I realized I'd been instinctively taking steps back, but as I hit the island, I had nowhere to go. He leaned over me. My gaze immediately lowered, and my lids fluttered closed because good God, he was about to kiss me and Jesus Christ, I wanted him to.

More than anything else in my life.

"You should always anticipate if your date is going to kiss you, and when he's going to kiss you. You should want it. You should be desperate for it. That's what a good date feels like."

His voice was so low and soothing. I couldn't put together

all the words right away. The way he was talking, I wanted to believe this was real.

I tried to force my eyes open, but I couldn't manage it. He was so close. So damn close, and I could just feel him, and smell him, and God this was going to be a mistake, but I didn't give a shit.

"Okay."

I could feel his breath on my cheek. "And when he kisses you, your knees should be weak. You shouldn't be able to think about anything else but him. Certainly not me."

So he *had* known I was faking that kiss. I wanted to say something intelligent, something to tell him that I wasn't thinking about him when I kissed Jase, but all I could muster was, "Uh-huh."

And then he was leaning toward me. His lips, I could almost feel them. He was so close. Between us, as his hips made contact with mine, I could feel the length of him against my leg, and it was all I could do not to rock into it.

It terrified me to admit it, but right about then, I'd have done anything to have his mouth on me.

⚜

## Lucas

The bite of desire injected my blood, making me tingle all over.

Fuck, she was beautiful. I knew what I *should* do, but her scent of hibiscus and gardenias wove around me, intoxicating me, confusing me. Making it impossible to think straight.

*Don't do it, don't do it, don't do it.*

But even though the command was loud and clear, impulse

won out. I had to taste her. The moment our lips met, the blood rushed in my head.

She tasted sweet and hot, like summer. For a long moment, Bryna held herself perfectly still. But then she made a soft mewling sound at the back of her throat and melted against me. I slid my tongue against hers, groaning when she kissed me back.

Soo fucking good. Too fucking good. She wrapped her arms around my neck, her fingers slipping into the hair at my nape. When she scored the back of my scalp with her nails, I shuddered.

My tongue danced with hers, sliding, teasing, playing. Cupping her ass, I pulled her tight against me, lust drowning out the rational protests of my brain. My cock nudged her belly insistently when her full breasts pressed into my body. Sliding a hand into her hair, I fisted a handful, using the leverage to help anchor her head so I could deepen the kiss. With her tongue sliding over mine and her body rocking into me, I didn't give a shit about what a bad idea it was. All that mattered in that moment was how good she felt.

When she tentatively slid her tongue into my mouth, my tenuous hold on the strings of control slipped. The blood rushed in my skull, and I once again slid my hands into the fall of hair at the nape of her neck. The low growl in my throat as I deepened the kiss warned me that I was losing control. That I was going to take this too far.

All I wanted to do was take that kiss deeper, but if I went any further, I wouldn't be able to stop. Slowly I released the handful of silken tresses and slid my hands down her body. I had to find some fucking control from somewhere. My hands flexed on her hips, and Bryna arched into me. Dragging my lips from hers, I hissed. "Bryna."

"Yeah?"

"Are you trying to drive me insane?"

She raked her nails over my scalp once more, and a shudder racked my whole body. The growl started low in my throat before I kissed her again.

I turned our bodies to brace her against the fridge and bracketed both her hands over her head. When I canted my hips, her body bucked into me, and I answered with a slow roll of my hips.

With one hand securing her wrists, I slid the other up her torso. My thumb traced each rib until I reached the underside of her breast. She wrenched her lips from mine. "Lucas—"

I dropped my forehead to hers. "Yeah, Bryna?" Fuck, I was so screwed. Now that I'd touched her, could I go back?

*Do you want to?*

"This feels so..." Her voice trailed as she tossed her head back.

"I know. I feel like I'm on fire."

I slid my lips over hers again. She was so soft, everywhere, with skin like satin. I could spend hours touching her, savoring every inch of her skin, but her breathy moans urged me on. Sliding my hands up her torso, my thumbs grazed the underside of her breasts, and the rest of the blood in my brain migrated south. My cock throbbed painfully against my thigh and I bit back a curse.

I traced my thumbs over the lace of her bra to the taut nipples beneath. With a frustrated snarl, I picked her up and settled her on the counter. She started to quiver when I stroked my thumbs over her nipples. When I closed my palm over her full breast, Bryna slid her hands into my hair and tugged.

"Fuck," I'd tripped into the land of no return, and I didn't give a fuck. I just needed to figure out how to get her naked as quickly as possible.

⁂

## Bryna

Lucas's hands on my ass and his thumb on my nipple. *Yes, Virginia, there is a Santa Clause.* His hands were sure, his lips were soft. I felt safe, but at the same time, I felt like I was about to jump off a cliff with no net.

His thumbs traced over my nipples again, and I shuddered. "Lucas, I—"

The booming knock at the door broke through our hazy spell.

For a second, we stayed like that. Locked in position, as if wondering who was going to make the next move.

Then Lucas's heat was gone. He was backing up. That frown I hated seeing on his face was back. "I—" He shook his head. "I need to get that."

"What?" I tried to blink the foggy haze clear.

He inclined his head toward the door. "Someone's knocking."

Knocking? But what about that delicious tingling in my nipples? Was I supposed to just pretend I didn't now know how that felt?

Quickly but gently, he readjusted my clothes since I was far too incoherent to do that myself. Lust had dulled my senses.

"God, all I want to do is kiss you again."

Hope flared but vanished when he bit his bottom lip and shook his head. Not going to happen tonight. Besides, I'd heard the knocking too. And maybe it's for the best. This wasn't even a real date, and I'd been ready to do him on the counter. I cleared my throat. "Oh, I guess I'll go to my room. Good night."

He nodded slowly, then added, "What you're feeling right now, you should feel it every time somebody takes you home. *Always*. Thank you for tonight. I had fun. Now get some sleep."

The hell I would. Lucas had just broken me.

## 23

I FELT LIKE A CREEPER. OUR 'MOCK-DATE' had been... intense. Surprising. Fucking perfect. But I had fucked up. Time to face the music.

She was already dressed and ready for class. Her hair was damp. As soon as she heard me, she stilled then turned around slowly. "Good morning."

Her gaze didn't meet mine. *Please fucking look at me. Let me see that it was real.*

Last night had been explosive. Some next level, off-the-charts shit, and we hadn't even had sex. But somewhere in the deep dark recesses of my mind, I knew that, in so many ways, it was better than sex.

I could still taste her on my tongue. I could still smell her, even though she was at least twenty feet away from me. I could still feel her warmth, and I wanted more of it. I wanted her back on that counter, legs parted for me, but this time naked, displayed in front of me, one leg hooked over my shoulder, with my mouth firmly planted on her sex.

*No, not helpful.*

My dick throbbed painfully, as if to echo the sentiment. *Not helpful at all dude.*

I cleared my throat. "Are you okay?"

She licked her lips, and my gaze focused on the tip of her tongue. "Yup, I'm fine."

I sighed. I really didn't want this to be awkward. It was already going bad enough because part of me knew that it was going to hurt. "Well, I'm not fine."

Her face fell then.

"No, I don't mean like that. Last night was..." What the hell was I supposed to say? Life changing? Or whatever? "Last night, I'm not sure I've ever felt like that before." I loved watching her skin flush a pretty pink.

*Don't get distracted.*

"But, for so many reasons, it's a really bad idea."

That hope I had just seen in her eyes vanished then. "Oh."

"Sebastian asked a favor of me, and for reasons I can't tell you, him believing in me, trusting me with that, is really important."

Her teeth grazed her bottom lip, then she nodded. "But why does it matter what he thinks?"

As much as I wanted to, there was no way I could tell her the truth. It wasn't public information. Her father might know, but as a member of the Regents Council it was confidential information to him, so no matter what, he couldn't out me. "It's a long story. And it doesn't matter what he thinks. This is more about me than anything else. I need to be the kind of man who doesn't take advantage of a situation. Who can see something through without thinking with his dick. I wasn't supposed to touch you."

"Is that what you think happened yesterday?"

I ran my hands through my hair. "I don't know what the fuck happened yesterday. But the truth of it is that you are my roommate. You needed help, and I overstepped the line. I shouldn't have. I just wanted you to have a good time and have a fun date."

She nodded as she pursed her lips. "And the next thing you know I'm sitting on the counter practically begging you to suck on my nipples."

Dick, hard. Tongue, desperate. I felt like I might die if I didn't taste her nipples. Fuck. I couldn't focus for shit. I squeezed my eyes shut and tried again. "Bryna, for once, I'm trying to be the good guy. Please let me. Believe me when I say, I want you more than I've maybe ever wanted anyone. But I refuse to be a dick. You need help. And a place to stay. I'm not going back to being the guy I used to be. Please." I wasn't above begging. I couldn't have her. And in the long run, she wouldn't want me. "I want us to actually be friends. No bullshit. And I promise to be a gentleman."

A furrow formed in her brow, but she nodded. "Okay. Right. None of it was real anyway. We both got caught up in the moment."

My gaze searched hers. I didn't want that to be the truth, but if it meant I could keep my word for once, then I'd take the lifeline and swallow the truth. "Yeah. Just a little carried away."

## 24

Two things kept running through my head all day. Sebastian's words, 'You wouldn't do anything to mess this up. This is
too important,' and the scent of Bryna's perfume.

Last night had been an exercise in flirting with disaster. I'd
been an idiot. I thought I could handle it. No problem. You
know, just to be that close to her, to feel her soft skin, to hold
her close, I thought none of it would matter. I thought I'd
be fine.

Rookie mistake. The truth was, I could still fucking smell
her. Hibiscus, gardenias, heaven.

Hell. I wanted her. Had wanted her. I got it now, why
Roone and Marcus laughed their asses off when I said staying
away from her wasn't going to be a problem. They'd been able to
see what I couldn't see. I wanted that girl, and not in the way
that I wanted most, but in a way that was going to crush me if I
wasn't careful. I wanted her in a way that made me want to
laugh. I wanted her in a way that made me want to tell her
things, my secrets, my truths. I wanted to tell her everything.

Mostly, I just wanted to hear her laugh. That throaty, full-on laugh, I'd kill for that.

That was a goddamn problem because guys like me didn't get to have that. If she had any idea who I really was, she'd run for the hills. She'd run so far and so fast, her head would spin. Not to mention Sebastian had asked me for one goddamn thing; to not go there. *Way to go, Rookie. You screwed up.* Getting that close to her was like asking for trouble, because I wanted more than to touch her. I wanted her to touch me and my soul. And given who I was, she was going to get hurt.

"Where's your guard?"

I whipped around at the sound of the quiet, lilting British accent behind me.

"Jesus fucking Christ. Why are you so damn silent?"

Matthias Weller just shrugged. "Where is your guard?"

I pointed at the coffee cart. Marcus had taken the shift today, even though it was supposed to be Roone's. Roone, it seemed, was still pissed at me. Which was fair. I was intentionally making his job more difficult. And last night, I would have said that it was well worth it, but now, now I didn't know.

Matthias shook his head. "There are a lot of people between you and him. What if I had intended to do you harm?"

I squared my shoulders. "Even before Roone got a hold of me in training, I was never helpless."

There was something in Matthias's eyes then. Respect? Acceptance? I don't know what it was. Frankly, I didn't care. "What are you doing lurking around anyway?"

"You asked for privacy. You haven't exactly been alone, mate. Last night was a risk too. You're lucky the Blake Security guys were so good. Oskar almost took out three guys last night, all because they got a little too close to you."

I threw up my hands. "Jesus Christ, all of this is fucking unnecessary."

Matthias's gaze narrowed. "No, it's not. If for nothing else, your mother and her husband are involved with some shady-ass shit. Some dodgy characters like the Melina Cartel."

I stared at him. "Are you shitting me right now?"

Matthias shook his head. "Nah, mate. That last job you did, the shit you stole was worth well over $300,000."

I whistled low. I only got a fraction of that.

"Those diamonds were supposed to be payment for a Melina courier. Now your stepfather and your mother are in deep with them. They need to pay off their debts."

I crossed my arms. "I'm not going back."

Matthias shrugged. "I don't think you should."

Even though he was quiet, there was something about him that said he wanted to say something. "Spill it. I'm guessing you have an opinion about the whole situation."

He handed me a flash drive. "Take it from someone who knows. Leave your past where it is and fast. You don't invite them into your future. They'll go fucking up all the good that you did. I should know. I know you're worried about your old lady, but mate, she made her bed. She made her decisions. Don't let her drag you back in. The Melina Cartel, they're not screwing around, and there will be collateral damage."

"Yeah, I hear you."

And I did. It was the same conclusion I'd come to myself. Mom and Tony were on their own. The problem was she was my mother. She was family. And despite all her faults, she loved me. Okay, maybe not as much as she loved Tony, but she was still my mother. I couldn't let her twist if there was a way out.

Matthias frowned at me. "I can tell from the look on your face that you don't plan on listening."

"Nah, I hear you mate. I do. But she's my mother."

Matthias shook his head. "If only people would ever fucking listen. Okay, deal with it how you will. If you're going to see her, I suggest you take an army, because she's going to pull you back into it."

I watched him walk away just as Marcus was heading back. I turned back toward Marcus to make sure he wasn't within earshot. When I turned back a second later, Weller was gone. Jesus Christ, the guy had the feet of a ninja. He had a point though. I should leave it well enough alone. I should walk away. I should leave her to her own devices, just like she'd left me. The problem was I knew I wouldn't be able to do that. Because like it or not, she was still my mother. If there was something I could do to help her, I needed to at least try.

I took out my phone and tapped out a quick message.

**LUCAS**: *Mom, I know you're in town. Where Tony is, you are. Meet me at Prohibition Bar tomorrow. 9 p.m.*

Marcus rolled up with my coffee. "Everything okay? I saw you talking to someone."

"Yeah, just a guy from class."

Marcus's narrowed gaze told me he didn't believe a word of what I just said. But he let it go, which was fine by me, because there was no way I could allow he or Roone to accompany me on my little family reunion.

❦

## Lucas

"I need to head into the Academic Building for a second to see a professor, want to hang out here?"

Marcus lifted a brow as if I should know the answer to that by now. I never really noticed how intrusive it felt having Marcus or Roone around all the time. I never really had consistent friends who weren't marks when I was a kid, so I thought it was great at first. Now, I saw. As much as I might like them, they were not here to fuck around. They were doing their job. And right now, Marcus was being a pain in the ass. I rolled my eyes. "Fine. Suit yourself."

I hit the stairs two at a time and heard Marcus mumble something behind me. When I turned my head, I wasn't looking where I was going and bumped into a pretty brunette. Her hair was long and flowing and hung down her back. She smiled up at me. "I'm sorry, I wasn't looking where I was going."

I shook my head. "No, my bad, totally."

"You're Lucas, right?"

I frowned. "Yeah, why?"

"I'm in your Marketing Management class."

She was? How the hell had I never noticed her before?

*Because you're always so focused on Bryna.* "Oh, small world. Well, I hope you're okay."

She frowned slightly, as if I'd said something wrong. But then instead of letting me pass by, she stepped directly in front of me. "Well, I know you already have a partner, but I was hoping I could run some thoughts by you. I know it's your last term. Someone was saying you're a senior, and you have some fancy gig in the works, but I was just hoping I could get some input from you."

"Sure. Um, my email is in the class roster."

She shifted on her feet and bit her bottom lip. That's when the alarm bells went off. I knew that look. Oh, she didn't want future job help. She was trying to get me to ask her out. Behind me, Marcus cleared his throat. I ignored him though. "Sure, we can maybe work something out. You know, go over some notes."

She beamed at me. "That's perfect."

Christ, that was almost too easy.

"I'll get your number from the roster."

She shook her head. "No. That's the house phone. I mostly just use that for my parents." She pulled out a notecard, scrolled something on it, and handed it over to me. "That's my cell. I'll talk to you soon, Lucas."

Marcus chuckled as she sashayed away. "Man is it always so easy for you?"

I nodded slowly. "Yeah, I guess so."

"You're not even humble about it."

I shrugged. "Yeah, whatever. It is what it is. She wouldn't like the real me anyway. She just wants a little walk on the wild side."

"Let me guess, you're willing to help her?"

I threw him my best devil-may-care smile at that point. "Never let it be said that I'm not a giving person."

Marcus just chuckled. "When I grow up, I want to be like you."

"Well, you can study, but there's only one Lucas."

Marcus rolled his eyes.

I didn't want to ask her out. Not really. She was beautiful, of course. She also had a striking resemblance to Bryna. But, as I couldn't have Bryna, it might not be a bad idea for me to wear some of the tension out. After all, turning my attention elsewhere, I wouldn't end up thinking about my sexy-as-hell roommate.

I TOLD myself I didn't care. But to hell with it, I cared a lot. Last night had been...magical?

God, no, I wasn't that naïve. But I'd felt something, something deep. Lucas could pretend all he wanted, but we'd truly connected for the first time since I came to live with him. Despite his charm, there were parts of him that were so honest and so raw.

He wasn't at all what I thought, and I'd had a hard time wrapping my brain around it at first. I'd thought he was a heartless player. But while he might be a player, he was so much more than that. And it was reflected in the people we'd met last night. They all cared about him and the feeling was mutual and genuine.

Once I chipped away at the exterior, the show, underneath, Lucas was someone I could talk to. And then there had been that kiss. My toes were still curled damnit. I had felt it to the center of my chest.

But now he wanted to go back to before. Before I knew what

it was like to have his hands on me. Before I knew what it was like to have his tongue coax mine into a dance. Before I knew what it was like to have his body pressed to mine.

I wasn't sure I could do it. *Well you don't have any choice. He said it wasn't supposed to happen.* That he hadn't meant to touch me. He said he'd gotten carried away.

What hurt the most was I'd let myself open up. I'd let myself feel with him. He seemed like it was tearing him up. But he was trying to be the good guy.

What the hell was so wrong with me that I kept picking the wrong kinds of guys.

Last night had been more fun than anything I'd done in so long that I could barely remember. Everything I'd ever said about him before, about how I didn't see the appeal, how I didn't find him charming in the least, and how he was really trying too hard, was lies.

*All lies.*

He was right though, he wasn't someone I could entertain. I'd made my deal-breaker list. At the top of it, sincerity. Next on the list, a non-awkward situation which, hello, I was living with the guy.

Third on the list, must not be a member of court. My list was fucked. I'd made my own damn list. Why couldn't I keep up with it? Why couldn't I keep it together enough to remember these little rules I made for myself?

It said a lot that I'd never been on that kind of date. It said a lot about me and the guys I'd previously dated, though granted, it's not like I had a whole sea of experience.

I don't know what possessed me, but I picked up the phone and made a call.

It took three rings, but he finally answered. "Hello?"

"Braxton? It's me, Bryna."

There was a beat of silence. "Bryna? What the hell happened to you at the ball? Last I spoke to you, you were supposed to save me a dance at the wedding. What happened to that?"

"Sorry about that. I had to make an unexpected departure."

"You don't say. Well, are you in town? We should do something. Talk."

"No, I'm in New York, actually. You know what, I just have one question." I wasn't sure I wanted to do this.

"Yeah, shoot."

"Why? Why did you go out with me? Propose even. I'm realizing now you never really seemed like you were particularly interested."

He was silent for a moment. For a second, I thought he was not going to answer me. But then he surprised me when he said, "Honestly, this isn't to hurt your feelings or anything, but your Dad still has a lot of power. It was simple, easy even, angling for the two of us to get together. So, I just followed suit, I guess. I mean, you're pretty and all that, but not really my style, you know? I needed someone way less uptight. And I didn't want to get married, but the old man threatened to cut me off if I didn't settle down, so I proposed."

*Ouch.* Well, I had asked. "Uh, thanks for your honesty, I guess."

"But hey, that was then. Maybe you've loosened up since then."

"What do you mean, 'loosened up?'"

He chuckled softly. "You know what I mean. You were always a bit, you know, serious. You weren't really that much fun to be around, Bryna. I always figured we could have a good time if you'd ever let yourself cut loose a little bit."

*Wow.* Okay, yeah. I'd done myself a real favor by calling him. "Yeah, thanks for that."

"Anytime."

As if he'd done me a huge favor. I hung up, wondering what I'd hoped to accomplish in that conversation. I was pretty sure at that point that I felt worse, not better.

I got ready for work. I had an early shift at the bar to do inventory and cover the lunch rush. When I arrived, Ellie was already in the storeroom. "There you are. What's up? How is it going?"

"You know those moments when you know you shouldn't do something, and you know it's only going to be harmful to you, but you do it anyway, and then later you wonder what the hell you were thinking?"

Ellie stopped what she was doing and nodded. "All the time. Did you go ahead and fuck your roommate?"

I stared at her. "What?"

She blinked rapidly. "Oh, I thought that's what we were talking about."

"No. I did *not* fuck my roommate, thank you very much. I did happen to call my ex." I left out the part about how said roommate had kissed me so good, I thought my bones might melt.

She winced. "Ouch. That's never a good combo."

"No, I don't know what I thought I was going to get out of it. Maybe just some answers as to why the hell I always felt like he was doing me some kind of favor by going out with me."

"Ugh, that's the worst. Why did you ever go out with him?"

"I don't know. I guess he was convenient. You know, just

always there. Little did I know that he was not enthused about dating me either, which I guess is fine. I just—" I sighed. How much should I tell her? She was my only friend here, so I didn't really have much to lose. "About Lucas..."

She grinned. "Oh boy, I knew he was involved somehow. Do tell."

We carried our clipboards with the inventory sheets to the front of the bar, and I started with the bottles on the bottom shelf. "We hung out yesterday. It was actually fun. It was an all-day thing. We went to look for apartments for me, and then I told him that I'd never been on like a real date, you know. Everything else always felt sort of manufactured and a result of proximity, not because I was super into someone. So he offered to take me on a practice date."

She grinned ear to ear then. "Oh yes, 'practice.' Did this practice end with hot boning? Because I'm a fan of hot boning."

"No, it did not end with hot boning. I mean, we uh, kissed, but that's where it ended."

She groaned. "Oh my God! I cannot believe you didn't lead with that! You're just a tease."

I laughed. "It didn't go further. We—uh, got interrupted. Someone was at the door. A little more time, and I'd be calling in sick from bed."

This perked Ellie right up. "I approve of this plan. Please give a girl some details."

I laughed. "I will say, the man can kiss. It's illegal how good he is. That and he has really big hands."

Ellie fake-fainted. "Well honey, I promise you, you were not the only one who went to bed frustrated. He looks at you like he can practically taste you."

I lifted a brow. "I mean, I'm not sure why it didn't go any

further. I'm embarrassed to say it, but it was pretty clear that I wanted him. It's not like I was playing hard to get. I wasn't being subtle. There I was, eyes all closed, lips all parted, looking like a caricature for a romantic comedy. This morning he said we should just be friends."

She snorted a laugh. "Oh man. Maybe he recognizes that it's going to be awkward. You guys are roommates. Maybe he doesn't want to screw it up." She snorted. "See what I did there?"

I couldn't help but laugh. "Maybe, I don't know. The whole thing was just... I was frustrated and confused, hence I called the ex. Spoiler alert, it did not make me feel better."

"It rarely ever does." The door to the bar opened and Ellie called out. "I'm sorry, we're closed right now. We're going to open in another hour and a half."

"I won't be here long." I knew that voice. I whipped around and groaned.

"Mom, what are you doing here? How did you even know I work here? You know what, never mind."

"I was worried about you. I was worried you'd be looking for money. Imagine my surprise when you'd already found a job." Where was she getting all this information from?

Of course, probably Lucas. "Mom, we have a lot to do, so if you could just—"

Ellie glanced between her and me, and back again. Then she said, "I'll just um, go recount the bottles in the back."

I gave her a tight shake of my head, begging her not to leave me, but she still scooted around me and made it to safety. I turned back to my mother. "Mom, this is ridiculous. What do you want?"

"I want you to come home. Or to the flat anyway. This is absurd. Where are you staying?"

"What do you mean, where am I staying?"

"I went back to that awful apartment of yours to try and talk some sense into you. And that horrible girl, the one with the dog, she said you moved out. She gave me no forwarding address, and I was really concerned. So then I had your father make some calls, and they led me here. This is madness, Bryna. You could be in a lap of luxury at the moment. You know, you totally look like you could use some time at the spa. Just come home."

"That would make you happy, wouldn't it? If I came home and had to admit failure?"

"I do *not* take pleasure in you failing, Bryna. But you, at a bar, a pub, or whatever they're called these days? Honestly, what would everyone say?"

"What they would likely say is that I'm independent and that when the chips are down, I know how to figure out a solution. If they have anything to say other than that, I'm not really interested."

"Well, at least tell me where you're staying."

"So you could ruin that for me too? No. Mom, you and Dad took money out of my account so that I would be forced to do what you wanted. I'm not gonna make it easy on you. Don't come here again. If you do, I'll have the owner call the cops."

That was an exaggeration, of course, but she didn't know that.

My mother left in a huff, as was her nature, almost as if she left in a cloud of smoke. A cloud of indignant smoke, to be honest. As I watched her, it occurred to me Lucas had kept his word. He hadn't told my parents where I was, which led me to think that maybe the reason he backed away last night was something other than him not wanting me. Maybe Ellie was right. Maybe he had his own demons to slay. Perhaps I'd misjudged him, because he'd been true to his word. Maybe I should actually look at him as a viable option. Heat pulled low in my core as if my body was saying, 'Finally, you're catching up to the game.' Well, better late than never.

*  *

### Bryna

My feet hurt. My whole body hurt. After my shift that morning and the unexpected visit from my mother, I went straight to class. Then I was called in to cover someone else's shift that afternoon. By the time I trudged off the elevator, I was feeling every single minute of the day.

I met Marcus as I walked past to the garbage chute, and I gave him a smile and a wave. He waved back, but I could have sworn I saw a wince accompanying his smile.

What was his deal anyway? He and Lucas were always together, but they didn't seem entirely close. In my head, I concocted some crazy fantasy world where Marcus was in love with Lucas. I couldn't really pinpoint why I thought that, all I knew was that Marcus was always watching Lucas like a hawk. Lucas couldn't even get up to go to the bathroom most times without Marcus angling himself to watch him. As far as I knew, Lucas was straight. So that was going to be one hell of a heartbreak for Marcus.

I opened the apartment door to find the smell of garlic and

something delicious in the air. Immediately, I sniffed. "Oh my God, did you cook?"

My stomach grumbled, reminding me that I'd only eaten a cold slice of pizza for lunch, and I needed to eat something more substantial.

Lucas stopped short as he was stirring the sauce on the stove. "Oh, you're home."

I nodded. "Yeah. I do live here, at least for the time being."

"Oh, I just—the bar called and left a message on the main line about you covering a shift tonight. I assumed you'd be working."

"Yeah, I was. Now I'm off."

Lucas winced. "The thing is I kind of have a date tonight."

It shouldn't have hurt. It really shouldn't have. I had zero expectations about Lucas, but it *did* hurt. So much so that my stomach bottomed out and then cramped as I considered him on a date, actually kissing some other girl. "Oh, I didn't realize. I'll just grab a quick sandwich, and I'll be out of your hair."

"Sorry, I didn't realize you'd be home."

"No, it's your apartment. I'm just a guest. I'll make myself scarce, I promise."

I don't know how I kept my voice even because I could practically feel it cracking in half.

With the scent of some delicious pasta and sauce wafting all around me, I made myself a quick cold turkey sandwich, grabbed a bottle of water and my books, and then headed for my room.

Lucas sighed. "You don't have to run off like that. It's just—"

"I get it. You have a date. No big deal."

"Are you sure, because after last night—"

"I know what you're trying to get at, but I wasn't going to go there. I had a mistaken lapse in judgment. It's fine. It won't be happening again. We're good." I escaped to my room and made an immediate call to Jinx.

"Lay it on me."

"He has a date."

"Wait, I thought you went on a date with him?"

"Well apparently it was only a mock-date."

"Honey, didn't he already say that?"

I knew I was being irrational, but I didn't care. "That's not the point. The point is he has a dat, after we went on this incredible mock-date yesterday. What am I supposed to make of that?"

"That the man has a date. Honey, you can't let this upset you."

"It wouldn't upset me if he hadn't kissed me."

"Wait, what?"

"Yeah, I mean, I texted you that I had a date yesterday. It was with Lucas."

Jinx sputtered. "Dude, you left out that very important detail."

"It wasn't supposed to be a real date, but it felt real. We had a great time. We came back, and things were all tense and crackly. And then he kissed me. And he's seriously skilled in the kissing and foreplay department, because I was ready. Like so freaking ready. And he was, uh, touching me. But, then someone knocked at the door and interrupted us."

"Let me guess, no continuing where you left off?"

"Nope. As a matter of fact, this morning he acted like it never happened. Said he wants to be friends."

On the other end of the line, Jinx cursed. "He's a twat."

"Yes, I agree."

She continued, "Actually, he's worse than a twat. He's a twat's ass."

I giggled. "I know right? It's one thing to give great date. Fine, okay, I get it. He's very good at it. He's clearly had a lot of practice. But you know, he made that shit feel real. I know the type. He seemed sincere, but then you peel back a layer and there's nothing really there. I don't know. I just feel duped."

"Okay, so he's going out? You should go out there in your skimpiest outfit when the girl arrives and just lay on the couch, refusing to move until they go."

I barked out a laugh. "Oh my God. You're terrible. But they're not going anywhere. She's coming here for dinner. Imagine me walking in. Lucas was cooking, and I immediately thought it was for me. Then he tells me he has a date."

"Wait, he's bringing a date to the house?"

"Yeah, before you say it, I know. I need to move out. I'm working on it. I'm considering reporting my roommate and her damn dog. I'm telling them the situation is untenable and I can't possibly go back. But I don't want poor Rufus to be without a home."

"There you go again, worrying more about other people than yourself. You need a place to stay. You can't keep staying there with Mr. Sex-on-a-Stick. It's going to give you sleepless nights."

"Right? This is my own fault for even getting my wires crossed. I know guys like him. None of it is real. It's all about the illusion."

"Oh my God, what is his deal anyway? Why do you keep attracting these losers?"

"I don't know. I'm not sure what gods I angered in a previous life, but this is hardly fair."

"I mean, it's like you have a special case of bad luck. But there is always payback."

"What am I supposed to do? I already went on a date, remember? I kissed the guy in front of Lucas. I don't exactly have Jase clamoring for a second date. He never even called me. I didn't even get a chance to turn him down." Though, he could probably tell I was more into pissing Lucas off than actually kissing him.

Jinx was quiet for a moment, and then she chuckled. "Well, there is one option."

"What?"

"It's a little extreme, but it will also get the *don't bring dates home while I live here* message across."

"Ugh, extreme. Let's hear it, because I'm still really pissed off."

"All right, are you ready for this? Because this is gonna take full commitment. You have to make sure you're up to the challenge."

"Oh, you better believe it. Let's talk payback."

"Oh my gosh, I love your apartment. I mean, how did you even get into a building like this? It must have cost a fortune."

*This is a bad idea.* I'd known it the moment I asked her out, but I'd done it anyway. Then the moment she arrived, I just wanted her gone. Not that there was anything wrong with Jessica, per se, it was just that she wasn't Bryna. And she talked a lot. She seemed more fascinated by all the cool shit than by getting to know me. Not that I'd actually let her get to know me, because, well, I had no intention of anyone ever getting that close. But still, as we sat on the couch after dinner, I just kept wondering what the hell Bryna was doing. Was she listening? Could she hear us? Was she upset?

*You are so whipped.*

I knew she wouldn't understand that technically, this was for her own good. I wasn't the kind of guy she wanted. She'd made that abundantly clear, so why was I bothered by that?

*Because for just a moment, you thought maybe you could be that kind of guy.*

And I'd let myself open up, just a little bit. It was stupid, a dumb, foolish mistake. Now that I had started to feel, there was no turning it off, really, which was a problem. The kind of things I'd done and the kind of places I'd been had taught me pretty early on not to feel a thing. If you let feelings creep in, you'll make mistakes. Mistakes can cost you everything.

Jessica cuddled closer, and I resisted the urge to pull back. I could use some emotion and show her a good time. It's not like I had to talk to her again after this.

The door to Bryna's room opened, and I couldn't help it; my gaze automatically shifted over there. Jessica's did too. In that span of seconds, my breath caught. I couldn't breathe, couldn't get any oxygen in. I couldn't believe what I was seeing. There was no way it was real. It was my mind fucking with me, making me crazy, trying to tell me I was seeing things, and I wasn't. The problem was Jessica saw it too, because her gaze flickered back to mine, and then back to Bryna.

Oh shit. It was not a dream.

*Mayday, Mayday, this is not a drill. All systems will shut down.* My brain screamed to me, but I couldn't help it. I drank in the sight of her.

Bryna, without ever shifting her gaze toward us on the couch, merely stalked into the kitchen as if she owned the joint, wearing nothing but attitude and a smile. She stood in front of the open refrigerator door completely naked with the interior light highlighting that insane silhouette. She got herself a yogurt and sauntered over to the drawer to pull out a spoon. Then, happy as she pleased, she sauntered right back into her bedroom as if she hadn't even seen us.

The problem was I had seen *her*. And the image of Bryna Tressel walking naked in my apartment was one I would never forget. As a matter of fact, I'm pretty sure it was all I was ever going to see for the rest of my life.

≛

*Bryna*

That was insane. I still couldn't believe I had done it. When Jinx had suggested it, I thought she was crazy. And she was. My bestie took no prisoners. And neither had I. The moment I walked out, I could feel his gaze on me. I'd almost turned around and run back. Who the hell walked around naked? But once the door was open, there was no turning back. I deliberately did not stick around to hear what his date might have to say. I went back in my bedroom, ate my yogurt, and then headed straight for the shower. Then I went to bed, wearing my earbuds so as to drown out any noise. But no doubt, there would be retaliation. There would be payback, and it would be painful, so, so painful, but I was ready for it. This was more fun. This was easier. I knew how to do this. We'd draw our battle lines and take our corners. That was a dynamic I understood. Me wanting to feel Lucas close, to feel his arms around me, that *wasn't* a dynamic I understood. As a matter of fact, that dynamic freaked me out, so this one was good.

I opened my bedroom door the next morning and sure enough, Lucas was all about payback. He was shirtless, which wasn't that unusual, but he wasn't *just* shirtless. He was in his boxers. Boxer briefs to be exact. He was just walking around, happy as he pleased, looking like a fucking underwear model. How was that fair?

*Do not react. He is looking for a reaction. Simply get your cereal, make your lunch for today and get the hell out of dodge. Easy.*

Yeah easy. Just ignore him.

But Lucas was not going to be ignored. "Bryna."

His voice was low, soothing, engaging, meant to hypnotize. "Yes Lucas?"

"Wanna tell me what last night was about?"

"What? I wanted a snack."

"Bryna, you came out here naked. My date was pissed."

"Oh, that's a shame. Did I ruin your date?"

His brows drew down. He looked pissed off, but there was a hint of mischief in his eyes.

I went over to the cabinets to grab the cereal and pulled the boxes out. When I turned around, Lucas was directly behind me. I noticed his expansive chest blocking my view. "A little close, aren't you? What's your deal? What do you want?"

"I don't want anything."

"You're too close." He backed up a couple of inches. I gave myself away the moment my gaze landed on his shoulders though. It wasn't my fault. Anyone who'd seen his shoulders would understand. They were divine. I wanted to do nothing but spend time touching them and testing the muscles. I was weak. I knew it. Unfortunately, he knew it too.

"Bryna that felt like you were throwing down the gauntlet. If you're mad about our mock-date, you can just tell me."

"I'm not mad. It was fun." I swallowed hard.

"Fun, but?"

"No buts, it was fun. That's all."

"Are you mad we were interrupted?" His voice lowered an octave. "Are you mad I didn't take if further? That I didn't drag you to the floor and fuck you until neither of us could walk?"

Holy hell. My core pulsed. "No." God, I sounded like I was mad. It occurred to me how wrong this could go. "I wasn't trying to pin you down, Lucas. Get over yourself."

"So you walked out naked when I had a date?"

"I told you, I was hungry."

"Okay. Well, hey, if you don't mind naked days, then I don't either." Then he took another step back, hooked his thumbs in his boxers and dropped them.

*Do not look. Do not look. Don't look.*

Spoiler alert, I totally looked. And, wow...

Yes, okay, fine. I'm not proud of it, but there was staring. And I'm pretty sure my mouth fell open. At that point, Lucas bent down, picked up his shorts and grinned. "I am so glad you're also a secret nudist. We could have grand naked days every day. I'm up for the challenge. Are you?" Then he sauntered away, and I further damned myself because I couldn't look away. I stared at his bare ass and wanted him even more.

# 27

## LUCAS

Maybe that morning hadn't been my finest hour or the best decision I'd ever made, but apparently, I was full of bad decisions. So, whatever. Roone still wasn't talking to me. He just treated me like I was more of a job than his actual friend. And that shit was starting to irk me.

I tried to get through to Roone as we drove to the office. I knew I'd have to hit the ground running when we arrived, so there wouldn't be a chance to talk later. And I wanted to clear the air. "So, you're not gonna talk to me?"

It was funny. I'd never noticed how subtle Roone was about his job. He somehow managed to walk in front of me everywhere, prepared to take all the dangerous hits first, his gaze sweeping from left to right, always shrewd, always watchful. For Marcus, I knew it was all about the job. But Roone... somehow, I'd shoved him into the friend box and hadn't noticed he'd been doing a job, which meant he was probably very good at it.

"I don't know what you're talking about."

"You've got your panties in a twist."

He frowned. "I don't wear panties. Besides, they're called knickers, mate."

"Knickers, whatever you call them. You're mad that I went off script."

He sighed and rounded the corner heading toward the office.

"Lucas, we don't have to do this. I've drawn the line between friendship and work. It won't happen again."

"Fuck, I'm sorry, okay? I broke protocol."

"You think I'm pissed off? You think I'm too tough with you because you took the piss?"

I frowned. I still haven't figured out all the British terminology, but I was getting there. "Why don't you do us all a favor then, and tell me why you're pissed off? Then I can buy you a bottle of scotch and be done with it, right?"

"No, not right. It wasn't just about you going against protocols for the day. I don't know how many times everyone has to remind you that your life is in danger. There are people out there in the world that want you dead for bigger reasons than fucking their girlfriend. There are actual life-and-death stakes at play here. And your brother, the king, put me in charge of protecting you. That is how important you are to him. And to have you completely disregard that and just do as you like, yeah, that pisses me the fuck off."

*Shit.* "Roone, shit man, I didn't mean it like that. I just—"

"No. Shut your mouth and listen for once. If you don't give a shit about your life, fair enough. Your father gave his to protect you and your brother and sister, but whatever. You certainly didn't give a shit about my job and what that would do to me or Marcus if anything happened to you. No, you were just thinking about yourself. So don't act now like we're gonna be mates, because you completely disregarded everything that is important to me. I am not here to hang out with you. I'm not up your ass because it's fun. I am doing a job. When you fuck with that, we don't get to be mates after."

He parked in my assigned space then left me in the car as he marched over to the elevator. All I could do was stare after him. But honestly, he only got about four steps when he realized I wasn't following him, and he came back for me. "Out."

Oh no, he didn't get to throw a hissy fit without me saying anything in response. "Roone, I know I fucked up."

"Mate, it's not up for discussion. I have a job to do, and you're it. And if you think—"

"Fuck, I'm sorry okay? I just wanted a day with Bryna to myself. Since everything happened and you were assigned to me, I've been mostly good. I know Sebastian was a problem; there are legends about him. And because you're my mate, I don't wanna put you through that. I know it's a pain in the ass." I sighed. "Since this whole thing happened, I haven't felt like myself. I haven't felt like I am *me*. And sometimes I just wanna break out and *be* me, even though that guy was an asshole. Sometimes I just forget. I am sorry. It won't happen again."

I wasn't used to apologizing, and I wasn't sure how long I stood there waiting. Roone's shoulders relaxed slightly, and he gave me a terse nod before turning back around. "We need to go."

I wasn't sure if I was forgiven or not, but at least I wasn't catching the waves of hostility now. It might take a while, but he'd warm up. At least I hoped he would.

We entered the elevator, and once we hit my floor I went left toward my office. Roone had no choice other than to keep close, but when I stepped into the small office, there was someone in there waiting for me, someone unexpected. "Mom?"

She looked exactly like I remembered her. Blond hair, sun streaked, slightly frizzy, lightly curling on the ends as it swung around her shoulders. She was never one for getting styles or blow outs or anything like that. Her eyes sparkled, and her skin was sunkissed, as always.

"Lucas, I got your message."

I glanced around. "What the fuck? How the hell?"

She moved a hand. "Did you really think I'd meet you at an open bar like that? Life is a little complicated right now for me and Tony. Going to a place like that is asking for trouble."

"So you don't say anything, and you just turn up here?"

"Well, you summoned me, didn't you?"

"How much trouble are you in? Is it money? I can—"

"You think I want money? There's no way you'd have enough."

"I do. I still have the core of what I fenced. If you need it, it's yours."

"Are you kidding me, Lucas? We owe six times that. That's why we're back. Tony wants you to do one last job."

I shook my head. "No, that's what you said last time. I had to leave UCLA. I took a semester off and came down for one last gig. I saw the way he treated you. I mean, the things he had you doing..." I shut my mouth. I inhaled with deep breaths trying to swallow it down. "You were sick, and he still had you running cons. I was the one who took care of you when I came back, made sure you had your meds. I had a way out for the both of us. All you had to do was show up. But there I was at that private airstrip, waiting. I suppose I should be happy that you didn't send Tony and his goons after me."

"Don't be melodramatic, Lucas. I couldn't leave. I had a life."

"What life?"

I immediately dropped my tone. I didn't want Roone running in here. "What life? The way you were living? It was like the old days all over again, always one job away from starving. Tony though, he sure as hell had a fine ride and nice clothes."

"Those are for the jobs, and you know it."

"Do I?" I spat, the venom and hatred from my childhood spilling out.

"Listen, baby, I just came to ask you to do this. Just one last time."

"It's never just one last time. You still haven't told me how you found me."

She laughed. "What? You think you're slick? Using his last name? Wow, that was original. I didn't expect you to go back to it."

So she'd figured it out. "I always liked him."

"Yeah, I know you did. And that was always your problem. You wanted to believe that the pretend world was real, where somebody would come in and save you from yourself, save you from me. It's never going to happen kid."

Michael Newsome had been a mark of my mother's when I was about seven. He was successful, wealthy, and handsome, and she and Tony had worked that mark for three years. She'd married him. For those three years, I'd had a hint of stability. I'd been well taken care of, even loved.

Michael Newsome took care of me like a father should. It was only after he asked to adopt me that my mother and Tony knew it was time to end it. I never thought I would take his last name. And when she walked away from that marriage, she walked away with a cool two million dollars.

And I had walked away with no father, save the stepfather I hated. Michael Newsome looked genuinely distraught that I was leaving. He begged for visitation rights to see me, and my mother promised that she'd allow it. I'd been forced to go along with her, of course, and I never saw him again. But I looked him up months later.

Tony caught me researching him and beat the shit out of me that day. It was the last time, though, because I put up one hell of a fight.

When I made my escape after the last job in Mexico, I took Newsome's last name, as an honor or some shit. I don't know. The point was, she'd been able to find me because of it. "I'm not doing that job Mom."

"You have to, because if you don't, I'm going to die. And I didn't beat cancer just to have the cartel kill me."

"Mom, I have money. Take it. Take all of it. And I have something else in the works. I don't how it's all going to pan out, but it could be fine. It could be *great*. Then you'll have access to even more money. Just walk away."

I strolled forward and took her hands, because at my core, I just wanted her to be my mother. I wanted her to love me more than she loved him. Even though I knew what the outcome would be, even though I knew it would hurt, I still did it anyway.

I begged.

"Mom, please just stay with me. We'll get you a place. I'll take care of you." She glanced down at our hands, mine clutching on to hers, holding tight, and she pulled away.

"No. He loves me. We love each other. And I need you to do

this because you owe me. They're going to kill me if we don't get them their money."

"Why can't you see what he's done to you, Mom? Every job, do you see any of that money?"

"He takes good care of me. You know that."

I knew how this worked. When they pulled off a score, Tony would shower her with gifts and attention for a good, solid month, sometimes two, maybe three. And then his little gambling habit would make it so that they'd have to start taking shit jobs again while he built up to the 'big one.' It was a pattern I'd seen all too often. "I'm not going to help you dig yourself in deeper. I'm just not."

"You owe me. You think this new life you have for yourself is real? It's not. This is a fantasy. The sooner you realize that, the better off you'll be. You have my number. Call me when you change your mind. We have our differences, but you're not going to let me die." And then she walked out, leaving me to stare after her.

There were moments in my life when I truly hated her.

I wasn't sure if this was one of those times. I also wasn't sure if I hated her because she was wrong or because she was right.

* *

### Lucas

By the time 7:30 hit that night, I was rubbed raw. After my mother's visit, things just went from shitty to worse. After my mother left, my meeting with the board didn't go well. One of the other charity directors wanted to know why I was looking into fund allocation. So much for keeping shit quiet.

Then in one of the classes I TA'd, I realized that Jessica was sitting front and center. How had I not noticed she was in my class before? *Because until she shoved her tits into your face, you didn't notice her at all.*

Great, so now I'd gone out on a date with a student. It was one of the larger lecture halls in economics, and there she was with a short skirt and a thong that I could clearly see. There would be serious ramifications if it became public knowledge that I had taken her out. Luckily, I didn't think she was in for all that, but she was making it clear that she was still interested.

And after Bryna's little stunt the other night, she was clearly trying to regain my attention. It's not what I needed. At the end of class, I just avoided her. I met up with Roone at the back of the class and headed straight home.

I had a lot to think about and a lot to plan. I'd been dead serious when I told my mother that I wanted her to have the money. I'd give it to her, free and clear. I didn't want the ill-gotten gains anymore. It was one thing when I thought my mother and I would use it to live on and to start fresh, start our new lives. It was another thing entirely when I was the only one holding the bag. It felt like blood money. Like I'd sacrificed my mother for that cash. It wasn't true, but it was a lie that snuck in when my defenses were down.

The truth was I'd given her everything, but she still always chose him. And there I was, still trying to figure out how to rectify the situation for her.

I unlocked the door to my apartment and inclined my head. "Are you coming?"

Roone lifted a brow but then slowly nodded. "Yeah. Let me grab a shower first. And let me order some food because I know you only have like a yogurt and an avocado in the fridge."

"That's not fair, man. Bryna lives here now. She buys food. *Real* food."

"Let the poor girl keep her food. I'll order from that East African place."

My stomach grumbled immediately. "Oh God, that sounds so good, but they take forever. "

He checked his watch. "The game is not for an hour. Go take a bubble bath or something. I'll check in later." At least things were getting a little bit better. He was still a bit stiff and cool, but since we'd had that talk earlier in the day, it had been better. Baby steps. I'd pissed him off, and he was right about that situation. Sebastian had trusted him to keep me safe. The world may not have known who I was yet, but there were people already looking. So for now, Roone and Marcus were actually necessary. I just had to figure out how to meld the necessity of their protection with me living my life.

I opened the door, ready for a naked attack from Bryna, but no, this time she was in sweat pants and a midriff tank.

It was odd. She was more covered, but somehow infinitely sexier like this. And with my edges raw and exposed, I wanted to devour her, which obviously was not going to happen.

"Oh hey, there you are," Bryna said.

"Here I am." My response was terse, muttered through clenched teeth.

She rolled her eyes. "What, pray tell, have I done to you this time? First you complain that I'm naked, so I sit out here fully clothed, and you're still complaining. What's wrong?"

"You know what? You're my problem. Your girly shit is everywhere. Candles... I don't even own candles. You've burnt more candles than anyone I know. Different scents too. I walk in here and the smell of girly, and pretty, and—" I was being a dick.

I like that smell. It smelled better than sweat. Before she showed up, as nice as this place was, it tended to be sparse. And I never smelled like vanilla, or rose water, or whatever the hell that candle was. Then she showed up, and suddenly there were candles. A lot of them.

"Is your problem my candles now? Look, the sooner I get a place of my own, the better."

I dropped my bag on the counter and leaned into it. "You know what? You've been threatening to leave for a couple of weeks now. Are you actually going to get up and do it?"

Her jaw unhinged, but it was the quivering lip that really got me. *Shit.* I'm such a dick. She pushed to her feet, grabbed her book, and started stomping toward her bedroom, but I caught her arm. "Wait."

She wrenched her arm free. "No, I will not wait. What the hell has crawled up your ass and stung you? I haven't done anything to you. And let's not forget that you strolled into my apartment and demanded that I come and stay with you. And for your information, I have been looking. There's just not a shit available that I can afford. Whatever. I'll call Ellie and tell her I'm crashing on her couch for a week or so until I figure myself out. I might be going back to student housing. You won't have to put up with me for much longer."

I sighed. "Stop. I don't want you to move out."

"Yes, you do. After what you just said—"

"I'm sorry, okay?" *Fuck.*

"What the hell is your problem? You run so hot and cold. You won't look at me. You bring randoms by the house."

Fuck, couldn't she tell how desperate I was to touch her? "Shit, you're still upset about that? I knew you were pissed."

"I wasn't pissed. It just felt..." she exhaled with a puff of air.

"It felt reactionary. Like after hanging out with me and having a great day, you just wanted to show me that you didn't give a shit about me by bringing some girl to the apartment. That girl looked like me, too."

I opened my mouth to say something and snapped it shut because she was right. It had been a reaction to that great day with her. Once again, the two versions of Lucas had to fight their instincts. "Fuck, I'm sorry. It's been a shitty day, but you know I can't be with you, right?"

"You know, you say things like that, but I don't even know what that means."

"You think I don't see you with your big doe eyes, looking at me like I'm Christmas morning?"

"My God, you have such an inflated sense of self. I do not look at you like that."

"You sure? Because that night we kissed, you sure did."

"You're such an asshole and so completely full of yourself. I swear to God, guys like you—"

"Oh my God, here we go again. 'Guys like me.' Honey, you don't know the first thing about me. You've never known a guy like me before in your life. You've dated a bunch of eunuch Ken dolls, and you dare compare me to them? Yeah, right princess, you should only be so lucky."

"You are such a cocky, arrogant bastard."

I chuckled harshly. Little did she know. "Oh my God, yes. You are absolutely right on that one."

"You're a dick."

I rounded on her. She was standing there looking beautiful and innocent, and tempting, in her low-slung sweats and her cropped tank, the soft skin of her belly on display, and the scent of flowers wafting around her. And she was giving me that look, part hellcat, part soft, appealing and completely touchable. "I am *not* a good guy Bryna. You can't just package me like you do your little Ken dolls, call me out when you want to play with me, and then expect me to go back in my cage. Once I'm out of my cage, that's it. I'm not going back in. I am not the good guy here, so don't look all hurt when I try to protect you from myself."

She jutted her chin up. "When I need protection, I will tell you. What is it you're hiding, Lucas? Why won't you let me see the real you? For the love of God..."

My world slowed. I knew what her tone was like when she had a full head of steam going. And part of me welcomed that, but the other part of me wanted to show her that she was wrong. I wasn't good. She didn't want to know what I was hiding. And God, when I was exposed, once everybody found out, she'd be the first to run right back to the safety of her parents and the circumspect guys she'd dated.

She would know that I was the kind of guy she was looking for all along, and I couldn't stand the idea.

She continued her rant. "God, are you about to kick my ass? Drag my ass from hell to breakfast by the roots of my hair again? Because I have better shit to do."

"What have I done to you? From the moment we met, you have disliked me. I'm not even sure *you* know why."

"Oh, I know why. You think y—"

I'd had enough. I wasn't listening to anymore of it. So I kissed her.

The air changed around us, and I shivered. I knew I couldn't fight it right now when I was feeling so raw. My brain gave one command but, before I even registered it, I was tugging her against me.

I gave her no chance to pull back. I just pulled her response from her. It wasn't fair. I knew it. But fuck, I wanted her so bad I couldn't breathe.

I slid my arms around her. My lips were demanding. Hers didn't yield at first, but finally with a whimper, she parted them for me, and her hand fisted in my T-shirt.

A spike of electricity flared between us, scorching my lips when her tongue met mine. With a low groan, I shifted our angle, kissing her deeper and ripping a moan from her as she started to melt.

I didn't have the defenses to fight off these feelings. Somewhere in the far recesses of my mind, alarm bells rang, starting as a low buzz, but quickly intensifying to a sharp clang.

With a strength I didn't know I had, I pulled back. "This is why I can't touch you. Because every fucking time it's like napalm. I'm not the good guy Bryna. I'll only hurt you."

I forced myself to turn my back on her. To keep walking for that door and to go across the hall. If I stayed, I might not be strong enough to keep my hands off of her.

## 28

LUCAS

As IT TURNED OUT, staying the hell away from Bryna was easier said than done. Everywhere I went, I could smell her. Vanilla and roses, like a calling card left all over the house to torture me.

I figured things might be awkward for a while, but I was serious about helping her find an apartment. I had to figure out her budget, and then I'd certainly make it happen. Somewhere safe where I wouldn't worry.

*You have it so bad.*

Yeah, so what if I did? For once I got to be the good guy, even if she didn't see it that way.

I was working my way back onto Roone's good side again, so I'd brought beer over to the apartment to watch the Heat play the Knicks, and he was busy shouting at the screen.

"How do you even have any skin in the game? You're British. You guys don't have basketball."

"Oi, mate, Samson Wickham, he's British. I've come to support my guy."

I rolled my eyes. Marcus had zero interest. If it wasn't rugby or cricket, he didn't care. Of course there was football. He thought European football was king. But he couldn't even get into basketball, which was just disappointing. So on nights when Roone and I were watching it, he watched TV in his room.

My phone rang, and it was an unknown number. The hairs at the back of my neck stood up in attention, and I frowned. Even without looking at me, Roone picked up on my mood immediately, and he paused the TV. "What's up?"

I shook my head. "I'm just going to take this over to my place. I'll be right back."

When I unlocked the door to my apartment, Bryna was nowhere to be found. Maybe she was at work. *Or maybe she's just avoiding you.* My phone kept on ringing. "Hello?"

"Ah, the prodigal son answers the phone."

A chill ran down my spine. "Tony, I already told you, I'm not doing the gig. I'm not helping you. I'll give you my cut from the last job, but I want nothing to do with you. I'm not part of this... whatever you've got cooking."

"Your mother said that. How could you say no to your own mother? You're only hurting her, you know?"

"You can say what you want. It's still not happening. As if I don't know you, as if I haven't been dealing with this all my life. Whatever job you've got lined up, however many people you need, find someone else."

"You know, I had the feeling you'd say that. You will do this. If you don't, I will hurt her."

I ignored the twinge in my gut, because he knew how to play me. He'd been doing it for years. "It's still not happening. Find someone else."

"I see you're still stubborn. Well, I guess I'm just going to have to find another way to motivate you. Your pretty new roommate, that girl you've been traipsing all around New York with, I can tell you want her."

Cold seeped out of my veins, and my voice lowered to barely above a growl. "She's got nothing to do with this."

"No. She doesn't. She's just an easy mark. I don't know what you've got going with her. The point is, I can easily twist you. I taught you better than that. No personal attachment. It's like you learned nothing. Now someone like me is going to use it against you. If you don't want to help me, to help your mother, fine, suit yourself. But I can't guarantee that something won't happen to that pretty little roommate of yours. Maybe she'll even find out exactly the kind of man that you are. I'll blow your shit open."

I didn't care about him blowing up everything about my past, but I did care about Bryna. "You stay the fuck away from her." If I had to, I'd get Blake Security involved. *Or you could do what he wants.* Not happening.

"Testy, testy. Oh God, did you break another cardinal rule? Falling for the mark? You are such a disappointment."

"So you keep saying."

"All you have to do is say yes. One job, and I'm out of your hair. I don't want to see your ugly mug anyway."

The insult rolled off my back like water. After all, I'd heard much worse over the years. "If I do this, you stay away from her. Leave her alone. She has nothing to do with any of this."

"If there was honor among thieves, I'd go ahead and make you a promise. But you and I both know there isn't, so let's just say this; Consider your debt paid if you do this."

I didn't want to do it. I was free. Finally fucking free. But he knew about Bryna. And if he was throwing that shit out there, he would do whatever he could to fuck up my life and hers. I'd told her earlier today that I would protect her from me. And I meant it. "Send me the details. I swear to God, if I ever see you after I do this, I will kill you."

"Yeah, you wish you could."

Little did he know that it was more than a wish. I certainly was capable. And if he did anything to hurt Bryna, I really hoped my diplomatic immunity would hold, because I would put it to the test.

❦

## Bryna

To say things were awkward, would be downplaying the situation. Awkward didn't even begin to cover it. Like when I woke up and caught a partially clothed Lucas out in the living room.

Shirtless is one thing, but he only had on loose boxers that showed off what he was working under the soft gray material.

The man was mouthwatering. But that wasn't the point. The point was now shit was uncomfortable. It had been three days since the hottest thing to ever happen to me in my life and two-and-a-half days since the backpedal to end all backpedals.

*It's not like he said he didn't want you. He just said he was being the good guy, not an asshole.*

Except he had been sort of an asshole by making that decision for me, as if I couldn't be trusted to decide for myself what I wanted.

I had decided he wasn't a bad guy. Who was he to tell me that he was? All that sounded like maybe it was his problem, not mine. So, I'd had some serious sleepless nights. I didn't even know how it had happened, but somehow, Lucas had become the guy I shared everything with. Not just an apartment, but my family problems, everything. I'd gotten used to coming home and having him explain basketball to me.

Honestly, did it really make sense? Somehow, Lucas had turned out to be the first real guy-friend I'd ever had, completely by accident.

Half the time, I didn't even like him. But if I ignored all his bravado and his charm and all that extra stuff, it was easy to see that he was actually a really good guy.

He took time trying to explain things. Fuck, he didn't have to help me find a job and he didn't need to let me stay here, but he had done that out of the kindness of his heart. He kept talking about the guy he used to be. I never wanted to meet that guy. But the new Lucas, when he was keeping it real, was someone I could talk to.

Regardless, Lucas Newsome no longer wanted to make out with me. So despite the throbbing between my thighs, I could just get over it.

I had to. I had to move out. *Coward.*

I didn't want to move out. I liked it here. Not just the fantastic location, and hello, penthouse apartment, but a girl could be lonely on her own. I liked the company, despite myself.

Squaring my shoulders, I unlocked the penthouse door only to find that it was dark. Fantastic. All that angst for nothing. I turned on the lights and found the mail on the counter as always. It's not like it was my permanent apartment, but I was pleasantly surprised to find something addressed to me.

It was a very fancy envelope with gold embossed letters and

little delicate embellishments, and the return address was *The Royal Artistic Trust Charity Ball.*

I'd called my old mentor to ask her recommendations for a job. She'd asked me for my new address. I didn't think I'd given her this one, but she must be the reason for the invite.

I pulled out the heavy card stock.

*To Miss Bryna Tressel and Guest.*

Oh, fantastic. I needed a date.

My mind, traitor that it was, wandered straight to Lucas. He was admittedly delicious in a tux. But despite being friends, there was no way was I going to open myself up to that particular brand of torture or rejection. I'd made the mistake of getting too close to him once. It wouldn't happen again. I couldn't stand it.

No. Maybe I'd take Ellie. She seemed like she'd get a good old laugh out of the whole see-and-be-seen charity set.

It might actually be fun. Sometimes these events would have date auctions to drive excitement. I might actually volunteer. Lord knew I wasn't having any luck the good old-fashioned way.

I stared down at the envelope. Maybe it was about time that I rediscovered a little bit of the old Bryna. New Bryna was great too. New Bryna was independent. But old Bryna occasionally had some fun. Maybe I didn't have to give myself up completely to become a new and improved version of myself.

THE PRESENTATION LECTURE hall was half full.

I shifted in my seat. Meeting here like this was risky. It was a tax symposium about the future of charitable giving for corporations. It was just boring enough to make sure Marcus and Roone were more interested in covering the exits then actually flanking me. I could feel the hairs on my neck stand up as soon as Tony sat down one row behind me. Why, after all of these years, did he still affect me like this? *Because he taught you everything he knows.* Hatred was definitely the emotion that poured out of me as soon as he spoke.

"I have to tell you, golden boy, I'm actually surprised you showed."

I didn't turn around. I made no indication that I was even speaking. "Hand over the plans. That's the only reason I agreed to meet you."

"Oh, touchy, touchy. Afraid some of your fancy new friends will know where you actually come from?"

What friends? Friends get you caught.

"I don't give a fuck what anyone else thinks of me."

Tony chuckled. "Of course you don't. Just your new room-mate, right?"

I said nothing to that. I wasn't going to give him any more leverage. As a matter of fact, the more distance I put between me and Bryna, the better. As much as I hated for her to go, I *needed* her to go. But the look on her face was going to be brutal, so I needed to find a way to be gentle about it.

"Plans."

"Oh, easy does it. I want to hear this interesting chat on the future of charitable giving. A bunch of rich fucks with too much money. I'm sure it will be fascinating."

I ground my teeth. "If you're here to bullshit, I'm leaving." I started to push out up my chair, and he tsked.

"Sit your ass back down, boy."

"Then get to the goddamn point, because I don't have time to waste."

"Oh, you think you're badass now. This con has fucked with your head, because you're a believer. Your rich friend from last year, the one you were photographed with in the papers. Seems he's a king. Got me thinking that maybe you were trying to cut me out of the job. I want a piece of that action."

"There's nothing to get in on. It's not a job. I'm doing this one gig for you. If you change the terms, our deal is off. I'll take my chances with Bryna."

He was silent for a moment. I figured he was contemplating, but he finally relented. "Fine. Under your seat, I already taped the flash drive there. It's got schematics of the building, all the exits, our egress points for the getaway, and the storage boxes for the jewels."

"What's the target?"

"The Royal Artistic Trust Charity Ball. We have men on the inside who work there. There's going to be an auction, and the event is going to be dripping with everyone's mama's and grandmama's jewels. I cannot wait. We're going to go with the Leaning Tower of Pisa con."

*Holy fucking shit.* "What? We're going to rob a charity event?" He wanted me to steal from Sebastian?

Tony nodded. "You bet your bottom dollar, we are."

"They're raising money for the poor."

"If you believe that, then I'm the Easter Bunny."

I could hear it in his voice, the ambivalence, the indifference.

"Besides, I don't care. And you shouldn't either because as soon as I have what you owe us, you won't ever see me again."

And all I had to do to get that was betray my brother. "Good. Because I really will kill you. It's not an empty threat. If you come after someone I love, then I'll go after someone you love."

"Who, your mother?" His chuckle was harsh.

I pushed to my feet. I didn't bother to look at him, but I muttered low, "My mother made her choice, and now I have to make mine." Then I headed up the stairs to the exit.

Marcus followed. "Where are you going?"

"You know, I was super excited about this, but it's kind of lame. Let's roll."

He sighed in relief but eyed me suspiciously.

*Suspect me all you want, but you will never make me crack.* At least I hoped not.

∗ ∗

*Lucas*

"Ow, ow, ow, ow."

After the symposium, I heard Bryna's cries of pain in the other room. I'd have to try and school my expression before running out to check on the problem. Trying to mask how I felt about her was getting more and more difficult. And since I'd been the one to put a little halt on things after that scorching make out, I needed to be the one to be cool. When I opened my door and sauntered out, I was anything but cool when I saw her limping.

She was shuffling to the island, attempting to reach her foot to take off her shoe. I ran over and tried to give her a helping hand.

"What the hell happened to you!" It came out more of a bellow than a question.

Bryna winced as she startled. "Jesus Christ, Lucas. My head."

I forced myself to take a breath. "Sorry. But what the fuck? You look like a mess, and you're limping. Why are you limping? Why is your make up smudged?" I narrowed my gaze. "Is that a fucking bruise on your jaw?"

My heart hammered against my ribs. I ignored the ache in my jaw from my clenched teeth. I had to keep it together for her. When she was okay, then I'd go and find out who the fuck had hurt her and annihilate them.

I was going to kill whoever the fuck had touched her.

"I'm fine. I'm not the first person to get mugged in New York City."

I stumbled back. "Holy fuck, you were mugged? Are you hurt? Tell me if those fuckers hurt you."

Bryna drew back, her gaze scanning my face. "While I love the effect of that growly voice, maybe you could just dial it back a notch."

The first thing I registered was that she liked my voice like this. Great, I'd store that for later. I also forced myself to take several deep breaths. "Okay, why don't you tell me what happened."

"Honestly, I don't' know. I was taking out the garbage at work because it was in my way. The busboy, Greg, was nowhere to be found, so I took out the trash. Then this guy came out of nowhere."

"Fuck."

She reached out and grabbed my hand. "I'm fine. He wanted money. I said I didn't have any. He yanked off my chain with the charm from Jinx. He'll be real disappointed when he discovers it's costume jewelry." She sighed and winced. "So anyway, then he pushed me down, and I thought he was going to hurt me or something, so I tried to wrench away from him and did something crazy to my back."

I stared at her. She could have been killed. "Did you call the police?"

She nodded. "I'm not a total Island newbie. They took a statement. The bar has security cameras, but the guy stayed just out of range of them."

"Motherfucker."

"Yeah, my sentiments exactly." She sighed. "The paramedics came, and not a hot one out of the bunch. It was very disappointing."

"Seriously, is this the time to joke?" I scowled at her.

"I take my paramedics very seriously."

I refrained just barely from rolling my eyes. "How's your back feeling?"

"Sore, tight. Twisting like that flared a ballet injury from years ago. I throw it out sometimes. It's a recurring thing. Usually it just takes a day of rest and some ice, but I don't have time for that. The charity event is in a couple of days. I need to do something about my nails, my hair, all that good stuff. And I can't walk right now."

"You're not going. Not after what happened today. How the hell did you make it home?"

She scrunched her nose and pursed her lips as she gazed up mischievously. "A police officer drove me home. He wasn't cute either. The doorman, Fred, was very helpful. But once I got up here, it was like the Green Mile or something. Shuffle, shuffle, wince, wince... you know, not fun."

She was so blasé about getting mugged. Maybe it was shock? I shook my head. "You have got to be more careful. I'm not ready to lose my pain in the ass roommate yet. Just come here. What helps?"

She groaned. "Could you not jump on me about the mugging. It's not like I asked to get mugged." She sighed. "Usually lying flat on my back and doing nothing helps. Ice. Advil. If it's not better tomorrow, then I may take a muscle relaxant and head to the chiropractor. But I don't have one here yet. Ow, ow, ow."

"Stop it. Stop moving right now. For now, we don't have to talk about anything you don't want to." I bent down and removed one shoe, gently lifting her foot as I did so, and then repeated the process with the other foot. Then I wrapped her arm around me and helped her wobble over to the couch to lie down. "Stay here. I'll bring you Advil and some water, and something to eat so it doesn't hurt your stomach."

"Oh my God, you don't have to take care of me. I swear, I'm fine."

"Says the woman wincing, even as she tries to get more comfortable."

"Now is not the time to lecture me. The time to lecture me is five days from now, when I feel better."

"Sorry, it comes with the territory." I entered the kitchen to get her some Advil, and I made her a quick sandwich while I was there. She really needed to eat before she took it.

When I brought it to her, her smile was soft. "Careful Lucas, your good guy is showing."

I cleared my throat at that. "If you tell anyone, I'm sorry, but I'll have to kill you."

She laughed and immediately winced. "Stop it. Laughing hurts."

"No one asked you to laugh. What else do you need?"

"Can you grab my phone? I need to call the nail place and cancel. There's no way in hell I can sit up right now."

"You have a nail appointment?"

She nodded. "I don't really go for the big mani-pedi things, but I do need a color change. I guess, I'm going to the charity thing with chipped nails." She sighed.

I glanced down at her sock-clad feet, and I got an idea. "Stay here."

"Oh, that's cute. Where am I supposed to be going?"

I went to her room and called out, "What color is your dress?"

"Blue. Why?"

"Don't worry about it."

I found the only nail polish that would possibly match, some sparkly situation. Then, I went to the bathroom for Epsom salt.

When I had everything I needed, including a towel and the nail polish, I grabbed what looked like nail tools from her bathroom vanity.

When I came out, she was frowning at me. "What are you doing?"

"Well, if the lady cannot get a pedicure, the pedicurist is going to come to her."

"Are you serious right now?"

"Sure, why not?"

She scrunched her face. "I don't know. It's weird?"

"It's not weird, I swear. Come on. Relax. Walk me through this, because I have no idea what I'm doing."

"You've got to be kidding." She tried to push herself to sitting, and I helped her.

"What are you doing? You're supposed to be lying down."

"Yes, but you brought the bowl thing, I feel like I have to soak in it."

I glanced down. "Oh, I see what you mean. Actually wait, I'll fix this."

I went back to the bathroom. I got a foot scrub and more towels and wash cloths, and then filled the pan with water and came back. "Now, you lie down. I got this. You just tell me what I need to do."

"I don't know. You have to take off the nail polish first. The remover is right there."

I got a cotton ball and the polish remover and then winced at the alcohol scent. "God, this is acetone."

She laughed. "Yep. How do you think nail polish comes off?"

"I never thought about it before."

"Typical."

I chuckled. "Well, I never really wore nail polish before, so how was I supposed to know?" Then I scooted to the edge of the couch, pulled her feet into my lap as gently as I could, and proceeded to start with her nail polish.

I grabbed the remote and turned on the game. She made the best sound and sighed contentedly. "Thank you, Lucas."

I shrugged, trying not to look back at her because I didn't want her to see how I was feeling. How this felt unfair. How I was having a real hard time being a good guy. Yeah, somehow, I was finding a way to be aroused by her feet in my lap.

There were a couple of games on, and so I watched as I removed her nail polish. She nibbled on her sandwich and then sat back against the pillows.

"I didn't know you did ballet."

She nodded. "Yeah, for ten years. I was never really fond of the cachet that came with it as opposed to actually liking it as an art form or a sport. Mother never seemed enthused about my performances."

"Did you like it?"

"You know, at first, when I was little, yeah, I loved it. The idea of looking like a prima ballerina and twirling around was great. But no one tells you that your body will go through hell. I didn't know. As I got older and I realized how strong ballerinas have to be, I really did enjoy it. Then, well, my back injury happened. I was trying to do a lift, and I landed wrong and twisted it. It's never been right again, and that ended my illustrious career as a ballerina."

"Do you miss it?" I made the mistake of looking at her as I

asked. I was wiping off the scrub from her feet using the wet wash cloth.

She was staring at me as my hands worked. "Yeah, I miss it. But I'm not sure if I just miss the consistency of the training."

I nodded in understanding. "Yeah, sometimes things become a habit. Then when they're gone, you almost don't know what to do with yourself."

"Exactly. I mean, I did enjoy it. I loved it, but when it was gone, the thing that I missed the most was... I don't know, just knowing that it was part of who I was, even if it wasn't *all* of who I was. But later on, I just had to figure out what I was going to do for me, you know?"

I reached for the lotion and then started massaging her feet. I didn't know why I thought this was a good idea, but just running my thumbs over her arch and hearing that long drawn out moan was an instant turn on. *Fantastic.*

Then I glanced back over at her. Her eyes were closed, her lips were parted, and her head was thrown back, and she looked blissful. There was no way in hell I was stopping.

After ten minutes, when I finished one foot, I started with the other one and the moaning and looking sexy as fuck commenced again.

I was so done. I was so totally going to lose it.

"You said before that you've never had a girlfriend."

I tensed. Where was this line of questioning going?

"No. I moved around a lot. Not ideal."

"Oh yeah? Where?"

Ah, so she was on a fishing expedition. I knew the lies that I should spill for her, but I didn't. Instead I told her the truth, as maturely as possible. "All over. Denver, Boston, Miami, but I mostly grew up in Baja. Then my Mom and stepdad moved us to Phoenix for uh, a job that was long term."

"That must have been sad. It's hard to make friends."

I nodded. "Yeah, it wasn't the easiest situation, but I managed. Turned out just fine, didn't I?" I winked at her.

She wasn't even watching me. This time she was wiggling her toes in my hand, silently begging me to keep massaging, so I did. Anything to keep that look of pure, decadent bliss on her face.

"I know we've talked about this a little, your complicated relationship with your parents. Why do you think you put up with it for so long?"

She sighed, but not in that contented way as before. This was more of a resigned sigh. "I don't know. Maybe it was easier. Maybe I was afraid of the worst thing happening." She shrugged. "And now it has. My mother is too emotionally fragile. All the reasons, all the excuses, so it's actually hard to sit down and talk with her. It always blows up."

"How toxic. I'm sorry."

When I opened the toe nail polish, she smiled at me. "Oh good. I was going to pick that color."

"I'm psychic. I can read minds."

Completely deadpan, she leveled her gaze on me. "Don't go picking around in there. It can be scary."

There was a hint of flirtation in her voice, and I couldn't help it, I took the bait. "There's nothing you've got going on back there that I've never seen before."

As I carefully painted each toe, I could hear her sigh of relief that I was doing a good job. And then she gazed up at me with her big brown eyes, and she smiled. "Thank you, Lucas. I couldn't have done this without you."

One smile from her and I felt a thousand feet tall. I wasn't sure when it happened, but I'd completely fallen for her.

&

*Bryna*

Lucas was in the middle of doing something delicious to my feet, when the doorbell rang. He was blowing on my toes gently as his fingers still caressed and massaged my arches. One spot he touched sent a spasm to my lower back. It hurt at first, but then it released and felt really good, like it loosened whatever the hell I'd done to myself. "Oh my God, again."

He blew some more on my freshly painted nails to dry them, and then he moved his thumb again, pressing insistently, massaging his knuckle back and forth.

"Oh my God, seriously, that is... *amazing.*" I groaned.

"The way you said that, it's almost like you're having an—"

He didn't finish because the doorbell rang insistently. He gently set my feet aside and gave me a look I now recognized to be his don't-you-dare-move look.

When he yanked the door open, I could almost feel the tension snap up his back, forcing his shoulders to square immediately. "What are you doing here?"

The next voice that came was one I recognized. "The king will hear about this."

I lifted my head. "Dad?"

My father marched in with his too-fast, too-brisk step. "Get your things. We're leaving."

I frowned as I tried to sit up. "What? Dad, how did you—"

He interrupted me. "Young lady, you will get your things right now."

Lucas closed the door behind my mother, who sauntered in, looking smug. Her eyes darted around, taking everything in as if calculating just how much Lucas was worth.

Lucas joined me back at the couch, wedging himself between me and my parents. "Bryna, you stay where you are."

Then he turned his attention to the two of them. "She can't move, so I guess you're shit out of luck if you need her to go somewhere."

My father frowned. "What's wrong with her? What did you do to my daughter?"

"You two don't need to talk about me as if I'm not here." I tried to sit up, and pain wound around my lower back and shot down my leg. While Lucas had managed to loosen it significantly, quick movements were still totally out of the question. "I'm right here. I can speak for myself."

I pushed into a sitting position despite the pain. Lucas's gaze pinned on me, and he gave me a sharp shake of his head. "I'm fine. Thank you, Lucas." I turned my attention to my father. "Dad, I'm not going anywhere. I had a tough situation and Lucas was kind enough to offer me a place to stay."

"You wouldn't need a place to stay if you would just stop being so stubborn and stay with your mother. We have a place in the city. That was always the plan."

My mother nodded. "Your father is right. What are you doing here staying with the likes of—"

My father cut his gaze to her and gave her a sharp shake of the head. Immediately, she snapped her mouth shut. He, however, continued on her behalf. "You don't even know him. While King Sebastian said he could be trusted, he's still a stranger. So you *will* get your things, and you *will* come with us. We're your family."

After what they'd done? "Stop it. Stop it now. For weeks since I've been in the city, you've shown up and tried to dictate exactly how things are going to go. And every time you do, you resort to your manipulations, to blackmail, and to all the things that tell me you don't actually care about what I want or need."

My mother's mouth fell open. "Of course we do. What a horrible thing to say about your own parents."

I sighed. "If you were listening, you would know what I'm saying. I needed to do this. I needed to move to this city, be on my own, go to work. And more than once, you have done whatever you could to deter me. First with Braxton and having him propose on my twentieth birthday. Honestly... putting me in positions where it was impossible to say no. When I finally *did* say no after I caught his ass cheating, you let everyone ostracize me. When I told you I was going to start my internship, you smiled to my face, you said I could go, and then, you basically kidnapped me to Europe so I'd miss my start date. Thank God I was able to defer."

My mother tried to interject. "Now young lady, that is not how it happened, and you know it."

I pushed against the arm of the chair, trying to stand. Lucas bent down and helped me. His skin was warm, familiar, soothing. "What I remember is you lying to get me there. To my face, lying and telling me that my grandmother was sick. Then, when I got there, you confiscated my passport."

"She was sick!" My mother persisted.

"She had *bunions*, Mom. Hardly ill. And then, when I attempted to leave on my own, you wouldn't allow it, so you can see how I wouldn't trust you with my future. Then you tried to force another engagement with the same man who cheated on me. I wanted out so bad, I snuck out a window at a wedding. I climbed right on out to escape you."

My mother rolled her eyes. "You've always been so dramatic. None of that was really necessary. If you had just spoken to us..."

"Spoken to you? And said what exactly? 'I don't want to marry this douche nozzle?' Like I said before? Or how about, 'I want this internship. It's important to me.' Would you have listened? Would you have let me just do it?"

She sighed. "You are always so prone to melodrama. Sometimes you don't know what's best. You don't make good choices."

My father shook his head. "You are our daughter, and you are supposed to do as we tell you. We have your best interests at heart. If you don't see that, we'll have to agree to disagree."

I shook my head. "You almost had me fooled before. But I am done with your manipulation. If you ever decide to start treating me like an adult and respect my decisions, I'm willing to hear it. Until then, get out."

My father's mouth hung open. My mother sputtered. "B-b-b- Bryna, how can you talk to us that way? I just can't even believe it. What has gotten into you?"

Lucas spoke up then, subtly blocking me from their view. "You heard her. Time to go."

My father glared at him. "How dare you?"

Lucas crossed his arms. And then his voice went low, deep, barely above a growl. "Are you refusing to go?"

My father might try and bully, but if someone was strong enough to stand up to him, he would back down. He peered around Lucas to glare at me. "Bryna, this conversation is not finished." He pointed a finger at Lucas. "Careful, boyo, nothing is official yet."

What the hell did he mean by that? What wasn't official? Was Lucas's job in danger? "Let me be clear. You retaliate against Lucas in any way, and we're done for good. He did what you asked. He kept me safe, looked out for me, which is more than you ever did."

Lucas went to the door and opened it. He said nothing as they stormed out.

With my hands shaking, my knees wobbly, and adrenaline rushing in my veins, I eased myself back onto the couch, and then I covered my face with my hands and sobbed. I had zero fucks left to give that Lucas was seeing me cry.

But instead of freaking out about it or being uncomfortable, he just eased down next to me, threw his arm around my shoulders, and pulled me close. "I'm really proud of you. That couldn't have been easy."

And as if I hadn't already fallen for Lucas Newsome, that completely sealed it.

AN HOUR after her parents left, Bryna called it a night. She tried to hang in for just a little bit longer, but she tapped out. "Thank you so much for helping me. I think I'm going to clean my face now and make it an early night."

Helping her get ready was torture for me. But she clearly needed it in more ways than one. I averted my gaze and helped her, even though I already knew exactly where her moles were, how she tasted, and how she smelled right behind her ear. I should be nominated for sainthood.

My phone rang when she was in her room. My gaze darted to the door, but I didn't take any chances. I knew who was calling. To make sure she couldn't hear me, I walked into my own room and closed the door behind me. "What?"

"What the hell do you think you're doing with my daughter?"

"Lord Tressel, I'm sorry that it panned out the way that it did, but it was her choice."

"What choice are you talking about? You have taken my daughter from me."

"Well, for starters, she's not a toy, and I haven't done anything to her. She kicked you out of her own volition today. She knew what she wanted, and she knew it wasn't you."

"I think you forget that you work for me."

Anger slid up my spine and held as I let the fury leak into my veins by drops. "I don't work for you. I work for the crown. And I'm pretty sure there are appropriate ways to refer to me, such as His Royal Highness, or Your Royal Highness. I'm not an errand boy. My brother, your king, is the one I answer to. Not you."

Never mind that Sebastian knew nothing about my room-mate situation. This was where Tressel was supposed to dial it down, step back, and take a bigger-picture look, but he didn't. "His Royal Highness, my ass. You would not *be* a prince if it weren't for me. You are nothing. Your mother is filth, and you are no more than a common guttersnipe."

"That might be, but you cast your vote. No take backs, asshole. You *will* sign when it comes time."

"If I don't?"

"I guess we'll see. What your daughter told you today had nothing to do with me. You made your choices. You made your bed. How you have treated her, that's all on you. Her refusing to let that happen again, that's all her. I had nothing to do with it. So, you can be an asshole all you want, but it's not going to change the fact that your own daughter wants nothing from you but to be left alone. She wants no part of what you're offering. You screwed up the moment you tried to manipulate her, the moment you tried to control her. She fought back, and it didn't end well for you."

"Your brother will hear about this."

"You know what? That's good. I'm pretty sure you'll find we'll be on the same page."

"You think you're so untouchable? The world will find out who you really are."

"You know what, yeah, there will come a time when I can't hide, when everyone will know who I am. But maybe they'll also see who I can be."

"You think he'll stand with you? When the king sees who you really are, when he really finds out all the nasty little details, he will cast you out, and you will be left alone."

I swallowed the bile in my throat and the fear of abandonment trying to claw through my belly. Sebastian knew about my past, but I history had taught me that you don't get to keep good things. I kept waiting for something to happen to turn Sebastian away from me. For my new life to go away. It was only a matter of time.

*No, it's not. You are the master of your own destiny.* I just had to remember that. One last job and I'd be free and then no one could ever threaten to take my family away again.

"If that's what it takes to ensure that Bryna gets to live her life, then so be it. She's my friend, and she deserves better than you. I'm going to make sure she has it."

"Lucas, what's wrong?" Sebastian's voice was gravelly, like I'd woken him up.

Shit. "I'm sorry, I should have checked the time. I mean for fuck's sake, you guys are in your honeymoon phase and I'm interrupting you."

My brother groaned. "If I was otherwise occupied doing something fun to my wife, I never would have answered. Not even if giant monsters were swallowing my kingdom."

"Right..." my voice trailed.

He was quiet for several seconds. "Lucas, what is it?"

I rubbed at the burning hole in my chest. "I—sorry. I don't' know. I wanted to talk I guess, but it's late."

He sighed. "You're in love with her?"

I choked. "What?"

"Bryna Tressel. The girl. You've been cagey as hell about her."

"Swear to god I haven't touched her... sort of. I mean we kissed, but I was trying to do the right thing. I swear to God."

Sebastian chuckled. "What's the current bet buy-in with Roone and Marcus?"

I frowned. "You knew they'd make a bet?"

"Well, yeah. They're assholes. Besides, I asked you not to go there with her because of the delicate nature of our relationship with Tressel. But if your preliminary reports are right, then Tressel might be a moot point."

I cleared my throat. I had to be sure. "So, you're saying I *can* have her?"

"Well I'm saying it's not ideal. And her father could still try to cause problems. But if you actually care about her, I'm not going to let matters of state stand between you. I worried too much about that. I might have lost out on Penny if I didn't say fuck all of that."

I wasn't sure if my sigh of relief was appropriate. "I thought you were going to be pissed. Tell me I had no business fucking with her."

"Well are you fucking with her or do you actually want her for real? Not because you're bored or she's off limits, but because of her."

That answer was easy. "I want her."

"Good, then what's your problem?"

I swallowed hard. "What if... what if I'm not good enough for her? She doesn't know anything about me. Who I was, or who I am now, for that matter."

"Ahh, that's part of the package, mate. You have to tell her. I made that mistake with Penny."

"But were a prince."

"And so are you."

I was quick to dismiss the new truth like always. "That's new. It's the old shit I can see her objecting too."

"You aren't your past. It's about the choices you make in the future. Every day is an opportunity for the new narrative."

"Man, you've really been taking the Bullshit Parable book I got you for Christmas seriously."

Sebastian's chuckle was low. "Basically, I'm saying don't be a dick now, and she'll be able to overlook who you were. That's if she's good enough for you."

"Oh, I think you and I have already established that she's out of my league. I'm the one who's not good enough."

"You are, mate. You just need to believe it."

Would he still believe it if he knew what I was going to do to him, to the trust? "You believe in me too much. Maybe you shouldn't."

He chuckled again. "Yeah, but you're my brother. Literally cut from the same cloth. If shit comes up ready to drag you back to that old place, I know you're smart enough to ask for help. It's like we used to talk about. You would never do anything to jeopardize your new life. You're too smart for that."

No, I wasn't, but thankfully Sebastian might have just put me on the right path. "That remains to be seen. But, thanks man. I guess I never really had anyone to call for shit before."

"Well, I'm happy to be number one on the speed dial. Unless of course I'm busy making my wife—"

"La, La, La, La." I cut him off. The last thing I wanted to hear about was him and Penny.

"Hey man, you could learn a thing or two. I have stellar technique—"

"Nope, got to go. Thanks and all that." I could still hear him laughing to himself as I hung up. He knew how to get rid of me.

He also had helped me without even knowing it. It was time

to call in reinforcements. As for Bryna, she might be better off not knowing who I really was.

＊＊

*Lucas*

"You want us to help you rob a charity event?" Noah Blake's gaze narrowed. "I thought you were retired."

"Not exactly right. I am *planning* on robbing a charity event. I want your guys to stop me."

Jonas Castillo slid a glance between me and Noah. "You guys know I used to be a cop, right? I can't casually sit by while you guys chat about a jewelry heist."

"Oh, come on, Jonas," said the tall blond guy at the end. He spoke with a slight German accent. "We all heard you and JJ playing cops and robbers the other night, and I'm pretty sure from what I heard that you were the robber."

Castillo's face flamed, and he launched himself at the gigantic German. Seriously, the guy looked like a Viking. Or like one of those Norse vampire dudes from that TV show. But luckily, it didn't come to blows, because Weller planted a hand on Castillo's chest easily.

Despite looking evenly matched, there was something way the hell deadlier about Weller. Castillo backed down even as the German cackled to himself.

Blake just rolled his eyes. "Ignore the animals. And you know we can't help you rob the event. It's for charity."

I shook my head. "My stepfather is back. He says this one last job and he'll be gone. But I know him. He'll never be gone. He's threatening Lady Bryna Tressel if I don't comply."

Noah sat straighter. "Protecting people is something we actually do. We can put a man on her for now."

She'd hate that. But she'd be safe. "I think that's a good idea. I also suggest you make that tail discrete. She's prickly."

"Can do. Delaney blends into the background."

The dark-haired guy in the corner rolled his eyes. "Not another debutante watch!"

Noah grinned. "But you're so good at them."

Delaney flipped him off but settled back in his seat. "The robbery is happening. There will be other members of the crew that I don't know. At this point, we're better off trying to catch them in the act than we would be trying to stop them this close to the event."

Despite himself, Jonas sat forward. "Who are the targets?"

I pulled out the plans. Tony had threatened to kill everyone I loved if I tried to double cross him. But I had to get him out of everyone's lives. Bryna would be safe. I needed to be strong enough to do this. "These are mine. There will be drops and couriers throughout the party, I'll have to mark the live targets as we go. The number one thing you want is to find the drops. That way you can make sure Tony never gets the jewels. If he does get any of them, he'll be in the wind."

Noah scanned his conference room full of badasses. Several of them were obviously keen on the idea of a good old-fashioned jewelry heist. "Okay, Matthias, Oskar, you're on."

The German dude stood and pumped his fist. Weller just nodded as if he'd expected it. Man, that guy was a cool customer. Nothing fazed him. Or at least it appeared that way.

I prayed the two of them were up for the challenge, because there was no way in hell I'd risk Bryna.

"All right then. Let me walk you through the set up." As I

popped everyone's jewelry-heist cherry, I tried to shut down the hum of excited electricity rolling through my body. I was not that person anymore. After this, *that* Lucas would be gone forever.

At least I hoped so.

# 32

LUCAS

It was time.

All I had to do to walk away from my old life scot-free was forget who I'd become in the last year.

*It's not forever. It's just for one night. Just forget. You can do it.*

For one night, I had to betray my brother.

If the knowledge of that wasn't enough, I also had to evade my Royal Guard. I would have brought at least Roone in on this, but as it was a significant risk to my safety, he'd have to report back.

And then in addition to the evasion of my security detail, I needed to make sure Blake Security caught my fucker of a step-dad. I sure liked to make shit easy.

But all in all, I didn't mind as much as I should. A part of me felt like I was stretching after a long sleep.

But the thought of what this would do to Sebastian... that burned. He trusted me.

*Never trust a con man.*

Tony had made a targets list. He knew exactly who and what they would be wearing, and we had a series of drop points throughout the venue.

Each of us was responsible for several individual targets. I was pretty sure that Tony had a scout watching my drop point. I didn't care. He would do everything to make sure that I didn't run off with his cash again. I got that. Fool me once, and all that good shit. I understood his world. I knew what to do. I looked the part. I was a philanthropist seeing after the king and queen's interests. But deep inside, I was who I'd always been. *A thief. A liar.*

But a damn good one. Even I'd managed to believe I was different now. The greatest trick the devil ever played was convincing the world he didn't exist, right?

With a quick survey of the room, I was ready. Willing. And then the hairs at the back of my neck stood in attention.

I sensed her before I saw her. When I turned, my breath caught.

*Bryna.*

She didn't see me right away. My heart raced at the sight of her, but years of training kept me on course. So what if she was here? All I had to do was what I'd done every day from the time I was six years old. Bryna didn't matter.

*What about you being in love with her? Does that not matter?*

As a waiter passed by with champagne, I took a glass and sipped. It wasn't so much that I wanted the champagne, but I wanted something to do with my hands. Plus, it made other people much more comfortable if you appeared to be having a good time.

In the far corner of the room, I saw my mother. For a

moment she looked younger than I remembered. Her smile was bright. She was on the arm of some older guy. He looked like old money, probably a new mark for access to this charity event, or maybe they were working on some bigger con.

*News flash. You don't give a fuck.*

Out of the corner of my eye, I saw Tony. He was alone, and his gaze was pinned on me. Suddenly, he smiled. But it was more like an evil baring of the teeth, really.

*Yeah, I don't like you either, asshole.* Then I realized he wasn't really looking at me, but instead, at something just beyond my shoulder. I turned, and that champagne lodged down the wrong pipe. Oh fuck.

*Bryna.* She was watching me, her eyes pools of melted chocolate. I was so fucked. But I had a mask on. It would take her a minute to recognize me.

In my ear piece, I could hear Tony's chuckle. "Easy does it now. No running off to warn your girlfriend. It's about to be show time. Do you understand? Remember your targets. You will only have a sixty-minute window when Emily Lorraine shows up. She's the event organizer and host. There will be sixty minutes of mingling, and then there will be a sit-down dinner. By the time the dinner comes, we want to be out. You got the plan?"

Did I understand? I wasn't the one who always had to change the plan at the last minute. "I understand. I'm not a newbie."

He chuckled. "So you think. I have to say, your roommate looks none the worse for wear after her little mugging incident. I'll bet you anything she ran into your arms afterward. You're welcome, you little shit."

Tony knew. He'd been behind it. I turned to find him in the

crowd, but he'd vanished. "Tsk, tsk, kid. Don't' lose focus. You can try and kick my ass later. Once you've paid me what you owe."

Maybe not today, but someday soon, I was going to make that bastard pay. As much as I wanted to tear the room up looking for him, I had a different task ahead of me. I had to do what I was doing, avoid Bryna, and figure out where the hell Tony's drop point was because the egress route they'd given me wasn't the real one, obviously. If I wanted any shot at Tony going down for any of this, I had to figure that out and tell the police where to go.

What Tony didn't know was that I had a little help from Blake Security in the crowd. Weller was some kind of an avenging angel. I had no idea what his plan was, but I knew he'd brought the German. The guy didn't blend in. How could he when he looked like Thor's brother?

I had to find Tony's drop points, alert them, and walk away. But if I fucked up, Tony would be in the wind. I kept my back to my sexy, beautiful roommate and kept my gaze trained on the door. When I saw Emily, I hit that little button on my watch. It synced immediately. She was here. It was show time.

First target, Jane Avis. Brunette, tits on display, gigantic pendant. Sixty minutes. That was all I had. I just had to be the old me for sixty minutes. Then I could be the new Lucas again.

⚜

## Lucas

Her pendant was off limits. As beautiful as it was, and it was gorgeous, what I wanted was her bracelet. But it wasn't just about a slip-and-grab. No. I had to replace it with what I had in my sleeve. Nobody who got robbed tonight was supposed to be the wiser, at least for the time being. Those were the most difficult kinds of con jobs because time was limited. Some would be simple slip jobs, slight of hands, that sort of thing. But some of them were far more complex. We knew exactly who was wearing what and which jewels needed to be taken and replaced. But time was the enemy. As long as I stayed out of sight of Bryna, I could do it. As a matter of fact, it was almost fun. *You like the old you.* I missed me.

Julie Weaving was easy. When I told her how much I appreciated her brooch, she'd sidled up to me and flirted. Within seconds, I had her bracelet replaced and in my inside pouch, but it required up close and personal "attention." At one point she slid her hands into my jacket and tried to drag me somewhere, but I made some feeble excuse.

Maria De Luca was the next target. She was slightly more difficult. It was her ring I was after. I had the custom replacement all ready to go. Working on her was going to be tricky because she was pissed I'd turned down her offer for drinks the last time Sebastian was in town.

"Ms. De Luca, you look stunning as always."

Her sharp gaze narrowed on me. "Do I know you?"

"Maria, don't be like that. You're one of my dearest friends." Lies. All lies.

She sniffed. "Are you sure? I feel like I would absolutely remember you."

I chuckled softly. "I have missed your sass."

"You look well, Lucas. You think you'll have time to drink with me now?"

"For a beautiful woman? Always." I rubbed her knuckles

gently. When I kissed her hand, I pulled her fondly against me, still holding her hand. "A woman as beautiful as you is completely unforgettable."

She chuckled.

It was easy because I'd been watching her already. She'd already had two glasses of wine. I kissed her fingers again and made the swap while she was laughing and grabbing more champagne. When I made an effort to admire the ring, I simply asked if I could see it in better light, and she nodded. "Just be careful. I declined the body guards that came with the thing, so I'll owe half-a-million dollars to them if anything happens to it." I held it up to the light and turned around, said something about clarity and cut, and then slid the replacement right back on her finger. She beamed at me. "Thank you for flirting with an old lady. You have made my night. Wait until I tell my husband."

"Well, it's my pleasure. I always love talking to beautiful women."

Yup, she would have a fascinating conversation with her husband once they realized it was a fake.

And on it went. What was really frightening was the ease with which I did this. As if the old *me* was always there all along. It didn't matter how much I'd dressed him up. I was still a grifter.

Out of the corner of my eye, I spotted Tony's scout. It was quick, but I caught their exchange, and I signaled to Oskar Mueller who he should tail. From the bar, Roone kept a narrow-eyed glare pinned to me. Did he know what I was up to?

I checked my watch. Fifteen minutes. In about no time, I'd be free.

I don't know what it was that kept me so focused, but I

didn't even notice when Bryna came up next to me. "Do you want to tell me what the hell you think you're doing?"

My smile fell, and the bottom turned out of my gut.

"Bryna? What are you doing here?"

Her voice was flat. "I told you I was coming here tonight. And mask or not, I'd recognize you anywhere."

I swallowed hard. "Same here. You look astounding."

"Don't flatter me. I saw you make the switch with that woman's ring."

I lifted my brows. "I don't know what you're talking about."

"Don't you lie to me. What's happening?"

She'd caught me, but the grifter's code is never admit defeat. "I'm sorry, sweetheart. You're mistaken."

But Bryna wasn't stopping. There was no way she was letting this go. "Come here, let's talk about this." She grabbed my arm. She was going to ruin everything if I wasn't careful.

"I'm a bit busy now, Bryna. Let's talk at home, okay?" I eased out of her grasp.

I had five more targets to hit. *Just keep grifting. Just keep grifting.*

"You will talk to me now."

And then I saw Tony. He was working his mark. He palmed the cufflinks so easily. He was so good, it was disturbing. And just like that, Bryna's gaze shifted over. But I didn't want her knowing about him, about who I really was, so I let her pull me away. "Fine, come on. I'll explain, okay? And then maybe you can let me get back to it?" What would I say? But there was no way I could let her see Tony.

"Whatever you have to say, that explanation had better be fucking good."

⚜

## Bryna

What the hell was happening?

"You can't be here. You have to go."

I crossed my arms. "I'm not going anywhere. What the hell are you doing?" I could only stare at Lucas as he paced and ran his hand through his hair.

"If you stay here, something bad is going to happen."

"What? What in the world could happen? You're freaking me out." He was always so charmingly calm. Nothing rattled him, but he was rattled now.

"You should be freaked out. That part of me I told you about, that part of me that was awful, you're interfering with it right now."

I didn't know what he was talking about. "What's happening? Why did you take that woman's ring?"

## 33

LUCAS

It was a no-brainer. I'd always choose to protect Bryna, no matter what. But I was out of options. Not telling her could get her hurt.

Over the crowd, my eyes connected with Roone's. I inclined my head to let him know where I was taking Bryna. His nod told me he'd seen me. His lips barely moved, but I could assume where ever Marcus was, he had me in his sights. How much had they seen? Anything? Did Weller or Mueller have their targets?

I turned my attention to the more pressing problem. "You are not supposed to be here." How was I supposed to tell her? How the hell was I supposed to explain what the hell was going on?

"I'm waiting, Lucas."

"This is so fucked. How do you even know how to do that? Most people can't see it. Most people can't see what's happening right in front of them. They never notice. Why are you so bloody shrewd? Why did my charm not work on you?

This would have been a whole lot easier if you would just be like everybody else." Fuck me. I was losing it.

She threw up her hands. "I'm sorry if that makes your life harder. But come on, talk to me. I thought you and I had a rule. We're going to be honest with each other."

Why the hell had I made her that promise?

That had seemed like such an easy thing to promise at the time because I got all caught up. "Look, I wasn't kidding when I said my family was all fucked up. I came from a family of grifters, liars, con men. It wasn't always like that. There was a point when my mother was a good person. I remember her singing these songs to me when I was sad, sitting up with me all night when I was sick. But she got caught up with my stepfather, and that changed. By the time I was six, we were running scams. Some as simple as getting a group of kids to steal fruit from vendors on the streets, to complicated Ponzi schemes, car theft rings, you name it, we've done it. But I specialized in long cons. I am what you call a con man. My face, my charm, all designed to work against people. They see me as trustworthy. Mom called my charisma my 'superpower.' It makes people want to tell me things. They want to share things. And in the case of women, they want to fall in love with me."

I could see some of the light draining out of her eyes. She didn't want to believe the truth, but she really had no choice because she'd caught me red-handed. I was telling her the truth. For once.

"So, what? This whole thing, you looking out for me... am I some long con?"

I paced. I needed to get the shit I'd lifted to the drop point. But what was the rush? If Oskar was on, then it might be okay. Tony had threatened to tell her, so I might as well come clean.

"No, you have nothing to do with this. Sebastian really did ask me to look out for you. It all just went sideways. I wasn't supposed to fall for you. Then everything got fucked up and I had no choice."

"Explain fast Lucas. Now, or I'm walking out of here."

My heart squeezed so hard that I thought I was having a heart attack. The racking pain that shot into my body was real and visceral. *Do not let her walk away from here. Do not let it happen.*

"I went to college at UCLA. After my sophomore year, my Mom called me home for one last job. One gig. That was it. I knew I shouldn't have really believed that, but I thought that I could convince her to come with me, that she needed to get away from my stepdad. He's bad news. I always told her that. He used to hit her. He used to hit me. I thought I could get her away. I thought I could help her. It was the first time she'd ever shown signs of not buying his bullshit a hundred percent, you know?"

She nodded. "I get that you want to support your mom, but what you were doing outside... I don't get that."

"I wanted to save my mother, but doing that meant doing one last job. A big one. We had a whole plan set. Mom and I had planned to meet at the airstrip, take the money from the con and start over." My hands shook. "She never showed. She chose him. Just like always."

Bryna's expression was hard to read. "And she just left you there? Did she ever tell you why?"

I swallowed, remembering how it had felt, waiting there, hoping yet knowing the truth. Once again, Mom chose Tony over me. "No. I finally had to just leave. I hadn't spoken to her since, not until Tony came back and started pressuring me to do another job. He knew all he had to do was mention her to make me come running back."

Bryna's brows drew down. "He threatened her?"

"Yeah. Right after I met you, my stepfather showed up in New York. He wanted me to do another job to pay him back. He came up with the usual threats to try and get me to comply, that my mother would suffer, and that he'd hurt her. I knew better now. I didn't listen." I scrubbed my hands down my face. Time was running out.

"Good, God. He sounds like an asshole."

"Yeah, he is."

She frowned then. "But, if you're here, and I just saw you steal a ring, then..."

I swallowed hard. "He had better leverage this time."

She frowned. "What could he possibly have on you? If you knew not to trust him with your mother, why would you trust him with anything else?"

*Fuck.* "You."

She frowned. "What?"

"He'd been following me. He had pictures of you, and after you were mugged, I just—I couldn't take any risks."

"You're doing this because of *me*?" Her brows lifted, and her eyes went wide. The horror on her face was so plain.

She could see it. I was a monster. That good guy she'd insisted lived inside me... there was no such thing. "Yes, *you.*"

"But why? What do I have to do with any of this?"

"That mugging was no accident. Maybe I suspected before, but he just fucking confirmed it. I wondered, but when he confirmed, I knew I was out of options." Here goes nothing. "He threatened to hurt you and tell you the truth about me, and I wanted to protect you." I was rambling now.

"I have so many other secrets it's like I'm a fucking pressure cooker."

"What truth? What could you possibly be hiding? If you're telling me this, what could be worse than this? Jesus Christ, have you killed someone?"

The pain sliced deep. "You think I'm capable of that?"

"No. But you're standing here looking worried and terrified and about to let this shit control your life. What could be so bad?"

I swallowed hard and then muttered the one thing I'd never said aloud except to one other person. "I am the lost prince. Sebastian is my brother. But before that I was a different person. I did things. Stole, lied. Anything I had to do to survive. If I didn't do this job, he was going to tell you about my past and hurt you. I couldn't risk it."

I could tell that it took several seconds for that to sink in properly. When it did, she blinked rapidly and stared at me. Her brows were drawn together in concentration, at first as if disbelieving, and then her eyes roamed over my face, my chin, the one I've been told looks so much like my father's, the one I've been told makes me look somewhat like Sebastian. Then she gasped and stepped back. But she didn't drop on a knee or some such shit. She just stared at me. "Oh my God!"

I didn't know which was worse, the prince thing or the thief thing. "You cannot tell anyone yet. Marcus and Roone, they're my guards." It was then that she surprised me, because I thought she was going to open the door of the conference room she'd locked us in and run. I expected to never see her again. But with her back pressed against the door, she merely sagged. "You're the prince."

I sighed and nodded. "Yeah."

"And you risked your new life to protect me? If you'd been caught tonight, it would have been a huge scandal."

I nodded. "Yes."

Her brows furrowed. "My father. He knows? He would have to vote. That's why he thought you would give me up and send me home with him. You haven't officially been named and signed in to the royal registry. All members of the council can refuse to sign and force another vote. It's only happened once that I know of from history class."

I nodded. I felt so weak. All I'd ever tried to do was protect her, keep her safe, and do what my brother had asked. But I'd screwed up left and right. I'd screwed up by being who I was, by falling in love with her, by not keeping my hands off her. Wait what? *Shit*. Love? When the fuck did that happen?

I didn't have time to examine my feelings right then, and all I could do was nod. "Yeah."

"This, tonight. Not your plan."

A harsh chuckle tore out of my throat. "No. I would never have agreed to steal from Sebastian. I tried to fix all of this, but everything just got so jacked up."

Bryna held out her hand. "Take my hand."

What the hell. "No. Bryna, no! I need to get back out there and see if any of this is salvageable. I had a plan to end it all, but I didn't count on you being here."

"Nothing you've told me is making me run. Let's face it. You need someone in your corner, not someone to run from. So, if you don't mind, I'm going to hold your hand, and then you and I will get out of here. Tell Roone and Marcus whatever you need to, but you're walking away. Just like you wouldn't let me cave with my parents, I'm not letting you cave either. Do you understand? Don't do this. Fight. Be the new Lucas. The one you *want* to be."

I looked at my pouch, the one where I'd been tucking all the jewels, and turned my gaze to her dark eyes. Then I did something I didn't think I'd be capable of doing again. I placed my pouch on the table, took her hand, and left it all behind.

We'd been quiet in the cab ride home. Marcus rode in the front with the driver. Roone followed in a separate follow car. When we left, I'd shot a text to Weller that I needed to get Bryna out of there. I knew I'd jeopardized everything.

Walking away like that... *Would they still catch him? Was he in the wind?* I'd walked away for her. My life could be in shambles back in the real world. But I'd deal with that later.

Tonight the woman I didn't deserve had asked me to walk away with her and I had. I'd deal with all the consequences of that tomorrow...*If tomorrow comes.*

We were silent as we waved to Fred then walked to the elevator. Marcus went up first to sweep the floor. The next one came down and we stepped in just as Roone marched into the lobby. He had his take no prisoners face on. Was something wrong? Was he still pissed off? There was no time to ask him what was happening back at the event. *Deal with it tomorrow.*

We stepped inside the elevator, leaving Roone in the lobby.

Gently, Bryna took my hand. I marveled at how soft her skin was.

She turned to me easily, and I couldn't help but wonder... Was this real? Was she mine? I tugged her close and dipped my head. Reckless and impulsive—that was my MO.

From the moment I'd met Bryna, I'd had some outrageous fantasies about her lips. How they would feel under mine, how they'd look around my—

She moistened her bottom lip with the tip of her tongue and I bit back a strangled moan.

"I'm going to kiss you again now, if that's okay."

She gifted me with a smile. "I think it might be okay."

The tip of her tongue peeked out to lick her lip again, and my cock jerked. Cupping her face in my hands, I pressed my mouth to hers, meaning to be gentle. Instead, I felt like I had electrodes molded to my lips, sending electric currents of need through my body. *Shit.*

She moaned, and I dragged her closer to me, unable, unwilling to break our contact.

My tongue coaxed a response, demanding more. When her tongue answered and met mine, need slammed into my body with such force, I thought I might explode.

*Holy hell.* But my body didn't believe that. I wanted her so badly my blood boiled. As our tongues danced, I lifted her so that her legs wrapped around me. I fisted my hands in her hair and could feel the heat from her core. Her soft moans urged me on—to sink deep inside her and never come up for air.

The elevator dinged, and we both pulled back. Her eyes were wide, her lips soft and thoroughly kissed. Her chest was rising and falling as she dragged in air.

I eased her down my body. The moment we broke contact, I

missed her. I took her hand and tugged her back against me. "Bryna—" I was quickly distracted by the long column of her throat. I kissed along her skin, and she shivered.

"Lucas, that feels..."

In the foyer I turned her around and backed her against the wall, bracing myself for the shot of electricity bolting through my veins. But when I dipped my head and our lips met, her return kiss was so tender it had me on slow melt. While my lips glided over hers in curious exploration, her tongue teased and coaxed mine.

Hard and fast was what I wanted—or thought I wanted. I'd gone looking for a flash of heat. My body hadn't bargained for this kind of slow and easy kissing. It burned just as hot.

Heat spread from the center of my body, rising to the epidermis and scorching my skin from the inside. Breath trapped in my throat, I tried to speed up the pace. The slow torture was telling me everything I needed to know about her. She was thorough. Took her time. Didn't rush things. She liked to be in control. It also meant she was confident and strong.

If she kept the slow burn up any longer, I would become a believer in spontaneous combustion.

Without breaking our kiss, I slid my hands down her arms and brought them up to wrap around the back of my neck. I mumbled nonsense words, more focused on getting her as close to me as physically possible. One kiss had reduced me to a horny teenager, and my brain couldn't compute.

Looking down at her, feeling her warmth around me, the soft curves of her body gently molded against me, I couldn't remember my own name. Couldn't think beyond what I wanted. Couldn't think beyond the need slamming through my chest.

Bryna arched her body into me and smiled. I couldn't remember why I'd ever thought it was a good idea to stay away from her. As I kissed her again, I thought I was branding her as mine, but it was her leaving an indelible imprint on me.

In the tiniest corner of my mind, a voice called to me to be careful. It tried to warn me that she was dangerous to me. That she wasn't mine. But I didn't listen. All I could hear were her ragged pants. All I could think about were those lips and where I wanted them. How much I wanted her to be mine.

She tasted like home. The flavors and scents of the islands wrapped around me. Intoxicating me. My hands tightened on her waist, and I nipped at her bottom lip as she responded with a shiver. My damn dick pulsed against the front of my tuxedo pants.

With every breath, shift and wiggle from her, I could feel the heat of her. I traced a path to her neck, inhaling deeply. She arched into me, pressing those full breasts into my chest. Needing to feel more of her, I slid a hand up to the V of her dress. Tracing the material as it clung to the rise of one perfect mound, I heard her sharp intake of breath and watched with fascination as her nipple puckered under the stretchy fabric. No bra. *Shit.*

Continuing to trace my finger at the edge of the fabric, I used the other hand to restrain both of hers above her head. She didn't struggle, only rocked her heat against me. Taking advantage of her arched form, I hovered my mouth for a moment over the puckered bud. I blew a warm breath, and she shivered again as her body arched even more.

Not one to disappoint a lady, I pressed my lips over the raised peak and suckled her through the soft material. Her breath came out as a drawn-out moan, and I tugged harder, trying to taste every rich flavor of her skin through the fabric.

Letting go of her hands, my fingers trembled as I peeled back the shoulders of the dress. One simple tug and it skimmed off her shoulders to her waist, baring the dark rose-tinted tips of her breasts. Another tug and the dress slid to the polished travertine of the floor. *Perfection.*

My brain stuttered. I'd seen her naked before. But that had been so brief. Now I could memorize her form with my hands. It had been a long time since anyone affected me. Since any woman had touched more than just my flesh. Bryna had managed it the moment I saw her. And now... Now she stood before me in all her naked perfection, and my mind completely fuzzed out on what to do.

Lucky for me, she knew what she wanted. "Lucas, I need this." She gazed up at me through thick lashes. "I need you."

I couldn't move. I'd had sex—lots of sex. Shit, I'd had all sorts of sex on six different continents. Never once had I felt truly connected. Not like I did now. Bryna reached for me, and I could only watch as delicate fingers tugged my crisp white shirt out of my tuxedo pants. She leaned in close comingling her scent with mine.

Her hands, delicate, but sure, moved inside the shirt, skimming my shoulders as she slipped it and my tuxedo jacket off. At the contact of skin on skin, my cock pressed against my pants, urging, begging me to love her. To slide into her soft warm depths and never come back up for air.

Heat flared in Bryna's eyes as my cock nudged her belly. As I felt the now-familiar shock of electricity, I eased her hands away from my belt. I grabbed a foil packet from my wallet before violently kicking off my pants. I left the boxer briefs on, tucking the condom in the waistband at my back.

For a moment, I saw the look of confusion in her eyes. My body finally surging into motion, I shifted her onto the antique desk in the entryway, hovering over her lips again like a starving man.

My hands took their cue from the roaring, pulsing blood in my veins and slid over her hips to her ass. Cupping her flesh, I levered her against me. "Put your legs around my waist."

When she complied, I cursed as her wet heat met the cloth covering the head of my straining dick. I braced her against the corner and slowly kissed her again. Taking my time, I teased her tongue into dancing with mine.

I traversed a path from her full ass to her waist to her breasts, never quite reaching the sensitive tips. Bryna moaned and rocked against me trying to get closer, urging me to take her breasts in my hands. When I gave her what she wanted, she moaned and arched her back, giving me better access.

Those breasts were a thing of beauty. I'd always been an ass man, and Lord knew Bryna had one that could win awards, but her breasts were quickly making me a breast man. They weren't much bigger than a B-cup, but they were high and firm.

Bryna arched her back as much as the confined space would allow. I took the hint. Dipping my head, I grazed first one nipple, then the other with my five o'clock shadow. I followed up with my tongue and with playful tugs with my teeth.

"Lucas."

I wanted to hear her moan again.

I growled against her breast. "I like it when you say my name."

She said it again on a whisper, and I sucked in a delicate tip.

With one arm wrapped around her for support, I slid my hand down the flat expanse of her belly. Only pausing to trace a circle around her belly button, my hand slid farther down, searching for her center.

When I found it, I hissed in a breath. She was wet. Slick. Teasing the entrance, I slid one finger into her moist core and she bucked. I buried my lips in her neck, inhaling the scent of her. She smelled like home. Gently, I withdrew then entered, withdrew then entered, in a slow, lazy rhythm that said we had all the time in the world. When in truth, we only had a minute before I spontaneously combusted.

Her hands fisted in my hair and she rocked her hips against my finger, trying to force me to increase the pace. I didn't. Instead, I inserted another finger and kept up the rhythm. *Nice and easy.* We had all the time in the world.

Bryna raked her nails up my back and I chuckled through a hiss. "You're making it really hard for me to take my time."

Doing it again, she asked, "Who said I wanted you to take your time?"

Hell, if that didn't wreak havoc with my self-control. Easing my fingers out of her, I reached around my back for the condom. With a series of wiggles, my briefs went the way of her dress. Getting the condom on in our current position took more effort than I thought, but when I was sheathed and my cock nudged her slick folds, I didn't care. All I could think about was how she felt against me.

"Lucas, now."

Her rocking motions caused her sex to rub against my tip.

I shuddered from the need. "I'll go easy."

She smiled. "There you go, trying to make decisions for me again. When I want easy, I'll ask for it."

With slow, tilting motions of my hips, I slid in to the hilt. We both hissed in breaths. Hers was an "Ahhhhh." Mine an, "Ohhhhh."

*Bliss.* I rocked my hips back, slowly pulling out, and rocked forward again. As my cock stroked the sensitive walls of her flesh, she dug her nails deep, scoring marks that a part of me hoped would become permanent.

She tossed her head back, baring her neck to me. Taking advantage, I nipped at the column of her neck even as I drew forward and the sensitive flesh of her core milked my cock, pulsing and releasing in its tight sheath.

"Lucas." My name on her breath was both a balm to the part of me that was always searching, always moving, and an accelerant to the driving urge for self-destruction. Even as our bodies moved together, mixing sweat and her perfume, I knew once wouldn't be enough. She was already under my skin. As I drove her higher and higher and felt the tingling at the base of my spine, I knew walking away from Bryna Tressel would be torture.

"Lucas. Please." Her delicate fingers twined in my hair, pulling me close.

"Come on, sweetheart." I drove into her with an increasingly insistent pace, no longer coaxing, but demanding she be my for a night, for a millennium. "I want to feel you around my cock as you come. Let go, Bryna. You're safe with me."

"I—" Her breath hitched.

I ground my teeth together. The tingle in my spine had turned into fire. I couldn't hold back. "Bryna."

Her body trembled in my arms, and I felt the quiver of her slick flesh against my cock. "Oh. Fuck. Me."

As she came, her body flooded mine and clamped tight around me, unwilling to let me go.

⚜

*Bryna*

I woke to the sun streaming in Lucas's bedroom window, and my body still tingled. Lucas lay snoring, one arm thrown over his face, and the other loosely thrown over me, sheets in a complete and total tangle.

I tried to scoot out of bed while keeping at least part of the sheet covering me, but that wasn't an option as Lucas was tangled in them. I eventually just gave up before grabbing a T-shirt from his top drawer. I glanced down at him and couldn't help but smile. He looked so sexy with his abs on display, an arm thrown over his head, and every muscle deliciously revealed.

I glanced at the clock on the bedside table and winced when I saw it was 5:30 a.m. I padded out to the living room to get some water. I couldn't help the sheepish grin when I saw most of our clothes strewn all over the living room floor. I stepped over my shoes, my dress, Lucas's tuxedo pants, his tuxedo jacket...

When I finally quenched my thirst, I filled another glass for him. I started to carry it back to the bedroom when I paused to pick up his discarded jacket. His wallet fell out, and I picked it up to put it on the counter. Several cards slipped out. I picked them up and meant to shove them back in.

I was not snooping. Totally not snooping.

But one quick glance and my breath caught. They were

IDs... several of them. Only one of them was Lucas Newsome. The others were for Lucas Beard, Jason Atkins, and Lucas David Anton.

I let them all clatter back to the kitchen counter with a sigh. What the hell was he doing with these?

*Stop. You know who he is. He told you everything about his history and who he was.*

And I'd chosen him. Last night, I told him that none of it mattered. And it didn't. I knew who he was. I knew him well. He would never hurt me.

So what the fuck was this?

He had five driver's licenses, each with a different name and address. I didn't want to invade his privacy anymore, at least not by going through his wallet, but I found credit cards in those other names too. If I kept digging, those addresses would likely flush out too. He'd have built a whole life with those names. Just in case someone like me came calling and he had to run.

*You gave him your word.* My heart started to race in my chest. The rapid *thud-thud-thud-thud* drowning out all other rational thought. Turbulent waves of emotion crashed through me. I just needed... Shit, what did I need? I couldn't talk to him. Not right now. I needed some distance, some time. I needed to filter and work it out.

I had made him a promise. I headed straight for the shower, and my brain still tried to make sense of what I'd just seen.

Pieces of last night's conversation kept coming back to me. All the things he'd said, every part of his confession played over and over again in my head.

He'd confessed to being a thief and a grifter, but that was in the past. He walked away last night from a job that probably would have been extremely lucrative. He told me who he was. I couldn't even imagine that kind of pain, finally finding his father and then losing him. He found out his father was a king, and he a prince, every fairy tale come true. And then to have that ripped out from under him...

He had reasons for what he did. He had to survive. And there would be consequences for last night, someone he'd have to answer to. It worried me how little I knew him.

*You do know him.*

I told this to myself as I climbed into the shower and let the hot spray pelt against my skin. He'd given me a job. He'd given me a place to stay. And he'd given up himself to save me. *That* was who he really was. Those IDs weren't him. Those were for survival.

When we'd come home from the event, I'd felt the kind of connection with Lucas that I'd only read about in books or witnessed in movies. That was real. There was no hiding from that. It existed. It was tangible. I could feel it and examine it. So I needed to find a way to deal with this. I loved him. We still had a lot to work out, but we could do it. I knew we could.

$P_{ANIC}$.

Not because I might have a bunch of psychos after me. Not because I walked away from my old life, not because I burned bridges, but because I woke up and Bryna was gone.

It took me several seconds to actually feel her side of the bed and realize it was still warm. She hadn't been gone for hours. If she'd run, it was only moments ago, and I still had time to catch her.

I recognized how desperate I sounded but I didn't care. Maybe she needed time, and maybe it was just safer for her to be away from me. After all, there would be retribution. I had my phone out, ready to call Roone, but then I heard the shower going.

*See dumbass? She's just having a shower.*

Except she was having a shower in the *other* bathroom.

*All her shower shit is in there.* We hadn't been exactly looking where we're going when we were aiming for the nearest bed for round two. We'd eventually made it to my bedroom.

*Where you fucked her like the animal Tony says you are.* I hadn't been gentle. I'd been out of control.

I ran to the bathroom door, and it took everything in my power not to thrust open the door and ask her if she was running. My instincts said she was, and I needed to know why. *After what you told her, what did you expect?*

*She recognizes that you're a crazy person, who'd made a whole career out of lying, and then you told her you were the prince? Oh yeah, that screams, 'You should totally stay with this guy.'*

But she'd promised she would talk to me. She wouldn't just leave me.

*Oh yeah, you believe that? She made you a promise between orgasms, and you bought it?*

Okay, yeah. That was dumb. I should have made her promise before I started giving her orgasms, held them for ransom.

It didn't matter though. I wasn't giving up. Even if she'd bolted from bed. I was going to be as understanding as possible because it was a lot to digest. So much. But I wanted to be better for her. I needed her I like I needed air, so I wasn't going to push. I was going to wait. I sat on the bed and tried to stay calm.

The water finally shut off, and several moments later she came out wrapped in a towel. She squeaked and jumped back. "Oh my God, Lucas, you scared the shit out of me."

I shrugged. "Sorry. I'm just returning the favor for when I woke up alone." The anger bubbled to the surface.

Immediately, her brows snapped down. "I was just in the shower."

"Were you?" I hated how that sounded. *Weak*, like I needed her. But who was I kidding? I *did* need her. I had completely fallen in love with her. She knew every single one of my secrets. There would be no recovery from this when she left me. And I knew it wasn't a question of *if*, but *when*. I just hoped that I would have a little more time with her first.

"I just came to grab a shower."

"Tell me the truth. Don't hide. Don't lie. You were running."

"I—" She shifted, her dark hair curling on her neck.

I shook my head. "Don't lie to me Bryna, if you're running, tell me now."

She sighed. "I just needed a few minutes to myself. Your wallet fell out of your jacket, and I saw your IDs and I just..." She shook her head. "I don't know what I'm doing."

I sat up. I wanted to go to her. I wanted to wrap my arms around her.

"Everything that happened last night was so visceral and emotional, and I just needed to mute things for a moment so I could think."

I ground my teeth and swallowed the pain like shards of glass in my throat.

"Second thoughts?" My voice came out low, almost inaudible, but she heard me.

She shook her head. "No, because I still know who you are. I'm just having a hard time understanding. For over a month now, you've been lying to me, lying to my father, lying to Sebastian, lying to everyone. It worries me how good you are at it."

She was right. I was a really fucking good liar. "I tried not to lie to you. Outside of keeping the secret of me being the prince, everything else I've told you is true. I worked with your father on behalf of Sebastian. Yes, I lied by omission. But several things I didn't have the authority to tell you. Not that I have the authority to tell you now, but considering I've been inside you, I don't give a fuck."

She swallowed hard. "You have such a fluid relationship with the truth."

"You said it didn't matter. I never would have touched you last night if you—" I shook my head and ran my hands through my hair. What the hell was I going to say? I was going to say whatever was needed to make sure she didn't leave me. I couldn't stand to have her walk away.

"Lucas it's not—"

I shook my head to cut her off. I couldn't stand for her to say the words. "I know. This is too much. I've asked for too much."

She sighed. "Stop. You haven't asked for too much. I volunteered for this. I'm just confused. I'm allowed to feel this way, right? Last night, I could feel it. Being with you feels right. But it's terrifying when I see five different IDs in your wallet. You could leave me at any moment, and I would have no idea where to look, or who to call, or what to say, or what to do, because this is what you do so well. And that's terrifying for me."

I pushed to my feet. "You think I'm not scared? Hell yeah, I am. Even one of those things I told you is enough to make you walk away, to make you run. Why did you stay? Why?"

She tilted her chin up. "I love you, you idiot. But those IDs... where are you going? Are you leaving me?"

What? She thought *I'd* go?

"I'm not going anywhere." I shook my head. "I considered it. I thought it might even work in your favor if I just vanished, you know? But I couldn't make myself do that. I need you too much." I exhaled and asked what scared me the most. "Even after knowing how awful I am, the things I've done, the things I was willing to do... do you still want to be with me?"

She opened her mouth, and I held my breath. I don't think I've ever waited so long for an answer in my life.

"Of course. This isn't exactly a choice for me. From the moment I met you, there's been this pull between us. I can't deny it. I feel alive, and infuriated and free, and giddy when I'm with you."

I needed to be honest with her, even though it was going to hurt. "I have no idea how to love someone right. I'm scared that you were exposed to the person that I was, exposed to bad people because of me and what I've done, and I don't want that. I'm also a man of my word. When I gave it, I promised you I wasn't going to make decisions for you. So if you're staying, then I'm keeping you."

Her smile was soft. "You are the master of my smile. I couldn't leave you. I'm not going anywhere."

I choked on a sigh of relief. It was all I needed from her. "I'm sorry you saw those IDs. I'm sorry you doubted for one second what I said."

She met my gaze levelly. "I'm in. I want you Lucas, always you. From the moment I saw you, I was in for the ride."

I didn't realize I'd been holding my breath until I finally let it go. She was really mine. And I would do anything humanly possible to protect her.

* *

*Bryna*

A deep chill woke me. I peeked an eye open and shut it immediately when the sunlight nearly blinded me. I reached for my blanket, came in contact with hard, searing heat. *Lucas.*

Memories flooded over me as I recalled the elevator, foyer, and eventually the bedroom. Our fight. Making up in the shower and again in bed. All of it in startling clarity. I bit back a moan as my tender flesh pulsed at the memories.

I'd been Lucas's to do with as he wanted, and I'd loved every minute of it. For me, sex had never been like that. Raw and dirty and so satisfying. With Lucas I could do anything with no fear.

I sighed when he pulled me close to him and turned me over in bed so we could spoon. As I nestled against him, the hard length of him nudged against my ass. He couldn't possibly...

"Hmmm, baby. You cold?" he whispered into my neck.

I nodded and murmured something noncommittal. I didn't feel nearly as cold now resting against his heat. I wiggled to get closer, and he growled.

"Damnit woman, I'm not a machine." But that didn't stop him from lifting my leg and shifting behind me to align his erection with my slick heat.

I felt him searching for something with his free hand in the bedside drawer.

"What's the matter?"

"Damn Bryna, I think we're out of condoms. I didn't think we'd go through them all."

A flush crept up my body. "Oh. I uhm. I've been tested in the last year, and I'm on the pill."

He hissed in a breath. "I had a clean bill of health at my last check-up. I'm pretty sure I have some more around here somewhere."

I shook my head. "I don't want to wait."

"Are you sure, Bryna? I—"

"Shut up and make love to me."

He chuckled and drew me back up against him. "Somebody sure is bossy. I could get used to this."

As he entered me with slow precision, I gasped. I hadn't thought my body could handle any more, but my flesh parted and stretched to accommodate him.

"You sore?" He stilled, waiting for an answer.

"A little, but don't stop."

"I don't want to hurt you." The twitch of his dick inside me wasn't voluntary, but the movement made me push against him.

"You're not... hurting me. Don't... you... dare stop," I breathed out.

He groaned but inched forward again. "What the lady wants, the lady gets." And he wasn't kidding. I felt every ridge and vein of him as he moved within me. The contrast of his soft, satiny skin against the hard column of his dick was enough to make me quiver.

We were in no hurry this time. He took his time. With aching tenderness, he kissed my neck and shoulder.

"Fuck. You are so fucking beautiful. And sexy. And damn mischievous. I will never in my life forget you walking out naked during my date. I wanted to spank you. And then I wanted to fuck you." He continued whispering words of love into my ear. He told me how beautiful I was, how much he loved being inside me, how much he needed to touch me. And how good I felt bare.

He reached around and stroked my clit, and I moaned as the pleasure and spasms increased. "Oh, God, Lucas." He wasn't far behind me, as he gripped my hips hard enough to leave bruises and thrust into me. I felt the warm flush of his seed as he came inside me, his dick twitching.

"Jesus, Bryna, I think you broke me."

"I'm just getting started Lucas Newsome..." my voice trailed. "What's your real name? It just occurred I might not know it."

His smile was soft. "It is Lucas Joninski. But I haven't been him in a very long time."

"It's nice to meet you, Lucas Joninski Newsome Winston. They are all you. And I love them all."

# 36

THAT AFTERNOON, Bryna took a nap. She looked so cute all curled up, hair a mess and falling into her face. I should take a picture of that moment and hold on to it forever. She was mine. For the first time in my life, I had somebody who loved me with no strings attached to that love, and I knew exactly who I was.

I also had Sebastian; I knew that. But our relationship would always be a little complicated. Besides, he came looking for his brother, determined to love him. Bryna loved me by choice, which, given who I was, was kind of amazing. Now all I had to do was be worthy of her love. I'd put in a call to Sebastian first thing after Bryna and I worked out how we were going to do this. He hadn't called me back yet, but I needed to fill him in on last night.

He'd be disappointed, of course. Furious, probably. But he was my brother. I hoped he'd forgive me, understand, and help me, because God knew I would need the help. Tony was going to come after me full on, which meant he was really going after

Sebastian and Bryna. I needed to protect them, so Sebastian needed to call me back.

I'd had a string of texts from Blake Security. Tony had slipped the net. He was in the wind. Which meant that Bryna wasn't safe and I still had a target on my back. It was fine. I could protect her. I wasn't leaving her side.

I'd also sent a text to my mother, asking her to meet me, and she'd agreed. I'd give her all the money I had, every cent of it, and she could do what she wanted to do. I hoped she would make the right choice, but at least I would have done everything I could for her.

I couldn't be pulled back into her crazy world anymore.

There was a knock at the door, and I half expected it to be Roone coming to read me the riot act. But it was the woman I'd been trying to save from herself for the last decade. Our doorman, Fred, escorted her. "I do apologize sir, but she insisted you are her son. She showed me a text message from you. I just—"

I nodded. "It's fine. Let her in."

My mother took one look at Bryna sleeping on the couch then stared at me.

"Are you insane? What are you doing? You should have skipped town already. He almost got pinched at the ball."

I dragged her out onto the expansive balcony. "Keep your voice down. She had a long night, and I really don't want her dealing with anything else."

"You're the one who wanted to meet."

"Yeah, I wanted to meet you on my terms and in a neutral location. You decided it would be best to just show up here unannounced. Let me guess. Tony's not far behind?"

She frowned. "He doesn't know I'm here. We caught the heat last night. He almost got pinched with his stash. He had to hide it. He assumed you would be laying low too. You know better. I worry about you. You have to leave. He's coming for you. I want you safe."

"You know it's funny, you toss that word around when it's convenient. But when I actually needed a mother, you know, to protect me, to give me everything I needed, you weren't exactly available."

She crossed her arms, her blond hair blowing in the October breeze. "I taught you how to survive, didn't I?"

"When I was a kid, I used to wish that you would have just given me up for adoption or something, so I wouldn't have to spend all my life surviving. I could have run away, but I loved you too much to leave you behind."

She winced at that, and I felt sorry for the bitter sting of the words. I wasn't bitter anymore. Now, it was just a statement of fact. "Look, I don't want to fight with you. I want to give you the money that I owe you and that you deserve. You can make your own decisions about your turd of a husband."

She blinked away tears. "Your whole life you looked down on me. Like someone was going to come and rescue you from our situation."

"Oh, I knew no one was going to rescue me. That was *your* job. For a few years, I thought it was mine to rescue you, to do what I was told, stay out of Tony's way. I tried to protect you. I tried to keep you safe. And all that has done is cause me pain. Especially as you *refuse* to leave him. I thought if I could just get through to you... but you don't want to leave. You're in this with him. It's a bed of your own making. And the sooner you realize that, the better off I'll be."

"You think you're so high and mighty in your fancy penthouse? I see the royal trappings, my son."

I didn't even flinch. "Why didn't you just let him take care of me? From what I understand, he wanted to. He wanted me to go live with him. He wanted me to have a *life* with him. And because of you, I never even got to meet the guy."

Her bottom lip quivered, and she bit it as if to steady herself. "Is that what you think? That your *Daddy* really wanted you to go live with him? That palace may look all beautiful and idyllic, but it's a viper's nest. His queen wouldn't have let you have a happy day. I know what it seems like now, but there's no way that would have happened."

"That's not true. I've met her, Mom. She was really kind to me when she didn't have to be. She would have embraced me as a child."

"You always had a flair for fantasy, Lucas. I'm just here for my money."

"Fine. Arguing with you is futile. You've never been my mother." I felt like I was swallowing hot coals as I added, "This is the last time you'll ever see me. Once you walk out that door, we're done. I don't want to hear from you. I don't want to get some 911 rescue call from you. We're done."

"You think you can just walk away? Tony is never going to let that happen, especially when the news breaks that you're a prince. He's going to be so happy to tell every single one of your stories about all the jobs you've pulled and every con you've done. He's going to ruin you. You'll never know when your life is going to get ripped out from under you. You need to run."

I shook my head. "No more running. I've already disclosed all that, and it doesn't matter. I'm safe. I'm clean." Blake Security had basically erased it all. I didn't exactly know how they'd done it, but apparently since I'd never actually been arrested, the proof was easy to disappear. Everything would fall on Tony. Or so I hoped.

I handed the check over to her. "I hope this helps you find happiness." She stared at me for a long moment.

"You actually have two hundred grand?"

"Yeah. I didn't touch the money that I stole from that Mexico job. I invested it. I also got a job. So, yeah, I can pay that amount. But there's no more where this came from. This is it."

Her frown deepened. "How did we get so far apart?" She shook her head. "As far as long cons go, this one has been a doozy. I couldn't have played this more beautifully if I had set it up myself."

I frowned. "What are you talking about?"

"This con, you, as the heir to the Winston Isles."

What the fuck?

"I am a prince. Sebastian found me. My blood has already been tested. You confirmed all of this."

That was when her eyes went solemn. "Everything you've been told, from the moment you asked about your father to this point, has been a lie. You are no prince of the Winston Isles. Years ago, I was in Italy. I was a starving actress. Someone paid me a lot of money and pointed me at the man who would be your father. I had a boyfriend at the time, but it didn't matter because they offered me a lot of cash. So yeah, I hung out with him. I didn't mean to care about him. That sort of happened by accident. But, you still happened."

I stared at her. "I don't know what you're getting at."

She held up her hand. "Let me finish the story. Well, predictably, he got what he wanted then vanished, and I found myself pregnant. The problem was while I was boning him, I was also boning my boyfriend, and I couldn't be sure who the baby belonged to."

*Shit.* My stomach bottomed out.

"He showed back up and insisted that my baby was his son. Those very same people that approached me in Italy, turned up not two days later offering me another boat load of money to tell him that the baby *was* his kid. I didn't ask questions back then. I didn't want to know. I needed the cash. The next thing I knew, the king of some island was asking to take custody of my kid. I got scared. It was real. Something was wrong with the whole picture. I didn't want any of that to blow back on me or you."

"I don't understand. Someone paid you?"

She nodded. "Things got really bad when he asked for a paternity test. I thought I'd get out of it. I thought I'd be cut free. I didn't give him a lock of your hair; I gave him a lock of mine. So you can imagine my shock when it came back that you were a positive match for him. The hair they tested, *my hair,* came back absolutely positive that you were his son. I knew the game was rigged. Someone was using me. Someone was *trying* to use you. So when he asked for custody, I told him no dice, and then I took you and ran. There was a reason you have been living under the radar your whole life, and it's not because I'm some horrible person. Your life is like this because I protected you. I've always tried to protect you. You might not like my methods, but they were all I had. When you called about your father, I told you the shell of the story. I thought maybe it might be okay. But now, I know better."

I shook my head, staring at her. "What the hell are you saying?"

"I'm saying someone paid me a whole hell of a lot of money to sleep with the King of the Winston Isles, and then they paid me a lot of money to keep it quiet. They tried to make it look like you were his son, including forging your records, and I don't know why."

Adrenaline fired in my veins. What the fuck was she saying?

I couldn't quite find the words, so I keep shaking my head. Finally, her gaze leveled at mine and she said the words that started whirling around, terrifying me.

"You're not the Crown Prince of the Winston Isles. In fact, you're no prince at all."

*To be continued in Bastard Prince...*

## WHAT TO READ NEXT!

Thank you so much for reading Royal Bastard.

Don't forget to pick up the epic conclusion in **Bastard Prince!**

Did you read Sebastian and Penny's story? No? Grab them now!

**Cheeky Royal**
**Cheeky King**

# ABOUT NANA MALONE

USA Today Bestselling Author, Nana Malone's love of all things romance and adventure started with a tattered romantic suspense she borrowed from her cousin on a sultry summer afternoon in Ghana at a precocious thirteen. She's been in love with kick butt heroines ever since.

Nana is the author of multiple series. And the books in her series have been on multiple Amazon Kindle and Barnes & Noble bestseller lists as well as the iTunes Breakout Books list and most notably the USA Today Bestseller list.